# HIDDEN IN THE LIGHT

## IAN CAMERON WOOD

**Copyright © 2020 Ian Cameron Wood**
First published in Australia in 2021
by MMH Press
Waikiki, WA 6169

Cover Design: by Bree Morel



National Library of Australia Cataloguing-in-Publication data:
Hidden in the Light/ Ian Cameron Wood
Fiction
ISBN: 978-0-6450521-9-0 (sc)
ISBN: 978-0-6450521-8-3 (e)

# WHAT PEOPLE ARE SAYING

Hidden in the Light is ostensibly written by the three Darling brothers – James, Andrew and Nathan. Confusion for the three brothers was created when their parents were 'saved', taking the boys to church twice every Sunday as well as to weekly Bible studies and prayer meetings. For James, Andrew and Nathan, this disrupted life as they had known it until that time. How each brother deals with the hypocrisy they see in the church is a fascinating feature of their individual stories which are written without any collaboration between them.

Each of the brothers distance themselves from the church because of leaders not living out the the teachings they preach so the brothers forge different paths from their late teens into adulthood.

James, Andrew and Nathan write their own accounts of the tragic events and horrendous abuses as well as their experiences of life and death. As harrowing as much of their stories are, they do introduce quirky and humorous moments as they struggle to find love and peace. They also reveal perspectives of each other which is an intriguing and enlightening aspect.

Ian Cameron Wood has crafted a thought-provoking, inspirational novel with Hidden in the Light

**Deborah Lloyd - Readers Favorite (USA)**


Hidden in the Light is deep, rich and ultimately, memorable.

**Matthew Crossman - Editor (Australian Community Media)**


This is one of those books I will remember long after having finished reading it.

It's a thought-provoking and provocative read.

**Dannielle Line - Editor and proofreader**

# FOREWORD
### by Derek Lenere (Journalist, Editor)

When I first suggested to Andrew Darling that he and his older brother, James, and younger brother, Nathan write their story, I knew there was a story to be told. However, I did not expect to receive three separate stories. I envisaged a collaboration in note form that I would edit into a final story. But their efforts prove that fact is stranger than fiction.

The Darling brothers have no writing experience, as is evidenced in this book. However, I have not interfered with their original expression. Rightly, I believe, I have kept almost all work as written by them despite what seems clumsy and even manic in their styles. They have individually woven anger with curiosity and meshed suffering with warmth and at times, threads of humour.

The Darling brothers are brought up together in a loving family environment. Childhood memories are for the most part positive and recalled with much affection. When the brothers were nine, seven and five respectively, their parents experienced what is called by some, a life-changing meeting with Jesus Christ. I am not convinced that such encounters exist and am therefore uncertain if this experience should have resulted in a sure foundation for the future of the brothers. If it was for this purpose, then for the most part, it failed.

I have spoken with and interviewed many Christians during almost four decades as a journalist. For the most part, I found them to be shallow at best, arrogant and disrespectful at worst. Christianity is a noble ideology spoiled only by the intrusion of its adherents—Christians.

Most Christians will in all probability not read this book. I would not be surprised if some church leaders warn their congregations against these pages, which contain scenes of abuse, violence and sex told with language they would label as offensive.

This book contains the stories of the three brothers. James, the more conservative brother is over-indulgent with words sometimes making sentences ponderous, perhaps even pretentious, but still revealing. I made the decision to leave the story in his original form, continuing this approach with Andrew and Nathan also.

Perhaps the writing of this story has offered him a release from who he attempted to be, thus allowing him to become who he really is. He admits that the process of writing his story, which did not come easily, has given him insights not only into his brothers but also into himself. But within his words remain hints of humility and integrity that have helped heal past wounds. He readily admits that writing his story has been of great personal benefit.

During the early 70's, Andrew lived the pop-star dream with his band. He enjoyed a degree of fame in Australia before they moved to London, aiming for further fame, but tragedy ruined that dream. However, he remains thankful for all that his life has been and is.

His writing is without ramblings or superlatives and is more precise. He has approached this task in the same manner he employed as a songwriter and a composer of music.

For nearly thirty years, I have had the pleasure of knowing Andrew. We have remained friends since I interviewed his band after the release of their first single in the early seventies. I also met with the band when they were in London. Andrew, Wally, Chris and I were together the afternoon the news came through that the band's drummer, Tony, who we were waiting for, had died of a heroin overdose. I reported on the tragedy which eventually led to the break-up of the band.

The worst of abuses became Nathan's cross to bear. Many Christians will consider him the greatest of failures, even a hypocrite. Yet the story of his suffering which led to great adventure from great anguish is remarkable. It is also a testament to his determination to find peace where others would have undoubtedly perished.

Nathan's writing is quite hectic at times, as though he is in a hurry. Whether it was a hurry to finish the memories or a rush to escape them, I am not sure. However, there is an addiction in the power of tragedy and the thrall of surprise he exposes in these pages.

As graphic as some of Nathan's story is, the greatest of evils are sewn with threads of humour into these unlikely and entertaining stories. We are introduced to memoirs from more than fifty diaries in which he wrote of daily events. He wrote poetry and anecdotes to express the deepest of regrets and the darkest of sorrows.

Regardless of the mental, emotional and spiritual confusion that Nathan has endured, he has hung on with a tenacity that raised him above the darkest depths in which he could have so easily been swallowed. The 'lost years' of Nathan Darling are extraordinary in many ways and represent a magnificent struggle to not just survive, but to do so with some self-respect.

Of course, this does not change or excuse what he has done or what was done to him. The result of his abuse and his response to it detached him from his family for twenty-seven years. A fugitive constantly running from God with the hope of finding Him again, Nathan becomes a perplexing mystery. His life is disjointed and separated not only from his family, but also from himself and the life that promised so much and from the God he expected to always be there.

One does not need to understand the enigma of this man to enjoy the richness of his personal history. His story will acquaint you with appalling indignity and deplorable human error. But the dark humour encompassing all of this brings many delights as it shines a light to dispel shadows from the gloom to finally reveal what was hidden in the light.

Unfortunately, so much abuse in the church is covered up or ignored by the institution itself, holding a light for all to see but turning it off for so many who seek justice for crimes and abuses committed against them. Hidden in the Light therefore seemed an appropriate title for this book of three individual stories that eventually weave into one at the conclusion.

I am not a Christian and I do not want to become one, but if I ever decide to pursue that path, Nathan Darling will be the first man I contact. Not because he represents what I believe Christians should demonstrate, but because he is firstly, a genuine, open human being.

'Hidden in the Light' is not like any other story or stories I have ever read, but I am grateful to have had a role in the publication of this remarkable book

# INTRODUCTION
## *by James*

There is no account I can write to prepare you for the narrative in these pages. The story seems innocent, even innocuous at first. Although containing pages of cold dampness, it nevertheless delivers a degree of occasional warmth and even humour. For myself, I think the cold has finally thawed, allowing me to enjoy the accompanying beauty and surprising delights that weave into the writing of my life and the lives of my two younger brothers.

The warmth is most welcome and eventuates in surprising ways. Equally, grief and abuse also penetrate unexpectedly. This has been my experience journeying through these recollections and observances of Andrew and Nathan, as well as my own.

Overall, our stories contain some victorious dignity despite the darkest moments. That we do in fact have life is a dilemma to contemplate or an opportunity to savour both in its joys and tragedies.

The thought of writing my autobiography had never been a consideration until my brother, Andrew, and his long-time friend and journalist, Derek Lenere approached me with the idea that has eventuated as this book.

There was little in my life that I deemed worthy of attention. Now, everything that has eventuated in my life has brought me to my part in the story of the Darling brothers. I am bewildered at much of it and I yearn for my life to be returned as it once was, easily understood and easily lived. But I am uncertain if I should now entertain such expectation. Life presents unexpected tragedy and unexpected fortune leading me to ponder the question: What is the opposite of a 'miracle'?

From a young age, I often speculated what I should do and what I should be, but none of my considerations ever seemed entirely appropriate. Mostly, it seemed that no conclusion I reached regarding my future was correct. All options were mulled over many times. Paralleling this was the irrational sense that I could not become what I desired to be. Indeed, I accepted that I did not deserve that which I desired. Mentally, I remained in a place where I deemed myself unworthy of attention and certainly, therefore, of any honour or prestige.

Nevertheless, for three decades I maintained a successful career as an architect. I managed many projects from the initial discussions and drawings, through to final plans and successful construction. However, none of my buildings included accompanying plans for the demolition of what would be built. I understandably reasoned that my life was inclined to the same premise: there was no plan for the demolition of my life or of those who lived it with me.

Incongruous though it seems, I rarely had any assurance about most things in life. Nonetheless, I prospered as I emulated the architectural career path of my paternal grandfather out of my respect and awe of him from childhood.

I accorded no significant thought to whether God or my upbringing in a Pentecostal church environment had in any way fostered a role in my success. Except for weddings and funerals, I have not attended church regularly for over thirty-five years. I was in no way convinced that God even frequented churches. The qualities I expected to abound in the God of Christians, I assumed, would also flourish in His people, yet I witnessed little evidence of such behaviour.

Although I have some favourable memories of my early years, those recollections are now infected by the virus of a few, so-called 'men-of-God.' Their suits, ties and neatly ironed shirts impressed a certain value of wisdom and holiness, but they were at best charlatans loosed upon an unsuspecting, even naïve assembly of faithful minions.

*** 

*During the writing of our stories, we have been made aware of overwhelmingly joyous news. Wonderful circumstances have come to light which contribute abundant hope. There is reason to celebrate, but I remain unconvinced that God has had anything to do with these occurrences.*

*My admission, or confession, is that I consider myself totally inadequate to cope with either the tragedy or the fortuity in this story and therefore, in my life. Fortunately, I realise I am not expected to cope with either alone.*

*Nevertheless, there remain some truly remarkable events which will be revealed through the pages of this book. I am content to let the story of the past remain in the past after I have related my contribution. Nathan inclines toward the premise that these extraordinary events are 'miraculous' in nature. I choose not to debate his position.*

*** 

*Our story commenced with pleasant childhood memories before disappointment and anger entered, which preceded the surprise 'arrival' in our family. However, it is now converted to an unexpected contrast with the beginning. On this occasion, a most dire circumstance has burrowed into our world, unpredictable to Andrew and me but not to Nathan, who has had to shoulder this burdensome pressure alone for nearly twenty-seven years. Hopefully, we can be of assistance and support him, but I do not know how this can be accomplished, or even if it will be possible.*

*I seem to be back in my place of uncertainty, but I now know what the opposite of a miracle is.*

# INTRODUCTION
## *by Andrew*

For me, life has always been great. From a young age I lived with the thought I would be famous someday, and this gave me great confidence for my future.

I have some wonderful memories of my childhood, from my years at school and to everything that led to a successful and rewarding career in music. My life has been very satisfying, and its rewards have continued through the years.

But that is not the entire story in these pages, even though I offer some interesting background and anecdotes. These pages contain scandal, abuse and tragic events that stabbed the heart of our family. I feel stripped bare and dirtied by what has been revealed. I have discovered some of those responsible for the destruction spread the stench.

Unfortunately, there was a man in our church who committed gross evil against two innocent young girls. Lust and greed and his narcissistic desire to control others motivated this man's wickedness. This man was not only known to my family, he was our uncle, my mother's younger brother.

Instead of being brought to account and convicted, other men in 'ministry' protected this wolf in sheep's clothing. Some of these men hold important positions today. They are highly regarded nationally and one, internationally. Any rewards they have gained from their self-importance will never pay the price for the destruction they covered over. They covered over a multitude of sin and cast the victims on the dung heap. They are spiritual wankers, pleasuring themselves with their own self-importance and 'holy fame'.

We have decided that in this book we should not give too much information about these men, because these bastards are still alive. The belligerent arrogance of two of these ungodly 'men of God' has led them to make threats. Both have threatened legal action against the Darling brothers, but most disturbingly one has 'advised' Nathan that his life is in danger if he speaks out. To God be the glory?

Severe anger had never been part of my life until I was made aware of these facts. I often wonder what 'the God of love' thinks about this individual, one who claims 'valid ministry' with upraised hands in the pulpit, yet would protect his 'holy' position by devising the fatality of a brother in Christ. My anger, indeed, rage is a perfect match to the madness of this minister. I want to name him but cannot do so here. But be assured, I will not be silent for long and he will face justice and criminal proceedings someday, unless he is silenced by one of his victims exacting revenge as justice. I can only hope.

I am sure this book will not be found in Christian bookshops, but perhaps it should be. Nonetheless, there remains some worthy testimony to the 'blessings of God', if that is what they are. Will I ever go back to church? I do not think so. In some way, I still believe that God loves me, but I struggle with the 'teaching' that God has a plan for our lives. I have seen too many plans go awry for too many well-intentioned people. Life is so fragile, so uncertain, so fleeting. Conception is a random chance with no predestined assurance.

* * *

*As this story by James, Nathan and myself was in progress, some remarkable events have occurred. One is especially beautiful for Nathan, and I think it saved a large part of him. Did God have a plan or was it just an afterthought for His holy amusement? Either way, it has brought a delightful twist and something none of us could have imagined, not even Nathan.*

*After re-reading the first part of my introduction, I can see that it was written mainly in anger. I decided not to change it because the anger is justifiable. But the amazing, even 'miraculous' arrival has given me a new perspective. But maybe it is not new at all, just revisited after many years.*

*Perhaps it is God's way of getting my attention, but how unlikely it seems. I always thought if God was going to intervene in my life to 'win me back' he would probably do it through some tragic event. But I do not think tragedy would have served to turn me back to the 'faith'. But this wonderful 'gift' or 'blessing' at least gives cause to contemplate the possibility of thanking Him.*

*There has also recently been what might be 'divine intervention' in other members of my family. Maybe the words that Pastor Tom used to say many years ago are becoming real. "God is good, God is good all the time."*

*There is a verse in The Bible saying that God's goodness leads us to repentance. Is this the catalyst that will cause me to return to the 'faith' I 'abandoned'? Although I am not yet convinced, I think it is possible. My cynicism no longer supports my apathy.*

* * *

*Now there is another complete change to the story. Starting with the joys of childhood, through to a great career and family life, and finally to the exposure of evil that none of us knew about. From there we went forward to great blessing as life (or God) seemed to work further 'miracles'. But in the end, it finally crashes down again. I do not know what to say.*

*My inadequate response is this. Not only is conception random chance, but perhaps all of life's activities are. But then I would have to concede 'evil' as chance also and I can't do that.*

# INTRODUCTION
## *by Nathan*

*(Editors' note) Throughout some of Nathan's story, he has inserted writings taken from the hundreds of pages of notes he wrote during the "lost years" as he so often refers to them.*

*These writings from Nathan's life accurately portray him as a disturbed and enraged victim who made a tragic decision resulting from the horrendous experiences he witnessed or suffered.*

*We have also decided to leave Nathan's text for this book as he has written it: with '&' instead of 'and', numerals instead of words.*

*His mostly short, staccato-like sentences also remain unedited. To 'correct' his method and style of writing would compromise its power and effect. (Derek Lenere)*

* * *

Ever heard the saying, "What does not kill you, will make you stronger?"

What about this one? "When you weather the storm, you come through stronger?"

What bullshit! If you get through the storm at all, you're just a survivor. If you survive without killing yourself, or someone else, good for you, but you're not necessarily stronger.

I survived. I reached the point many years ago where I had a love/hate relationship with my life. I loved what it used to be but hated what it became.

How often did I contemplate, even plan suicide? Too many times. I still think about it. I'm breathing, but I have no life. My pulse beats, but my heart is cold. I cry tears that burn inside like red-hot drops of molten metal, searing into my inner being.

Something horrible was done to me. But I also saw a 'horrible thing' done to a friend when she was about 11 or 12. I had no idea how the witnessing of this would lead me to greater horror many years later.

But what I went through eventually brought other sewage to the surface. Now the truth is being told. There will be repercussions & regrets. So what? Regret has been my constant, unwelcome burden for many years. I have been a dark shadow cast by darkness. It shut the light out of my life. A tragic end to a life that should have lived what was promised.

I'd only been 'saved' a few months. My life had become a wonderful place. There was so much to look forward to. I had a beautiful Christian girlfriend. She was joyful & effervescent. I loved being with her. I loved her. I felt like I was in heaven.

I'm not 100% sure what I will reveal in this story, but years ago there was a tragic accident. It happened so quickly. Nobody could have saved him. The police, the press, his family, & the people in the church I was attending, heard the story. They all believed it as I related it. But that was the greater tragedy.

Fuck the official story. I was glad the bastard was dead. He was fat & ugly. He was evil personified. He was not just a mere wolf in sheep's clothing. No, he was a rabid werewolf feeding on the blood of virgin innocence.

As human beings, we are not designed for hatred & bitterness. We are not designed to take revenge. I ignored the design. Had some good reasons, too. You'll find them in this book. You may or may not agree. Too late now though.

Anyway, I watched the last moments of the bastards life. I saw terror in the eyes of his pallid, white face. Now, nearly 30 years later, I still look back sometimes & laugh. But sometimes I'm horrified at what happened. Horrified that I was there. Horrified that I was there & that I've had that in my head for so long. I don't think Christians can be more fucked up than me.

I can't bring the fat bastard back. Who'd want him, anyway? His evil son will join his father in the depths soon enough. He will drink the bitter cup of his own acts of perverted destruction.

Perverted, because what they both did was inhuman & ungodly. Destructive, because the church allowed such bastards to hold positions of leadership & authority. Further destructive because they were never brought to account for any of the accusations. Instead, their victims were labelled evil. The victims just wanted to tell the truth. No one listened to them.

The evil continued to flourish. Darkness & light side by side in oblivious harmony. Neither caring nor taking any responsibility for what the other was doing. Keeping themselves secret from each other to protect the 'ministry.'

*"Oh, come all ye faithful..."* unless you've been abused by someone in leadership. In which case, *"Fuck off & keep your mouth shut."*

So, how the fuck did I, as a 'blessed' young man, become such a messed young man? You'll find out in these pages. Mine is not your usual testimony of coming to Jesus & living a joyful life. Oh no! This one sure is different.

I was reading from Proverbs one morning about 30 years ago.

I read one verse that stood out. It seemed to be in big, bold type. It compelled me to run away. Such is the power that biblical scripture can wrongly exert. But, after running away, I was a fearful outcast. I spent 27 years trying to get away from myself. 27 years of trying to 'get right' with God & trying to get away from God. I will reveal the verse later. I'm not ready to go there yet. There's a lot I'm not ready for. You might not be either. But don't let that stop you from reading further, unless you think your boat is too small for rough seas.

Despite all the hurt that has been lived through these pages, there is still hope. Strangely, I am still optimistic, sometimes ambivalent. But then I suddenly plunge into dark despair. A few days later I rise *'on wings of eagles'* with joy in my heart & praise to God on my lips. He hears me. He loves me. He comforts me. & then I scream, "What the fuck is it all about? Why did so-called leaders in the church fuck up my life?"

I am a friend of Job. His story in the Old Testament is parallel to mine in some ways. Not all. But this is another verse that gripped me.

*Job 10.1 - I loathe my very life*
*therefore, I will give free rein to my complaint*
*and speak out in the bitterness of my soul. (N.I.V.)*

***

*For years I agonised over what my life had become. Now it suddenly becomes something else. Is this God's way of saying everything is okay? Even in the middle of my personal torment, I am overwhelmed by this apparent goodness of God. If that's what it is. No one could have imagined such an incredible outcome. Not to such a fucked-up life. I call it my 'miracle'. The 'miracle' that God gave me to prove His grace, not just His forgiveness.* * * *

*I couldn't keep it a secret. I don't regret revealing what I concealed in dark, hidden places inside myself. I know it causes great heartache for everyone else. This is something I deeply regret. I don't know what happens now. Anyway, I don't give a shit.*

*If you've read this far, you're probably not a Christian. "Too many swear words, brother." "Not enough positive attitude, brother." "Tone it down a bit, brother." "Make it more acceptable, brother." Well, all I can say is, 'Fuck you, brother.' It was so-called 'brothers' whose evil attitude & words killed me. Brothers didn't tone me down. They turned on me. They kicked my trampled soul into the sewer. "What do you think of that...brother?"*

*Most Christians just keep polishing their shoes 'shod with the preparation of the gospel of peace.' They see their dark reflection in godly patent leather. Now we see through a glass darkly. Fuckwits! Light can be found in the darkest depths of anyone who calls out to God.*

*But most don't look in the darkest depths. They only see the surface. The surface is pitted. Often brutal. Unattractive. Don't get too close to them, 'brother.' Don't scuff your shoes.*

*I'm sick of hearing that 'hurt people hurt.' Hurt & hurting people are bewildered, in anguish, torment & pain. Romans 12.15 says, 'Rejoice with those who rejoice & mourn with those who mourn.' But Christians are only good at rejoicing with the happy & the 'attractive'. Often, they do nothing for those who weep or mourn, except to criticise them for weeping.*

*You can criticise me, & I'm sure there'll be plenty who do. But criticism is the easy way out. Criticism relieves you of the responsibility of trying to understand the person you are criticising. Sure, I'm fucked up. But I'm still here. Still trusting God. Still hopeful.*

*But what if the shit hits the fan in your life? Will you be able to hold on? For how long? Could you hold on for more than a quarter of a century?*

*What would you be like after all that time? 99.9% of you will never find out. Be thankful for that & stay the fuck out of my way.*

*Anyway, I lived through all this crap. You should at least have the guts to survive reading it.*

# PART 1

## JAMES

Sex in a Cubby House,
Architecture, Death, Depression

As the eldest of three boys, I often deliberated on my responsibility to be the protective big brother for Andrew and Nathan. If it was my responsibility, how should I perform such a duty? I had no idea and thought that I remained somewhat detached and aloof from them. Although we interacted well together, I assumed a difference between us. In retrospect, I see that it was a presumption based, not on clear facts, but rather by my own insecurities and dubious self-image.

Both Andrew and Nathan were very independent and much more confident and secure in so many more ways than I. My sense of detachment has resulted in a certain degree of guilt over Nathan, considering that we had no contact with him for nearly twenty-eight years. We had no knowledge of his whereabouts for twenty-seven of those years.

I apportioned blame upon myself, assuming I had made bad or wrong decisions as the eldest brother. If only I had been more caring, shown more interest or attempted to enter his world, perhaps I could have prevented Nathan's disappearance.

But for now, I will elucidate on more of my personal journey as I venture toward whatever closure I might meet. For now, I am uncertain of how my story in this book will conclude.

Grandfather was an architect and director of a large architectural company. I greatly admired and respected him and remember announcing to him when I was about thirteen that I'd decided to pursue the required regimen to become an architect. I will never know whether it was wisdom, expectation or insight that prompted his response, but I will never forget his affirming acknowledgement.

"Well, James my boy, I expected this to be the path you would choose and, I expect also that you will undoubtedly be an excellent architect," he uttered with pride as he put his large hand reassuringly on my shoulder.

He was a stately man of grace and dignity, but I did not consider him pompous or pretentious in any way. I idolised him and was distraught when he died a month before my eighteenth birthday and just four months before I commenced architectural studies. I determined to diligently apply myself in honour of his memory and perhaps become such a grand man as he. I became an architect but being grand in the manner of Grandfather Darling was not realised. Nonetheless, I am sure he would be immensely proud and gratified at my achievements, even though I never attained the eminent position he held.

Our maternal grandfather was a delightful man with a great sense of humour and was also the family dentist. His humour often bordered bizarrely on the absurd, but he never failed to delight us with his presence. I greatly enjoyed his company but had no desire for dentistry.

In our family, Andrew and I were always addressed by our full names, never Jim or Andy. Andrew and I used our full name when speaking to each other, but to Nathan, the youngest, we were Jimmy and Andy. He was the only one in the family to use those forms of our names.

There was only one other person who called me Jimmy, and that was Julie, the younger daughter of the pastor of the church we attended. I do not know why she addressed me as Jimmy when everyone else called me James, neither do I know why I did not ask her to stop referring to me as Jimmy. Perhaps it made me feel like her big brother. I had often pondered the niceness of having a sister and felt that I would have been a better brother to her than I was to Andrew and Nathan.

Nearly thirty-five years would pass before I would learn what she suffered as a young girl. I cannot imagine her personal anguish at such abuse as she endured. Poor Julie, and her older sister Robyn, endured through the darkest of evils perpetrated by the pastor of our church. I had no idea that my heart would be pained for them.

* * *

Our surname was always an inducement for much ridicule, and this taunting affected me more than my brothers. As a young boy, I would at times become disquieted or indignant at such teasing on account of my surname. Andrew seemed to shrug it off without bestowing it any consideration. Nathan, on the other hand, revelled in such provocation, introducing himself as Nathan D-a-a-a-a-rling, extending the name for an unnecessary duration. He actually exploited the surname to affront others by introducing himself as the 'Darling of the class', a brazen announcement being at an all-boy's school.

I had a non-admitted admiration for his daring and his disarming wit and charm. What to me was a dilemma or personal difficulty, became for Nathan, something to be transformed to advantage, either with humour, brazen disdain or both.

* * *

I was nine when our parents became 'saved' and commenced attending church every Sunday. I resented having to be present in this strange milieu, especially during the summer. It was an intrusive inconvenience, and I ceased my connection with church attendance when I was sixteen.

Coming to terms with the changes in behaviour and attitude in my parents was perplexing for my nine-year-old mind. Jesus became an intrusion in my world, and I blamed him and afflicting my parents with a religious zeal that supported no useful purpose. Our lives were disrupted. Mine most certainly was, but this encroachment was different for Andrew and Nathan. Perhaps it was their age or perhaps their personalities, and the fact that they also possessed a ready ability to adapt and easily engage with others.

But my experience, although largely negative, was not without some rewarding occasions. During some services, I would whisper secret prayers to God. I would pray quietly and furtively, but most of my prayers were self-centred. I prayed for things I wanted, which of course, I did not receive.

Neither I, Andrew or Nathan were overtly 'Christian' at church or at home and certainly not at school. I do not concede that we were rebellious though, rather, I contend we were more curious about that which our parents, and those around us, performed because of their faith.

Nathan's relationship with Andrew was a definite contrast to mine. Indeed, my rapport suggested more of an isolation rather than companionship with my brothers. I was self-absorbed, wrestling with the conflict between the grandeur of my expectations and the inability and hopelessness of knowing I would probably not realise any of them. This constant affray disrupted my uncertain passage toward my desperation to succeed. Unceasingly plagued by these travails, I thought I was quite insular and detached from Andrew and Nathan in numerous ways. They both disagree with my summation and were unaware of any such division. But I was entangled in my world of few delights and much confusion. Fortunately, my relationship with Andrew today is decidedly one of brotherly camaraderie and reciprocal admiration and appreciation for our respective successes.

Unfortunately, Nathan disappeared from our lives when he was only twenty-two. Dad and Mum received a few letters he wrote from New Zealand, but there was insufficient information until the final three or four. He wrote with the announcement that he had been 'saved', was attending a church, and in a relationship with a wonderful Christian girl.

Mum and Dad were elated at this welcome report and there was much rejoicing within the family environment and in the church, which I had not been to for over ten years by this stage. Although I was nonplussed and indifferent to this news, I was also respectful that Nathan had experienced that which neither Andrew nor I had fully embraced.

However, we would not see Nathan again for nearly twenty-eight years. We had no further communication, nor could we find a trace of his whereabouts. His sudden and unexpected reappearance many years later would bring an immediate joy. However, it delivered great anguish and heartbreak for Mum, for Andrew and for me.

Much of our family life was centred on the church. Mum's younger brother, Alwyn, aligned himself to the church and within a few months had assumed the role of pastor. It was a perplexing period, but I had no clear comprehension of the circumstance that developed at that time. I would not be privy to his treacherous nature until nearly three decades had passed.

I harboured an intense dislike of attending church on Sundays, especially in the summer. We resided in Hampton, not far from the beach, which to my reckoning, prevailed as a far more welcoming 'church'. I could 'praise the Lord' for the waves that provided an opportunity for using my surfboard, or, on those days when the water was clear and calm, I could 'praise the Lord' for favourable spear fishing weather.

My summer 'prayer life' alternated between requesting waves suitable for surfing and invocation for calm seas. I indulged summer holidays to either surf beside the Brighton Beach Baths or go spear fishing. Andrew and/or Nathan accompanied me on many of those occasions. These presented the Darling brothers with activities that I embraced enthusiastically, given that they were such adventurous pastimes where I delighted in being the eldest brother.

The beach was my escape, a refuge throughout the summer months of my younger years and well into my teens. Of course, the beach was also the locale for the potential encounter with girls, although for me it only provided increased opportunity for observing girls. I lacked the confidence to engage any of them in conversation. My habitual process was one of attentive observation with the desired expectation that an attractive female with far greater confidence than I would make the first strategic advance. I earnestly prayed that I would get lucky.

Late one balmy summer afternoon while the final touches of sunshine splashed reddening rays upon the edge of sand and the bluestone seawall, I did get lucky. Andrew and Nathan had taken leave of the late summer shoreline, returning home to assuage their increasing eagerness to consume whatever nourishment our mother had readied for our return.

I had been lying on my back and had not long raised myself to a sitting position, with the intention of departing for home when I recognised Robyn and Julie strolling along the beach toward me. They were sisters, the daughters of the pastor of the church we attended. At the time, Robyn was about sixteen and Julie about thirteen. They were both attractive but a little strange. Robyn did not converse a great deal, although I remembered her to be more effervescent and animated when she was younger. Julie always looked sad, but back then I had no perception, and certainly no suspicion of why these once vivacious young girls had become so sullen and detached.

At the time, I assumed it was related to the tragic death of their father. His death was manifestly traumatic for his family and to the church. But after a few months, Alwyn became Robyn and Julie's 'stepfather'. He also deviously intimidated his way into the role as the new pastor, but there were objections raised. Nearly forty years later, Alwyn would be revealed as the man who defiled the lives of Robyn and Julie.

However, the heart-breaking demise of Pastor Tom had occurred almost seven years previous to this summer day and early evening. It would summon no memory for me, of Pastor Tom.

The girls were each carrying a bag, and Robyn was also shouldering a beach umbrella. Undoubtedly, they had advantaged themselves the opportune leisure of whiling away a day of summer at the beach.

"So, how long have you been at the beach today?" I asked as they approached.

"Actually, most of the day. We were in the park under the shade of the trees with friends from school," replied Robyn, as she released her bag and let the beach umbrella fall to the sand.

She commenced to slowly unbutton her light cotton beach dress, allowing it to slowly slide down over her bikini top and then her hips. The movements she accentuated with her body greatly aroused my attention. I first ogled her bikini top, which outlined the hidden mystery of delightful breasts, punctuated by equally eye-catching nipples. My eyes delighted in every incitement of her sensual figure as they finally lingered on the mystery hidden by the lower piece of her bikini. All the while, she monitored my leering gaze as she stood before me, her long, lithe legs slightly apart. Robyn then pulled the bottom of her bikini higher, revealing an outline of female anatomy I'd only ever dreamed about. She then playfully ran her fingers provocatively over the front of her bikini, further accentuating the outline of her hidden anatomy.

I'd never witnessed such a display and was very hastily becoming aroused. She looked at the rising bulge in my bathers and then searched my eyes with a soft, seductive smile. Without saying a word, she slowly turned and walked toward the water, knowing I was watching the accentuating movement of her hips and beautiful rounded backside.

Julie was sitting next to me, but my thoughts and eyes were on

Robyn who was now standing waist deep in the water, looking toward me. After watching her very recent teasing actions, I ran down the sand and into the water and dived in, thinking this would impress Robyn.

Whether I was impressive did not enter my mind as I reached her. She smiled at me, said 'Hello' in a way she had never spoken to me before. I was mesmerised and gazed at her bikini top with the outline of her nipples as a shivering excitement rose within me.

"Hello," I replied, with what was much hesitation and no confidence. "So, what have you been doing today?" I continued, naively.

"James, is that what you really want to know?" she said as she lowered her head while holding my eyes with her alluring gaze. Before I could absorb the question and craft a reply, she continued, "Come to our place tomorrow after lunch and I'll play you a record that Mum and Alwyn don't know I have and then..." She paused briefly before adding, "We can maybe do something else if you like. Perhaps you might find out what you really want to know," she concluded.

As she spoke, she allowed her hand to glide gently over her breasts hidden behind her bikini top, then moved her hand down to the bottom half where she seemed to lightly caress herself. I wanted to see her naked, and my anticipation was evident under the clear water.

Obviously pleased with my noticeable reaction, she waded past me to go back to the beach. And as she brushed slightly against me, she looked down at my excited reaction and said, "Ooooh, I'll see you tomorrow, James," and she continued on her way.

I watched from where I stood in the water as she wrapped a towel around herself, picked up her bag and walked away with her younger sister. As she walked away, she turned and gave me a single wave with her hand while late afternoon touches of sunshine splashed gold and orange rays upon the waters of the bay and washed up glistening diamonds onto the sand.

At seventeen, I was not wondering how a sixteen-year-old girl, who was raised in a Christian family, could have become so seductive. Years later, with the added benefit of knowing what had happened to her, I felt a sense of guilt and sadness. But walking home along the beach that afternoon, my thoughts were concentrated on the exquisite pleasure that the next day might have reserved for me, wondering if perhaps my prayer was going to be answered.

The following afternoon, I sat on the floor of the family room where Robyn and Julie resided with their mother and Alwyn, neither of whom were home. Robyn played the record a friend from school had allowed her to borrow. I have no recollection of who it was because the latest of music trends was not high on my list of interests.

But watching Robyn and Julie listening to the music was fascinating. Most fascinating for me was the way Robyn was sitting and what she was wearing: a cream coloured cotton top with short, puffy sleeves tied with fine red cord. At the neck, the red cord that tied the top was undone. On the occasions she leaned forward, I could see the top of her breasts and saw she was not wearing a bra. I was far more interested in looking at her long, tanned legs that met at her mystery, which was covered by a pair of tight shorts that clearly outlined her anatomy.

The music finished, and Robyn went into the kitchen, returning with three glasses of orange juice.

"James, let's go out to cubby house," she said, as much with her eyes as with her alluring voice.

Pastor Tom had built it when the sisters were young, and we had been in and out of it over the years when we visited as a family. I had not been inside it for at least two years and it seemed lower than I remembered, but the pitched roof allowed Robyn to stand anywhere along the centre.

Julie stayed in the house, but outside in the cubby house, Robyn started telling me she thought I was a nice-looking guy and had always liked me from the days of growing up in the same church. Being in close proximity to her body had me aroused already.

"Do you think I'm pretty, James?" she asked while leaning forward for me to again see she had no bra on. My eyes were transfixed. I was seeing real female breasts and nipples for the first time. She stood upright and slowly lifted her top to reveal her entire upper body. She asked me to undress myself.

We did not have intercourse that afternoon, nor at any other time, even though she removed all her clothes. At the time, I was experiencing what most teenage boys dream about and I was elated at all that happened. A few minutes later, that elation pulsed through my teenage body and mind through Robyn's attention to my aroused anatomy with her hands. I considered myself to have leapt from the curious anticipation of adolescence to the impudent assumption of manhood, now evidenced by the experience of my first sexual encounter with a girl, a naked sixteen-year-old girl.

There were occasions after that experience when I tried to tempt Robyn for a repeat of our brief afternoon of pleasure, but she always brushed me aside. The alluring gazes ceased, the enticing sexuality she kept reserved, and she never again spoke to me the way she had spoken on those two days during that summer, nor did I see her delightful naked body again.

Nearly forty years would pass before this would disturb me with a degree of regret. I occasionally questioned myself about the incident. With the passing of the years, the restlessness increased and, unbeknown to me, for good reason. Robyn had been a victim of sexual abuse, as was her sister, Julie, long before my sexual encounter with her.

I communicated with Robyn to seek her permission to write

of this event and expected she would decline to be mentioned. Her response was not anything like I had anticipated.

"Honestly, James, I have no idea what you're talking about," she answered when I asked her.

When I repeated what she spoke to me that day, Robyn declared she had no recollection of anything I related from my memory of the incident. To me, it seemed she had disowned this segment of her past. Now, knowing of the abuse she was subjected to, I understand why.

"Write whatever you like, James," she continued, "because such things as this from the past hold no interest for me, in fact, they no longer hold me at all."

* * *

Although I was raised in a very loving family environment and had no reason to leave home, I moved into an apartment at the commencement of my second year of studying architecture. Michael was an architecture student with whom I had formed a good friendship in our first year at R.M.I.T. He lived in the apartment during his first year and I had been invited there on occasions.

We shared that apartment for two years, and it was a period that further diverted me from the faith in which I was raised. Many interesting and easily engaged people lived, worked and socialised nearby. I was fortunate to be stimulated and refreshed by the laughter, conversation and demeanour of such inspiring personalities dispersed in the vibrant milieu that was this part of South Yarra. Some remain important in my life to this day. Three of them became clients in my early career as an architect, inviting me to remodel or design buildings.

These experiences and interactions shaped who I became and the confusions I discarded. Prior to these two years I had felt lost, an oft-repeated phrase from the church I was glad to leave behind. From no church life at all up until the age of nine to suddenly being taken twice every Sunday and once during the week to a Bible study and prayer meeting, was unsettling. Now I was free of the restricting confines of thought processes I felt I had been pressured into.

Life had become more complex for me at nine as I attempted to reconcile the real and the perceived restrictions to what had once been my free Sundays. However, I sensed myself emerge into a clear, bright life of possibility from whatever clouds of confusion had surrounded me prior to my two years living in the apartment with Michael in South Yarra.

* * *

But for now, I must leave these fond memories to expose more recent events. I had been happily married for twenty-nine years, had two children, owned an admirable home, enjoyed a professional career and expected a future of contentment and reward. However, I have learnt that our existence is fragile, and dreams can be extinguished as quickly as a delicate candle.

For twenty-nine years I had been the most fortunate man in the world. My wife had remained attractive and vivacious and we held a strong physical desire for each other through those marvellous years together. On the morning of her fiftieth birthday, before we rose from our bed, I enquired what would most delight her as a memorable birthday gift.

She raised herself slightly, tilted her head back, brushed the hair from her face and looked me lovingly in the eyes and in the softest and sweetest lilt said,

"Let's make love forever, Jimmy Darling." I readily obliged, but 'forever' only lasted about twenty minutes that morning.

During those years of wedded bliss, we raised two extraordinary children who are now in their mid-twenties and following successful career paths. Miriam, whom everyone knows as Mitzi, is the eldest at twenty-six and is employed as an interior designer with a large London architectural firm. Michael, at twenty-four, has completed a law degree and is based in Canberra performing a minor role in the Department of The Attorney General.

I was in my mid-fifties, Barb had just turned fifty, I had a reasonably successful, yet small, architectural practice, some excellent investments and many years remaining to enjoy being with her. What more could I have wished for?

On the evening of her fiftieth birthday, I escorted Barb to dinner at a restaurant in St. Kilda for what was supposed to be a memorable evening. It was indeed memorable but opened the door to a darkness with which I was not acquainted. That was the last time I would ever see her zest and joy for life. Nine days later we buried that beautiful girl after an inoperable brain tumour seized the most desirable creation God had ever made, if indeed He exists and can be credited with such a masterpiece.

Returning home from dinner that February evening we laughed about the pending night of passion, playfully disputing who would make whom go first and who would be on top at that deliriously exciting moment. That moment never arrived.

"James, I have a strange headache," she announced from the other side of the bed as I began undressing.

I looked up and smiled and was about to comment, but the countenance of her face and the look of fear in her eyes signalled something different. She collapsed on our bedroom floor.

"Barb, Barb, Barbara," I cried as I hurried to her side and held her hand.

Even though I did not know what was wrong, I felt myself sinking into a dark place oozing with morbid dread. Grieving had already overwhelmed me and held me prisoner in a stifling gloom.

The ambulance arrived and rushed her to the Alfred Hospital, but she did not regain consciousness and I most regretfully, was never able to say 'Goodbye'. The fact that on the drive home we discussed our soon-to-be-realised sexual pleasures continue to exacerbate my loss with yearnings that can never be fulfilled.

Blackness closed around me, and a pain of immense intensity gripped my insides, tearing my life to pieces again and again and again. I cried for hours, for days, for weeks, sobbing with uncontrollable convulsions that caused unimaginable pain. Inwardly, I screamed in anguish and torment at my loss. There was none to console me.

My son, Michael, arrived home the day after Barb was admitted to hospital and Mitzi arrived two days before her mother died. The three of us were at her bedside most of the time, but Barbara never opened her eyes to acknowledge our presence.

They had tragically lost their precious mother and now, to them, it seemed they were suffering the loss of the father they had known me to be. They had the vital need that their father be a strength and comfort, but instead, were further bereft and bewildered by the dishevelled mess I became after Barbara's passing.

I do not remember speaking to any of the visitors at the funeral. There were many of our family and friends, many faces, but none held any hope, and no one could restore me to life.

But that day at Barbara's funeral, I saw one face that puzzled me. He was a sad, elderly, bearded man. I did not know who he was, and I thought he was perhaps at the wrong funeral and did not want to cause a scene by leaving during the service.

At the end, I noticed him watching Mum as she comforted Mitzi and Michael, but he did not come to the afternoon tea served in the room adjoining the chapel.

During my many days, weeks and months of incoherence, severe depression and daily anguish, there were only two faces I could easily recall: that of my beautiful Barbara and that of the old bearded man at her funeral. I could still recall his sad eyes and sometimes wondered what became of him and if his sadness was as ruinous as mine. I remember almost hoping his sadness was in fact worse than mine, in a useless effort to somehow promote a more positive outlook for myself. We would discover ten months later, *who* he was and the extent of his suffering and brokenness.

Two weeks after the funeral, Mitzi flew back to London, resigned from her position, packed her things and returned to the only home she had ever lived in. She tried so hard to cheer me up and to get me back to functioning normally, but she also had pains enough of her own to deal with now that her mother had passed away.

I had not returned to my office since Barb died, relinquishing all my duties and responsibilities to my staff of three. I never reconsidered a return to my work. I eventually sold the practice to Hayden, who had proved himself a faithful employee for eleven years.

Michael had gone back to Canberra but would telephone late in the afternoon or early evening every day, presumably before leaving his office to go home to the apartment he shared with his girlfriend. Mitzi had departed London, leaving behind her French boyfriend, also an interior designer, to return home and be with me. Her pain and sense of loss must have been far greater than I knew at the time. I will be forever grateful for the sacrifices she made to come home.

It was therefore a momentous joy for Mitzi when, three months after returning to Australia, the front doorbell rang early one Saturday afternoon to reveal the arrival of Raoul. It was an unannounced surprise to Mitzi. She squealed with delight and hugged him, laughing and sobbing as she buried her face against his neck and shoulder. Raoul and I looked at each other and smiled with instant acceptance. We became good friends in the days that followed.

I suggested to Mitzi and Raoul that they have the bedroom that

Barb and I had shared for twenty-nine years. I had been sleeping downstairs in the spare room since Barb had passed out of our lives. To this day, I have not slept upstairs in the room that my beautiful wife and I shared.

Sometimes I would hear Mitzi and Raoul laughing at night, and although I was contented for them, it only exacerbated the suffering of my bereavement. Six months after Raoul arrived, he and Miriam were married. My pride and joy overflowed that day, but so was my sense of sadness and loss because Barbara was not in attendance. Apparently, I managed an appropriate speech and enjoyed the glowing demeanour of the bride and her groom, but I have no recollection of the reception meal or accompanying flavours. I can recall few names and faces of guests, but I do not remember what I said, nor the proceedings of the day.

For ten months I had done no work, travelled nowhere, and socialised with very few people. I remained devastated emotionally and mentally, cocooned in an empty shell. I was hollow. Grief continued to rend my insides, shredding the man I had been, and on occasions, I would still cry.

The first Christmas without Barbara was only two weeks away, and I was distressed and apprehensive at the soon approach of a time that had previously delivered so much joy.

But I was about to embark on a momentous course of great consequence, and to this day I have no explanation for my spontaneous stroll, nor do I recall the motivation for such an out-of-character undertaking. Perhaps I will never have adequate insight, but Mum acknowledged that it was by the prompting of the Holy Spirit. For me, I did not 'feel' or 'hear' anything. Although I have no rational explanation, I could not consider Mum's response to be of sound reason. Regardless, sound reason does not, in this case, offer a reasonable answer either.

Late one morning I spontaneously ventured for a walk. It was a mystifying occasion for a walk because I had been preparing to have lunch and I have no explanation why I suddenly decided on this impromptu walk. Barbara and I would on many Sunday mornings indulge in a stroll to the beach, walking hand in hand along the shore in the summer months and occasionally in winter too.

However, this was the first time I had attempted such an endeavour without Barbara by my side.

Was I in pursuit of her memory? Was she trying to show me something? These questions and many others of equally unknown origin are what I pondered as I walked along the beach on that uncanny day. Where was I going? Why? I did not know. Nonetheless, I continued.

From my house in Sandringham, I walked down to Beach Road and crossed near the football ground, continuing until I could see the familiar water of Port Phillip Bay. I reminisced sadly as I passed places where we used to go spear fishing and beyond to where the Brighton Beach Baths once stood, beside which we would go surfing when conditions allowed.

But sadness was not my only companion on that day in early December. Walking across the beach toward the edge of the water in the new summer warmth was the old man I had seen at Barbara's funeral. His hair was a mess and his old clothes hung loosely on his thin frame. He had wooden beads around his neck and on his left wrist. His pale shirt was hanging loosely with rolled-up sleeves revealing tattooed arms that had obviously been weathered over the years. Wearing faded and frayed jeans, his appearance was that of a sad, old hippie.

He turned his head in my direction and our eyes met. He still possessed the same sadness I had seen prior, but there was also something else. Perhaps it was some ancient worldly wisdom; some time-worn knowledge accompanying the survivors of tragedy. Was he also marooned in a dark place or washed onto a hostile shore? Was it his sadness that afforded me a sense of connection?

I turned to look away, but he was walking toward me. Did he remember me from Barb's funeral? I looked at him again and the sadness in his eyes overwhelmed me.

His sad appearance reflected my own despair. Sobs rose from the empty places of my inner being. In the very place where many years earlier, I received my invitation to 'manhood' from Robyn, my tears were now surrendering any remaining masculinity to the sands of Brighton Beach. My mind was telling me to stop but also was projecting unfamiliar thought patterns.

I had no understanding what my response to this unlikely encounter should be. I was lost in a familiar place.

I continued sobbing, not daring to look up, hoping that the sad old hippie would meander past, but instead, he positioned himself in front of me without saying anything. I then felt his right hand rest on my left shoulder, and I cried even more. I could comprehend nothing of this unfolding happenstance. Was he transferring further sadness to me? Was this some strange phenomena of the 'laying on of hands' that was siphoning off the final remnants of my dignity, instead of conferring blessing or healing? And yet, strangely, I did not shrug his hand from my shoulder.

He was quiet and still. I found the courage to raise my gaze momentarily to search his face, only to see that he too was crying, so I quickly lowered my head. Concern within me was speculating whether anyone passing may be watching. What conclusions might they have judged as suitable to such an unusual public display? Unaware of anyone else, I hoped no one would recognise me. Why did I embark on this walk to Brighton Beach?

Once I had been someone; once I had dignity and composure; only a year ago I was alive. My pain, my loneliness and my despair seemed untidily massed against me like flotsam and jetsam abandoned against the seawall after a storm.

The old hippie spoke. It was not a question. It was a simple statement. There was no threat, nor menace, neither was there any comfort.

"James, I'm so sorry for your loss," he said, sounding so genuine and compassionate.

His unruly appearance had not affected his memory in the ten months since the funeral. His voice seemed to reverberate back through various childhood memories and then unexpectedly leap back to the present moment. I was perplexed and astonished at my condition, convinced I was losing contact with reality and about to slide off into some unwanted malady of the mind.

Still with tears in my eyes, I slowly raised my downcast face again.

"How… how do you know me?" I asked hesitantly.

With lament, he beheld me with his sad, tear-filled eyes as though searching my face for evidence of a long-ago buried treasure. He bowed his head as the wind further disarranged his wild, windswept hair, streaked grey and tangled. He bowed his head slightly and spoke shockwaves.

"I've always known you, James," he managed nervously, yet with an assumption that I should somehow have knowledge of this unlikely information.

"James… Jimmy," he cried, "I'm Nathan. I'm your brother."

And he sank to his knees in the sand as a tide of tears flowed into his straggly beard, which matched the dried black seaweed on the sand.

New waves of high emotion rolled in, cresting before breaking. Tremors of sobbing arose from deep within me. Like wild surf dashing to the shore, each wave crashed against me, dragging me out helplessly into a sea of guilt. Tossing me through loss and dumping me with a vulnerability that left me exposed to the harsh elements of what my life had become.

Yet, there was also indescribable elation. But what do I do now? What do I say? This amazing confrontation in the most surreal of circumstances heralded the unexpected re-entry into our lives of my long-lost brother. Was this a sign from God? I yearned for an explanation to leaving the house and taking this walk. Again, sound reason offered no answer.

Yet, I cannot offer words that adequately describe what I experienced in that early afternoon. It was an exploding cacophony of bewildering emotion: joy, sorrow, fear, anger, distrust, love, concern, anticipation. What joys might there now be following this extraordinary meeting?

But there is another undeniable marvel of this unthinkable occurrence. Nathan had woken that morning with the sudden desire to visit Brighton Beach. What makes this so implausible, even absurd, as we discovered later, was the fact that he was living in Warburton and had been there for nearly a year. Nestled in the upper reaches of the picturesque Yarra Valley, Warburton was probably a drive of well over an hour and a half, but Nathan had arrived on public transport. He paid the bus fare from Warburton to the Lilydale station, boarded a train from Lilydale to Richmond, and then a Sandringham line train to Brighton Beach. Nathan has no explanation for this escapade. He calls it a 'miracle'. Days later, he shrugged with a smile, saying he had stepped out to buy the Saturday paper.

Nathan gave no account or history of the missing years, nor did he offer at least a summary to justify or explain his absence for nearly three decades. There was no insight into where he had been, where he was now living, or what he wanted to do next. After we both gained some self-composure, I urged him to come home with me. He politely turned down the offer, saying he was compelled to leave, and he would telephone Mum the next day.

"Where are you going? For God's sake, Nathan, how can you just walk away now? Why didn't you say anything to us at the funeral? Come with me, we have to go and see Mum and Andrew," I implored.

"Not yet, Jimmy. Please bro, just wait until I call tomorrow morning. Please! Please! I know you don't understand, but I'll call. I will call Mum tomorrow morning, okay! I've got her number."

He begged me not to follow. He seemed very sure of something, but I did not know what it was at that time, and to this day, I still have no idea.

We hugged each other, and both cried again before he turned and walked back to the steps which led up onto Beach Road. I watched my long-lost brother crossing the road toward The Terminus Hotel and saw him running to reach the station before the arrival of an approaching train.

I hailed a taxi to take me home so I could tell everyone that Nathan had returned. What was I going to tell Mum? How could I explain Nathan's reluctance to return home with me? How was I to assure Mum that he would call the next day? Why did I not insist on further explanations of his whereabouts and disappearance from our lives? Why didn't he tell me where he was living? Why didn't any of us recognised him at Barbara's funeral?

What joys of reunion would we now experience as a family? What amazing story would now be revealed? Will this soon-to-be revealed news bring some wondrous remedy for the loss of Dad and of Barbara? Tomorrow was already too far away as I urged the taxi driver to hasten me home.

Although Nathan's return would usher in a time of sudden joy, there were distresses to come that would lash me in a different way and tear further strips from the remainder of what little sense of self I still had. More grievous than that, it would crush the wonderful life from the sweet, God-fearing woman who had been our mother for more than half a century. Although I would have anguish, it would not become a pain unto death as our mother would suffer.

As I returned home to break the news to Mum and Andrew, I wondered what had become of the brash Nathan I had known before he disappeared. What had taken place to dismiss his zest for life, his effervescence, his whimsical, carefree nature? Why had the years pounded and trodden his youth to such an extreme degree? He, being the youngest, was gripped by age beyond mine and that of Andrew. His visage was of a man ten years my senior, yet he was four years younger.

We were to hear what had befallen my poor brother, and we were unprepared for the telling. Life is not a preparation to enable us to deal with adversity. The ghastly features of tragedy or disaster are the insidious constraints applied to the entirety of our being and our life. Some people seemingly overcome them, but I remain to wonder if people in fact do overcome. There are incidents in life that we might never come to terms with, but we move forward despite the horrible circumstances. For many, this is easier said than done.

For Nathan, this was to be the beginning of his triumph. He had made contact, and for now, was satisfied with that.

The day after the encounter on the beach at Brighton, the much-anticipated telephone call was received. Mitzi and her husband Raoul were at Mum's as were Andrew and me. It was Mitzi who answered the telephone.

"Mum?" asked the quivering, emotional voice of Nathan.

"Is that you… Uncle Nathan?" asked Mitzi who was, as she admitted later, somewhat emotional herself because she knew who it was.

"I've never been called that before," was his quiet response. "Can I please talk to my mother?"

By this time Mum was already standing next to Mitzi, trembling with emotion. When she held the phone to her ear and heard Nathan's voice for the first time in twenty-eight years, she sobbed and wailed uncontrollably for several minutes, begging Nathan not to hang up. He didn't. He'd rung from a public phone in Warburton.

Christmas was less than two weeks away. Nathan had seemingly returned from the dead and everyone was busy accommodating his return to the family and looking forward with anticipation to what would assuredly be the best Christmas since Dad had died. What a joyful Christmas this would be, and what a tremendously astonishing surprise we had to share. I so much wished that Dad could have been partaking of this celebration. I craved even more for my beloved Barbara and her presence, not only for myself, but for Miriam and Michael too.

The following week, the Saturday before Christmas day, Andrew and I were invited to Mum's for lunch. Nathan had been staying with Mum since we travelled in Andrew's car to pick him up from his house in Warburton. Nathan had requested us to be together so he could disclose some reasons he hoped would assist in explaining nearly three decades of absence.

Mum sold the family home in Hampton at auction about ten months after Dad died and was now living just ten minutes away in a three-bedroom unit in Black Rock.

I arrived with four buns and some macadamia nut cookies I had purchased from a bakery earlier that morning. Mum was so excited about having 'her boys' home for lunch. At Nathan's request, it was an opportunity, even a necessity, for the four of us to gather and listen as he shed light on the much-anticipated story of the missing years.

Andrew's car was not parked in the street outside Mum's unit, so I assumed I was the first to arrive. Both Andrew and I had keys to Mum's unit in case of emergency, so I rang the doorbell and let myself in, as was my usual habit. Mum was in the kitchen slicing fresh fruit and appearing her usual neat and happy self. I placed the two brown paper bags of bakery items on the bench.

"Andrew just called from his mobile phone, James. He and Nathan will be here any minute," Mum offered as an explanation for why I was the only one of the Darling boys present.

"They went out a couple of hours ago to buy some new clothes for Nathan," she continued. "I say, it doesn't seem like he has purchased new clothes for a long time, does it, James?" she added with a hint of sadness as she busied herself placing sliced fruit into a glass bowl.

Mum continued. "I bought some lovely berry yoghurt to have for dessert, James. Now show me what you have in the bag."

I opened the bags to reveal the contents of my purchase. "Oh James, they look very nice, but I hope you don't eat too many of these."

"No Mum, of course not," I assured. "Only on special occasions."

My special occasions were every Saturday morning from about three weeks after Barbara died. She would not have purchased such delicacies, but my visit each Saturday morning to the bakery for coffee and cake had become a comforting ritual, not a serious attempt at rebuilding my life.

I must admit, however, that since Barbara had died, I had not been eating well. I did not care much for food anymore. I had not ventured out anywhere for lunch or dinner except for the occasional morning or afternoon coffee-break at the local bakery cafe. Of course, I had accepted invitations to dine with Mum at her unit and to Andrew's and to Mitzi's and Raoul's. Unfortunately, I always felt sad and desperately lonely at these times, even though everyone was eager to deliver some cheerful and light-hearted buoyancy to my world. Alas, I longed more for my soulmate, lover and wife to miraculously reappear and infuse my life with her laughter. But her memory was all that remained.

Although I could envisage no means of ever enjoying a happy life again, I certainly had no inkling of the unwelcome grief that would soon storm into our lives. This would unfortunately be the result of Nathan recounting the reason for his tormented years and the justification he expounded to explain why he could not return.

The information we gleaned from Nathan in the few days after his return heralded many more questions than answers. However, his brief explanations offered some insight into what can only be described as an amazing adventure of sailing the Pacific, its islands and beyond.

Nathan's story was more the lament of a broken soul. There was no immediate disclosure of anything from his years 'at sea' as he called them, but that day he revealed the ghastliness of what had been perpetrated against him. He also hinted at the possibility of a horrid and criminal event that stole his Christian girlfriend from his life.

While these abhorrent revelations shocked and perplexed Mother, Andrew and I, Nathan continued to appal us further with a stupefying revelation involving Alwyn, Mum's younger brother. There would be no happy Christmas this year.

# PART 1

## ANDREW

A Long Bike Ride, My Band,
Lost Brother Returns

There were many times over the years I thought of writing about my life. Mine has been an amazing journey. My career in music from the late 60's with the successes I've had in Australia, England and to a lesser degree in America, make for an interesting story.

I certainly don't have any bad memories. My older brother, James, thinks he was a bit aloof, but I didn't see him that way. He did seem to want to be alone more of the time than Nathan and me, but he was considerate of his younger brothers. I always looked up to him to a degree, as much as adolescent brotherly love allowed.

We had our share of arguments, but there were never any physical fights. Nathan, the youngest, was always a great source of entertainment for both James and me. He was daring, adventurous, and bold, and went a little crazy from the age of about nine, but at that time I had no idea why. Nathan would turn fifty before we would learn the truth of why his personality changed. But for the three of us, growing up in the Darling house was wonderful.

My brothers and I, together with our cousins, Glenn and Terry, spent years of fun-filled adventure exploring the coastal cliffs and shoreline not far from where we lived. On many Saturdays and numerous Sunday afternoons, and of course during school holidays, the five of us would more than likely be together inventing new adventures. In winter, we would gather driftwood along the beach and on rocks and huddle together in some makeshift shelter around a small fire at the base of the cliffs.

We often climbed the cliffs and clambered over rocky outcrops searching for fossils or flotsam and jetsam or articles of value left behind or lost to the beach.

The five of us met near the Sandringham Yacht Club early one morning during the summer holidays and scour the area for lost articles. Within a few minutes, Terry found something in the bushes that caught his attention.

"Hey, check this out," he called with wild enthusiasm. We eagerly ran over to inspect his find.

We all laughed at the sight of the used condom left in a bush and used tissues lying in the sand. Still at an age where we considered sex to be frivolous and naughty, our laughter seemed the only appropriate response. But together with the evidence mentioned, there was also a pair of shorts lying discarded, with one leg inside out.

Terry claimed the shorts as the prize for finding the 'fuck nest' as we called it, and from one pocket, pulled out a wallet. Inside was a driver's licence, two five-dollar notes and some coins.

"Ha, ha, ha, ha," laughed Terry. "This dickhead lost his pants."

"Yeah! He got into hers but lost his," said Glenn, as he fell on the sand, laughing.

"Wonder how he explained that when he got home?" said James, and we all rolled on the sand laughing and suggested making plans for returning the wallet.

"Oh shit, he lives in McKinnon," said Terry as he looked at the driver's licence and then laughed loudly as he added, "and his name is Bruce. No guy named Bruce could ever get a root," and we rolled about in absolute hysterics.

Continuing our jaunt along the rocky shoreline, in and out of the bushes and eventually to the beach, we devised an amusing way to return the wallet.

"Why don't we look him up in the phone book?" suggested Nathan.

"Yeah! Great idea, Nath," agreed Glenn. "And we'll ask him if his dick is still sore from last night."

We laughed again. I don't know why we assumed sex must somehow be painful.

"Hey, why don't we buy him a get-well card with his own money," I said, and the laughter exploded again. We walked back to our bikes to ride to the nearest public telephone box and find Bruce's number in the directory.

We found a number that corresponded to the address on the driver's licence, but the initials were different, so we assumed that Bruce lived with his mum and dad. By this time, it was after nine o'clock in the morning, so we rang the number. Glenn made the call. With Bruce's money, of course.

"Hi. Is Bruce home?" he asked. A brief silence followed.

"Aha! So, he's gone to work, has he?" Glenn nodded. "Has he got his pants on?" he enquired, and the five of us laughed with delight.

"Oh, bugger, she hung up," said Glenn, putting on a sad face and we laughed even louder.

"I think Bruce is very happy that we found his wallet and I'm sure he'd like us to buy some hot jam doughnuts," said James. We all agreed and rode our bikes all the way to the Dendy Beach Life Saving Club car park because we knew there would be a hot jam doughnut caravan there. We bought Cokes and doughnuts and sat on the beach congratulating ourselves at Bruce's expense.

There are so many escapades and adventures to tell, but we all had what I consider a wonderful childhood. One evening, when both families were together, we convinced our parents and Uncle Edmund and Aunt Claudia to let us ride our bikes to Grandpa's holiday house down at Mornington. Grandpa (Mum's dad) thought it was a great idea and agreed to drive down and await our arrival and stay with us the night and take us fishing the next morning.

It is a treasured memory, both the ride down, which took us six and a half hours, with stops for drinks and food. The following morning, we went out fishing on Port Phillip Bay with Grandpa on his cabin cruiser and caught lots of flathead, some snapper and some garfish. Arriving back at the blue-grey weatherboard holiday home, Grandpa taught us how to scale and clean the fish, then he made some batter and lit the BBQ. We feasted on fresh fish and orange juice, followed by ice cream with chocolate topping. We climbed into our sleeping bags on the bunk beds that evening very content with our achievement and excited about riding all the way back to Hampton the next morning.

It was at a family Christmas gathering a few years later that they informed us that Grandpa had watched our progress all the way to Mornington and all the way home again the next day. He would park out of our sight a few kilometres ahead and when he saw us coming, would then drive on a little further, repeating the process until we arrived safely.

Glenn, Terry, Nathan, James and I were outside after lunch that Christmas day and asked each other if we had noticed Grandpa along the way. None of us had, but I think each of us regarded ourselves as much loved and cared for.

In all the fun we had, and with few arguments between us, I still wondered how three brothers could be so different? We had the same parents, the same home environment and the same opportunities. We went to the same school and shared the same bedroom until I was nine, which was when the extensions were completed on the family home. Two extra bedrooms meant that the three of us each had our own room.

Our parents showed loving affection toward each other and toward their sons and reflecting on that, I recognise it as the foundation that gave the Darling brothers an emotional stability and security. Thinking back to those days, I realise our father was very liberal with his emotions and thoughts. One of my fondest memories was one Sunday afternoon when I was eight or nine. Mum and Dad had invited some people home from church for a BBQ lunch. James, Nathan and I were being our typical rowdy selves and trying to get some of the other children involved in our antics.

Alwyn was standing at the BBQ with Dad and said, "Listen to me Allan, I'm telling you, you've got to take a very firm hand to these boys of yours or they'll become unruly larrikins."

Dad made no immediate response, but after turning over a steak he looked at Alwyn with the slight hint of his disarming smile. Then he simply said, "Well Alwyn, when God starts taking a firm hand to me, I'll know how to take a firm hand to them."

Dad was the most amazing man I have ever known. I don't remember him ever showing anger or frustration. He was calm all the time. He could bring a sense of peace to any hostile situation with his charm and his gentleness. But it was a charm and gentleness that he used with such courage and conviction that made him the strong character he was. He earned the respect, trust and admiration of everyone.

Unfortunately, he died eight years ago, just two months after his seventieth birthday. He suffered a heart attack and was hospitalised but died four days later. I visited him one lunchtime, taking a break from a recording session at a South Yarra studio for an advertising campaign. He wasn't conscious, and I knew he would make no response, but I talked to him anyway and thanked him for being such a wonderful example as a father. As I was about to leave after spending almost twenty minutes with him, he opened his eyes and looked at me. He seemed bright and alert and spoke clearly.

"Andrew, my boy, Nathan's gone sailing," he said with surprised animation and clarity. "Tell Mum I'm going too, okay?"

He closed his eyes and did not wake again. Less than an hour later he died. After his death, we thought his cryptic reference to Nathan having gone sailing signified that Nathan was also dead, but we didn't know how or where he died. None of us would know how incredible these words were until Nathan returned after many years.

Dad's funeral had a much larger attendance than I expected. There were church people, neighbours, community leaders, colleagues from the advertising industry, radio and television personalities together with all the family of aunts, uncles and cousins, except for Alwyn, who we had not seen for many years. I didn't realise how valuable Dad was to so many people, and that the lives of so many were positively impacted, not just by what he did, but by the man he was.

That sad day was made even more so, especially for Mum, because Nathan wasn't there. We didn't know where he was. The last contact Mum and Dad had received were some letters from New Zealand about nineteen years earlier. The letters told of his experience of 'getting saved' and 'filled with the Holy Spirit' and 'speaking in tongues'. But after three or four months the letters stopped coming. Mum and Dad waited expectantly for nearly six months before flying over to look for him, but to no avail. We didn't know where he was or if he was dead or alive. The pastor of the church Nathan attended offered no clues, nor could the police provide any leads, and they returned broken-hearted after two weeks.

Personally, I thought he was most likely dead as he had no reason to cut himself off from us. We knew he had gone to New Zealand to be with a girl he met while he was at art school. He was a talented artist and was accepted into the prestigious National Gallery of Victoria Art School. The girl was at the nearby Conservatorium studying music and was an accomplished cellist.

With typical Nathan brashness, and accompanying exaggerated imitation of cello playing, he told me one evening that he loved her because any girl who plays with something between her legs has got to be fabulous. Nathan's comic portrayal of a cello-playing female had both of us in fits of laughter.

"What's so funny up there, you two?" echoed Mum's cheerful call from downstairs.

"Cellos, Mum," laughed Nathan in quick response. "We're laughing at cellos."

"I don't see what could possibly be so amusing about a cello," Mum called.

Nathan and I continued to joke about it for a short while before going to our rooms, James was not there because he was living in South

Yarra. I'm sure he would have initially shown himself to be above such vulgarity before cracking up with laughter too. I continued to be amused by Nathan's remarks after I entered my room and closed the door. He was a very funny brother, and I loved his sense of humour and ability to make fun of just about anything, even his new girlfriend.

The girl's name was Diana, and the relationship lasted nearly two years until she had to suddenly return to New Zealand to care for her much younger brother. Her parents were killed when their car ran off the road in bad weather. Soon after Diana returned to New Zealand, Nathan left art school and went to New Zealand too.

Mum and Dad had received letters from Nathan nearly twenty-eight years ago relating the testimony of his 'salvation experience'. They were overjoyed and lived in hope all those years, but Dad didn't live to see Nathan again. Now there are many times I wish Mum hadn't either.

We had no idea we would not see him for nearly twenty-eight years, nor did we know the turmoil that his unexpected, but very welcome reappearance would bring.

For twenty-eight years all I had were memories of my funny young brother. Sometimes I missed him greatly and would imagine him walking into my house with his cheerful, happy grin. He would probably say, *"Hi Andy-old-boy, have you missed me?"* and burst into fits of laughter at the joke of having been gone for nearly three decades.

Nathan, at times called me Andy-old-boy, and he sometimes referred to James as Jimmy O.B. or J.O.B., which stood for Jimmy-oldest-brother.

James was sometimes lost in his own world, which meant I spent more time with Nathan. This resulted in a relationship of great brotherly affection and we were best of mates as well. We laughed at everything, mostly because Nathan seemed to have the ability to find humour in every situation. He was very popular at school and even the teachers had a respect for his quirky antics.

When I was seventeen and Nathan was fifteen, he and I were laughing at something we had seen on television one evening. It was something quite absurd, and I suggested we form a comedy team and come up with some absurd riddles.

"Good idea, Andy-old-boy," he said enthusiastically. "You can be the straight man and I'll get all the laughs and attention."

"You already are, and already do," I answered.

"Okay then, let's get to work," he said as he jumped up from where he was lying on the floor, turned off the television and headed for his room.

The two of us sat in Nathan's room that Friday evening and spent two or three hours writing the most ridiculous nonsense and laughing until we were sore. Fortunately, if for no other reason than fond memory, I kept everything we wrote that night. Occasionally I would browse through what we'd written and smile sadly to myself and shed a tear for my beautiful little brother who once filled my life with such merry laughter.

Looking at it today, I can only wonder why we laughed. There are so many crazy riddles that make no sense at all today, but at the time they seemed hilarious. On the following evening we put on a comedy show downstairs so that Mum and Dad could gauge our potential.

"Why did the lawnmower ride a horse after visiting the dentist?" I asked Nathan.

"Because corn flakes don't grow on trees," he answered.

Mum and Dad looked at us quizzically as we both burst out laughing.

"I don't see anything funny in that at all," said Mum dryly.

"Okay then, what about this one?" I asked and continued, "Why did the empty red wine bottle buy a comb?"

"Oh, that's easy," said Nathan, and from a Simon and Garfunkel song he sang the line, *"She said the man in the gaberdine suit was a spy."*

Then I sang, *"Be careful his bow tie is really a camera,"* which was followed by Nathan asking a question.

"How many cameras are there in a packet of chocolate biscuits?"

"That depends which colour of the rainbow wrote a number one hit single for an old car tyre," I replied as I tried to keep from smiling.

We looked at Mum and Dad for a response and Dad, with his typical good nature, lovingly said, "Well, that's very good, boys. I think all you need to work on is actually making it funny, but apart from that your work is very obscure and a trifle cryptic."

Nathan and I weren't disappointed, but obviously we did not pursue comedy as a career. We wrote many more crazy riddles and I look at them with amusement but recognise that they are crazy and not really funny. But it was so much fun at the time.

During the years that Nathan was missing, James and I became closer as brothers. On many of occasions when we were together, James commented that perhaps he was partly to blame for whatever happened to Nathan.

I would counter his guilt by telling him the truth; that Nathan had always been a law unto himself. Nothing that any of us did or failed to do could have prevented whatever happened to our younger brother.

Tragically, what happened to Nathan could have been and should have been prevented if one church leader had been more attentive to abuse issues. Instead, like so many others in church leadership, he dismissed the claims of the victim and supported the 'poor' elder who was being accused.

Both James and I had become successful over the years. James, as an architect who had designed some great residential and commercial buildings, and I in music, film and television. During my mid to late teens, I developed a keen interest in music and reached a high standard, firstly playing the piano and then the guitar. With two of my friends from school, one guy I knew from church, and a younger guy we knew from our days hanging out at the beach, we formed a band.

After four years together, having two singles that sold reasonably well, touring all states of Australia, and to New Zealand, we decided to go for the big time and headed for London. It was a big risk and one that saw us break up after only eight months. Tony, the youngest, had become a heroin addict while we were in London and died of an overdose at twenty-two. We were devastated.

Wally, the bass guitarist, married a lady who was twelve years older and very wealthy. We all knew the marriage wouldn't last but we were wrong. They had three wonderful children and are still together today.

Wally has kept busy doing session work in England, France and Sweden and occasionally goes on tour with some very well-known jazz musicians. He also co-wrote a couple of big hits that charted well in the early seventies and has become a wealthy man in his own right. We catch up at least twice a year and always jam together just for the sheer joy and pleasure of making music.

My career in writing music for film, theatre, television and advertising has taken me around the world and although I've been very successful and to a greater degree, lucky, I haven't made the millions that Wally has made. Not that I'm complaining. I have a beautiful home in Beaumaris near the beach and have a very lucky or 'blessed' life.

Chris, the keyboard player was the quiet member of the group and today is a pastor of the lively church that Mum now attends. We catch up at least once a year, even though he only lives about three kilometres away in Cheltenham.

Mike, the other guitarist returned to Australia immediately after the break-up and went to work in his fathers' building company. Today he is the managing director of a land development and building company, but I haven't seen him for over ten years. Actually, I have no desire to see him again. He's become a total prick and made more enemies than he has dollars.

In our years together we had a lot of fun, got into some difficult situations and gave in to all the temptations of alcohol, drugs, groupies and easy sex. But in all that time I never saw Chris let go of his commitment as a Christian. Although I did not hold to the teachings I was raised on, I always admired Chris's courage and integrity. I think that is one of the main reasons why I still count him as a good friend.

But there is a greater impact that Chris has had in my life which will unfold towards the end of this story. A man of proven and tested faithfulness and integrity is most beneficial when you are desperate for answers during times of great stress or tragedy. These times were on the way, but we had no idea that they would wage war against our seeming, easy lives.

In 1976 I married Tanya, whom I first met in San Francisco in 1974. She had been a dancer with The Russian Ballet Company and defected during a season in New York and had eventually become involved in the theatre world in San Francisco. We have two beautiful daughters, Michelle who is twenty-four and Giselle who is twenty-one and we also have a nineteen-year-old son, Adam, who is at the National Institute of Dramatic Arts (N.I.D.A.) in Sydney.

James and his wife Barb were wonderful to our children. I think James tried to be the older brother to my son, Adam that he thought he had not been to Nathan. But Adam and Michael, James' son, had a 'brotherly' connection from a young age, despite their five-year age gap.

Over the years, as both our families grew closer, the guilt that James carried about Nathan still haunted him. I gave up trying to assuage his torment with encouragement. It was not his fault. There was nothing he could have done. There was nothing I could have done either. Nathan was 'sailing' somewhere in the afterlife and nothing could bring him back, just as no miracle could bring Dad back.

Of more concern though, was that James remained so distraught at Barb's death. He had been withdrawn and inconsolably depressed and I was concerned for his well-being. Fortunately, Mitzi was doing a wonderful job trying to ensure her father was at least eating properly. But we wanted his mental and emotional state to get back to normal.

The suddenness and tragedy of Barb's death had changed James to his detriment. He was living a sullen, lonely life of grief and I hoped for his sake that he would find another woman with whom he could enjoy the remainder of his life.

Sometimes 'suddenlies' disrupt our world: like Barbara's death, Dad's death and presumably Nathan's death too. But suddenly, about ten months after Barbara died, our younger brother, Nathan reappeared. It was an elation that saw me weep tears of absolute joy at Nathan's 'return from the dead'.

He had been back in Australia for over a year and had been living in a house up near Warburton. He had come to Barb's funeral service but said nothing to anybody and didn't stay afterwards. None of us recognised him, not even Mum. Our attention that day was on James, Mitzi and Michael. In the most unusual circumstances, James encountered Nathan ten months after the funeral. Now, after an absence of nearly twenty-eight years, we were reunited with our younger brother who looked much older than both James and me.

He rang Mum the morning after he had encountered James on Brighton Beach. I arrived just minutes before the call came through and after a while, spoke with him too. But I did not speak to the brother I remembered from so many years ago. He sounded different, even distant. We arranged to pick him up the next day and bring him back to Mum's for a while so we could catch up on why he had been away so long, where he had been and why he had not contacted us. That would prove to be a difficult process for him.

The following morning, I drove Mum and James to Warburton to get Nathan. He was back. It was as strange as it was surprising; it was miraculous, yet the 'miracle' would also bring some foreboding. It was so unbelievable that he had returned. But why had he waited so long to contact us? Why go to Warburton on his return to Australia after an absence of twenty-seven years? Where had he been all those years? We soon sensed all was not well.

He was quiet and morose and not the exuberant Nathan we had known and loved all those years before. There was no adventurer left. He was quiet and uncertain, and the bold confidence and brash daring had vanished, how long ago I could not tell. The drive back to Mum's consisted mostly of answering his questions about our lives while he mostly avoided answering questions we asked about his past twenty-eight years.

We had no idea how our lives would be changed by his sudden return. Nathan had come back to us but the cost we would pay for his return would be the shattering destruction of all that we valued of our early years in the church. All the service my parents gave, the sacrifices they made of their time, their money and their loyalty and faithfulness, was to be assaulted in a full-frontal attack.

It was less than a week before the Christmas that promised so much. Nathan was back, and although he was a very different person to the brother I remembered him being all those years ago, I determined to show him my full support, encouragement and love.

On the Saturday before Christmas, I took Nathan out to buy him some new clothes and some Christmas presents. He was unsure of himself and found it difficult to communicate or answer questions with any more than minimal sentences. I wanted to get information about the missing twenty-eight years.

Nathan had been back with us for over a week staying with Mum, and for most of that time he slept. The hours he was awake were spent watching television. He would constantly change channels with the remote control as though looking for something. He was morbid and sad and Mum was worried for him. We all were.

On our return from shopping to have lunch with Mum and James, I hoped to get some answers from Nathan about the lost years. We were all looking forward to lunch. Mum had prepared everything in her usual immaculate way and even though it was a casual lunch, she had set the table with her best dinnerware and cutlery.

When Nathan and I arrived at Mum's after shopping, James was already inside. We walked in to find James pouring glasses of Chardonnay for Mum and for himself.

"Oh, the boys are back," Mum said, beaming as Nathan and I walked into the kitchen. "Nathan, go and put on some of your new clothes before we have lunch together," said Mum as she carried a plate of sliced mango and avocado into the dining room.

Mum was so meticulous with every meal. When we were growing up, even breakfast was served with great care. Peanut butter and jam were spooned into small bowls to avoid 'unsightly' jars on the breakfast table; the milk was always poured from a jug on cereal or into a cup of tea, and a platter of fresh fruit was sliced and neatly presented in the centre of the table.

The lunch on this Saturday was typical of Mum's way of presenting an enjoyable meal for her three boys. But that day much of the cutlery would be left untouched, as would much of the food. We heard things, horrendous things, from Nathan that we were unprepared for.

# PART 1

## NATHAN

Art, Encounter, Boat Trip,
Abuse, Shark Attack

I could never see what all the fuss was about. Growing up was the easy part. Being a kid was an everyday adventure. But being a grownup was difficult, & despairingly so as I would find out.

I remember my childhood as the best part of my life. But that is now polluted. My manhood was stolen. With it went my faith, trust & confidence. I don't think I've ever been a man, just a boy. I can only hope that I will at least die a man. I will never be an old man. I will just be an aged decrepit. Perhaps my final brave, manly act will be to face eternity with great courage. A future-less life is a place for the dead.

Although my younger years hold many great memories, they contain one dark memory. It clouded my life. Sometimes it would be like a fog. Sometimes it would be a dark, thunderous billow. It wouldn't go away. No cleansing breeze blew strong enough. Years later, a darker storm would come. It would hail nightmares in my daylight hours.

The youngest of 3 brothers, I always seemed to be the centre of attention. For the wrong reasons, usually. Almost everyone thought I was reckless. I never saw it that way. To me, there were lots of exciting things to explore. The exploration took me to some exciting places. But a certain degree of abandon entered my life at 9. I went through some character & personality changes that began after I witnessed something no young child should see. No young child should be abused that way either.

Human beings are not designed for abuse, not to receive it, nor to inflict it. All-the-more-so for a minister in the church. His abuse destroys a human heart with irreparable damage. He injects an evil poison that circulates through the soul. It prevents the effectiveness of an antidote or a healing balm.

But first, I'll recall a good example of reckless exploration which occurred when I was 10. Some of my friends at school told me about the opening to an underground storm water drain between Dendy Beach & the Middle Brighton Baths. Apparently, you could walk up it for quite a distance before crouching down to go further. I told Jimmy & Andy, my two older brothers about it & suggested we should go to see it.

Their ready agreement was probably more for my protection than a real desire to explore the drain. They knew that I would go alone if they didn't come. So, one Saturday morning we told Mum we were going to the beach. We spent most of our summer on the beach anyway. But she had no idea where we were going that morning. We'd usually be away most of the day. Mum would make a few sandwiches or give us some money to buy lunch. That morning she gave Jimmy some money.

It had probably taken about half an hour to get there. But to me it was worth the ride. We left our bikes on the grass above the entrance to the drain. We jumped from the top of the sea wall to the sand. I peered triumphantly at the large opening. There was only a small narrow stream of water & a dank, stale smell.

The lure of venturing into the darkness & what lay beyond was all the motivation I needed. I went in first. My brothers followed. We walked up as far as we could before we had to stoop lower to walk up to where the tunnel became two smaller drains. Jimmy & Andy wanted to go back, but I was already on my hands & knees & continuing up the smaller tunnel on the right-hand side.

Jimmy kept telling me to come back, & I kept refusing. I had to keep going. The space was too small to turn around, so I continued to crawl forward. I became scared. It was dark & smelly. I was thinking about what would happen if the pipes got smaller again & I had to go out backwards. I think it was panic that drove me forward. But I also 'sensed' a dark evil close behind me. I had to get away. I knew who it was. I'd heard his voice before. I kept going faster & faster, getting hotter & hotter. I was becoming desperate for fresh air & light.

After what seemed a long time, I came to a small opening. I was looking out from gutter-level onto a street. I didn't know where it was, but looking further up the drainpipe, I could see another source of light. I had no choice but to continue. It seemed to take forever to reach this point of light, but I emerged from the drain near a railway bridge & climbed out of the drain to the street. My knees were bloodied from the constant pounding on the concrete pipes. But I hadn't noticed the pain until I got to the street.

I had no idea where I was but crossed the road to wash my knees at the hose in the front yard of a house. I started walking down the street to get back to the beach. An elderly lady pushing her shopping cart asked me what I'd done to my knees. I just laughed & told her that I'd be praying a lot. Evil had chased me through the darkness in the drain. But I got back to the light. I won.

I was about to cross over New Street when I heard Jimmy call out, "Nathan, you dickhead."

He was on his bike riding toward me. Because he was my big brother, I thought he must have come looking for me. But he was also on his way to Church Street to buy chips, potato cakes, dim-sims & Coke. Jimmy 'dinked' me up to the fish & chip shop. The man in the shop put everything in a box, which Jimmy put on the back of the bike. I sat in front of Jimmy as we rode back to the beach where Andy was waiting.

I remember that day with great fondness. It was one of those times I loved being Jimmy's little brother. With me holding on to the middle of the handle bars & Jimmy in control holding the handle grips, I felt safe. We got back to find Andy sitting on the grass under the shade of some ti-tree. He wasn't interested in where or how I got out of the drain. The three of us were hungry & we ate on the beach with our backs against the sea wall.

As we sat there, three of Jimmy's mates from school walked down the beach. I liked Jimmy's mates; they were big, rough, carefree & unruly, & they were my kind of guys.

Moose was the biggest & a lot of guys at school were a bit wary of him. He had been to our house on occasions & was always pleasant. He called me 'Twerp' & always said it with a friendly smile. Then there was Daks, who had a wild mop of black curly hair & finally Betsy-Lee, who apparently got his nickname from a story in a schoolbook.

It was Moose who first got Jimmy interested in spear fishing. Jimmy only had a home-made hand spear while Moose had a spear gun. Later that summer, Moose accidentally shot himself in the chest with his spear gun while he was getting out of the water. Fortunately, he survived.

"Got any chips for us?" asked Moose, as the three of them approached us, walking on the sea wall.

"No, we finished the lot," replied Jimmy to Moose's hope of a free feed.

"Oh, bugger!" he said, but with no malice. "Shit Twerp, what happened to your knees?" asked Moose as they jumped down to the sand.

"He crawled up the drainpipe & came out up near the railway line," replied Jimmy.

"Bullshit! Really?" said Moose.

"He did. I saw him & his bloody knees about to cross over New Street. He's a bloody dickhead," Jimmy added.

"I reckon he's a tough little bugger," commented Daks. "I reckon he'd even ride his bike along the top of the bloody sea wall."

I couldn't resist the challenge of winning their admiration. I ran down the beach to the steps. Then back along the path to where we'd left our bikes. I put my bike up on the ledge of the sea wall &

trying to look as fearless as possible, set off to see how far I'd get. I made it all the way to the steps without falling off. An act of bravado to prove that I was stronger than the evil I had seen. I had to stay strong. I have to stop the evil.

Rapturous applause & guffaws rose from among the guys as they stood to their feet & cheered. Even Jimmy was clapping & cheering. It seemed I could never do anything to please him, but that was a day that was different. I'll never forget it. Crazy really when I think of it. What an absurd memory of brotherly love.

The three of us went to an all-boy's school not far from where we lived. We would usually leave home together but arrive separately. I was always in a hurry to cram in as much fun before school started, which was always with morning assembly.

I did reasonably well at school academically. Always passed. Always got good marks in exams. My reports seemed to gloss over my antics & concentrated on my achievements. My greatest love at school apart from art was gymnastics. I'd train most lunch times with my best mate, Brownie. We started together in gymnastics because we were both shorter than a lot of the guys who played football & other contact sports. We figured we wouldn't get hurt in the gym. But we did. Many times, too. By the time we finished school four years later, we were tough balls of rippling muscle & felt good about our physiques.

My physique came in handy during my arts course at the Gallery School. Some students occasionally asked me to pose for them. One girl asked me if I would come to her apartment in St. Kilda one Saturday afternoon. She had some ideas she wanted to experiment with. I arrived one cold winter Saturday after getting the train to Windsor & walking the rest of the way. Her bed-sitter apartment in an Art Deco block was neat & clean & warmed by a large radiator.

We talked about art for a while & she showed me some of her

nude studies. I knew what she was going to ask long before I got there. She was just slightly plump, but not overweight. She had the greenest eyes & curly auburn hair. We didn't have a lot to do with each other at art school. We'd had lunch over the road in the gardens earlier in the summer months, but other than that there was no relationship.

"So Red, (my nickname at art school because my work mostly featured the colour red) would you mind posing for me?" she asked hesitantly after explaining the effects she wanted to achieve with charcoal & of all things, candle wax.

"Sure Rae, I'm interested in your ideas," I replied, although I wasn't really. "But do you mind if I ask you to do something for me?" I continued as I started to unbutton my shirt.

"Ask away," she said as I caught the look of triumph in her eye.

"I'll pose naked for you, but you have to be naked while you do the sketches," I proposed. I felt certain she would say no. I would have posed anyway.

"Okay, that's fair," she said, & started to get undressed. She threw her clothes onto the black satin doona cover of her neatly made double bed.

My eyes followed her every simple move. Her soft white complexion mesmerised me. I was already naked. Watching her undress had aroused me. We stood looking at each other.

Looking at my growing erection she smiled & said, "I can't draw you like that, can I?"

The way she spoke was so calming. Not judgemental & not offensive. Her calm, soft tone & the understanding look in her eyes gave me much confidence. I couldn't have been embarrassed. She came over to where I stood & gently kissed me on the lips.

Both of us stood with our arms by our sides as we kissed, moving our tongues around each other's lips & inside each other's mouths.

I'd arrived at Rae's apartment at 1.30 that Saturday afternoon & by 10.30 that evening we'd made love 4 times: on the bed; in the bed; among red, brown & cream cushions on the black shag-pile rug, & finally as she straddled me while I sat on a dining chair.

We drank a bottle of port together & some orange juice. We smoked 2 or 3 joints during our time together. & we laughed long & hard as we made jokes about famous artists: Pick Arso, Reppa Titian, Piss Arrow, Dove Inchy, Randy Whore Hole, Caravagina Oh!, Cuntstable, Self-Adore Darling, Rump Brand, Canned in Ski, Rootbens & Turn 'er over. We laughed a lot. It was a wonderful afternoon & evening. A day of memories I still cherish.

All afternoon & evening we remained naked as we drank, got stoned, laughed & screwed. We got into her bed about 10.30 that evening. We laughed some more & talked before finally falling asleep together. I still remember that day with the fondest memories. I often wonder what became of the lovely Raelene. She did no drawings of me that day or any other.

No one would have guessed the Darling brothers were from an evangelical Christian background. The 3 of us turned away from church & church authority. Mum tried to get us to go but Dad never made us go once we were about 15 or 16. He'd just say, "Don't worry Beth, just leave them in God's hands."

Dad was so confident in his faith. I greatly admired his strength, but I tried to get as far away from God's hands as I could. I was the last one that anybody would have expected to get 'saved'. But that was exactly what happened about 28 years ago, in New Zealand.

I'd gone to New Zealand to live with Diana. I'd met her during my first year at the National Gallery School while she was studying music at the Conservatorium. She played the cello. I thought we would be together forever. She was my soul mate but left me when I got involved in drugs after arriving in New Zealand. She has since travelled the world performing in orchestras. Apparently, she married a Swedish recording company executive.

Thinking about Diana saddens my heart deeply. I had her name tattooed in a heart on my left arm. I never got over losing her. That was the worst thing about my involvement with dope. She didn't like what it was doing to me, & I couldn't see that it was doing any harm. I was too blind to see that I was acting differently & treating her differently.

There were some other women I had relationships with after Diana, & 4 very extraordinary months with a girl I'd grown up with in Melbourne. Her name was Julie & she used to go to the same church our family attended. We laughed about the unlikelihood of our chance meeting. Neither of us knew the other was in the Solomon Islands at the time. But this chance meeting came about 7 or 8 years after my life had been totally fucked up.

After Diana, I thought there would never be a girl in my life with whom I wanted a permanent relationship. But about 4 months after losing Diana, I met Rachel one evening while I was walking around Auckland. None of my hippie friends were with me that night. I had left the house late that morning after taking LSD. Although I was coming down from my trip, I was still high.

I saw a fresh-faced, red-haired girl walking toward me. She looked so alive. It was as though a spotlight followed her every move as she stepped sideways to avoid other people.

Walking up to me, she nonchalantly asked, "What are you doing tonight? Want to come & hear some live music? I know a place where this guy is going to play guitar & sings his own songs," she announced with confident exuberance.

She was attractive in a very natural way. Light freckles dusted her cheeks below her hazel eyes & auburn hair brushed her creamy neck & shoulders. I was smitten. Everything about her made me weak at the knees. Her vibrancy, confidence, & boldness astounded me.

"Well, I'm Rachel, what's your name?" she said, looking up at me with eyes I thought would melt me before I could answer.

"I… I… I'm Red," came my stammering reply.

"Red? Wow! That's my favourite colour. Is it short for Redmond?" she enquired.

"No, it's short for Redgum," I responded, not too confidently.

My hippie friends in the house in Auckland came up with the name 'Redgum' because I was from Australia. It also followed on from the nickname I was given at art school.

We crossed the road & walked a short distance up a side street. We went into what looked like a bookshop. At the rear of the shop was a room that was about 30 x 50 feet. There were 6 or 7 tables with chairs around them at the rear of the room. There were shelves with books on them & a small kitchen area. To the left was an even smaller stage. There were a couple of girls setting up some folding chairs in rows facing the stage. The stage was about six inches high & only about 4 feet by 6 feet. A guy who looked to be in his mid-20s was setting up 2 microphones near a stool which was positioned centre stage. A black, 6-string Ovation guitar was on a stand to the right & on the left was a Maton 12-string guitar. In between the guitars was a cream, vinyl clad amplifier.

His excellent equipment immediately impressed me. I had started playing the guitar when I was younger (only because Andy played). I knew a few things about guitars. What I was about to hear would change my life. I would never be the same again after that night. I could not have imagined that a guy with a couple of guitars could introduce such power, majesty & peace in this small insignificant room.

There was no dimming of the lights. No spotlights came on. There was no formal introduction. Everybody seemed to know exactly when things were going to start. We were all seated.

There were about 40 guys & girls who looked like they were in their late teens to late 20s. As soon as everyone was seated, the guy with the guitar sat on the stool & picked up a book from the top of his amplifier.

"Come unto me all you who are heavy laden & I will give you peace," he read.

I turned to Rachel & whispered in her ear, "He's a bloody Jesus freak."

"Shh, just listen, Red," she said with a disarming hint of a smile.

Phil played & sang & quoted occasional verses from the Bible. He also told some amazing stories of the miracles Jesus had done in his life. Everyone seemed so enthusiastic. I remember thinking these people are either fucking crazy or they're right. At the time, I didn't care which. I loved the things Phil spoke of. I was sitting there with tears in my eyes but had no idea why. I didn't care anyway. This was the first time I'd cried in front of other people since I was a young boy. For some reason, it didn't seem to matter. There were others who seemed to be just as emotional.

I had been in church 100's of times in my younger years but had never experienced this. After about 45 minutes of playing, singing & talking, Phil asked everyone to stand.

"Let's pray," he said.

"Father God, we thank You for Your grace, goodness & love. Love us tonight Lord, extend your goodness & grace to all who are gathered here tonight. Dear Jesus, work your miracles in the lives of those here tonight. Amen."

Everyone said "Amen" & I noticed I heard my own voice among them.

Unstrapping his guitar, Phil got down from the small stage & walked toward me. I reached out my hand to shake his, but instead of shaking my hand, he hugged me. I started crying. No man had ever hugged me before. I remember wondering if perhaps I was a poofter & Phil was supposed to be my boyfriend. This couldn't be possible. I was too smitten by Rachel. I looked at her & noticed she was crying too.

"What's your name, brother?" asked Phil.

"Redgum," I said through my tears.

"Jesus wants to welcome you into his kingdom, brother with his love & forgiveness. Will you ask Him in?" he asked.

"Y... yes," I stammered.

He put his hands on my shoulders & asked me to invite Jesus into my life; ask for His forgiveness & for the promised gift of the Holy Spirit.

I heard myself pray in a way I had not prayed before, even though I had been brought up in the church. "Forgive me, Father. I have sinned against you. Please Jesus, come into my life & make me clean & new."

I don't know where the prayer came from. It wasn't something I remember saying in my earlier years, but I'm sure that's where it originated. No sooner had I spoken these words than I felt a great weight lift off me. I felt like I was going to float away. It was the most beautiful thing I had ever experienced. I knew God! Well, I'd at least been introduced. The elation was powerful, undeniable. Jesus really was alive & now He was alive in me. Phil continued to speak to me.

"Jesus wants to fill you with the Holy Spirit now, Red. You'll have a strange sense of unspoken words on your tongue. Speak them out, man, pray in your new heavenly language," he encouraged.

"Fill my brother, Lord Jesus, fill him now with your precious Holy Spirit."

I began speaking words in an unknown tongue. It was like I was filled with light & when I opened my mouth to speak, all that came out was light. Waves of joy & love washed over me like a continual cleansing shower. I knew my life would never be the same again. This was not a natural human feeling or emotion. I knew it was heavenly.

That proved true for the next few months as I grew in faith. I stopped doing dope, I stopped swearing, & I went to church whenever it was open. If something was on I'd be there.

My commitment to the church & my new family was one hundred percent. I went to the mid-week Bible study on Tuesday nights. Prayer meeting on Thursday nights. Youth group meetings on Saturday nights & church every Sunday morning & evening. After about 3 weeks, I had my long hair cut shorter & shaved off my beard, leaving a neat moustache. My hippie clothing, I gave to the guys I'd been living with. I moved into a bungalow at the back of Ross & Andrea's. Ross was the youth leader at the church. It was the same church that Rachel went to. We'd often spend time talking on Saturday nights after youth meetings & Sunday after church. Mostly we talked about what God was showing us.

Rachel's dad, Robert, was one of the elders in the church. He was an insurance salesman & although he was very traditional & conservative, he showed a very pleasant manner toward me. It was obvious to all that Rachel & I were more than just interested in each other. Robert's kind nature seemed to me to be a seal of approval. Rachel's mum was always full of life. Always cheerful & bright, always busy & always complimenting others, including me. Her name was Alice & she looked more like she was Rachel's sister than her mother. Her younger brother, Rodney, was a funny kid. He reminded me of myself.

Life was wonderful. I'd written a couple of letters home, telling Mum & Dad about my new life. They were very pleased. Dad wrote a lovely letter that I have kept all these years. I still read it occasionally & cry such bitter tears. At times, I break into uncontrollable sobs, wanting my father to be with me. But he died a few years ago, & I didn't know. How could I know? I hadn't been home or been in contact for nearly 20 years by the time he died.

But a joy-filled life can suddenly become a total tragedy as I would soon discover. The evil destruction of my life, my dreams, my hopes for the future, my relationship with Rachel, my commitment to my faith was about to unfold. I could never have prepared for it, nor would I ever recover. Rachel's life would also be fractured. She would fall into the abyss of depression as a result of what she suffered. But it would be many years before I would find out what had happened to her.

I was to become a wretched, lonely, & broken old man before I was 23 & would have no contact with my family or friends for nearly 28 years. What a tragic waste of time & of life.

Rachel & I had discussed the possibility that God meant us to be together. After a youth meeting one Saturday night, we decided to pray & ask God to show us if we should be together as man & wife. We did not tell anyone what we were praying. The next morning after church, Joe, who was a big Dutchman & an elder in the church, called me aside.

"Nathan, how vood you like to be makink some goot money?" he asked in his no-nonsense manner. "I tink you maybe gonna be needing some money, yeah?" he sneered as he looked toward Rachel & then back at me with a sly smile.

My first reaction was distrust. I sensed lust in his eyes for Rachel. He was a fat, ugly man with a ruddy complexion & I'd had little to do with him in nearly 10 months at the church. He made his offer the morning after Rachel & I had prayed about our future together. I thought that was evidence of God's answer to our prayer. Wrong!

Joe led the Bible study on occasions & often prayed aloud at the prayer meetings in his gruff, bombastic tone. His wife always looked sad & had a down-turned mouth & ill-fitting false teeth that made a clacking sound on the rare times when she did speak. Joe did not seem to treat her well, nor did her son, Mark, who was their only child. He was a suspicious character who studied people through his half-opened eyes. His arms were usually folded across his chest & the superior smirk on his face & a goatee beard made him look evil. How he got the position as leader of the younger youth group is a mystery I'll never understand. What he did to some of the younger girls is a disgusting evil. But this information was not made known until over 2 decades later.

Joe was a professional fisherman & would sometimes be at sea for over a week. Mark wasn't interested in fishing or boats. I'd been told about Joe's boat by Robert. It was well equipped even though it was more than 20 years old.

For 6 months Joe had employed a young guy in his early 20s named Don, who always accompanied Joe when he went to sea. He had come to church a few times but apparently did not enjoy it. Don was from Canada & lived on Joe's boat.

Early one morning, two boys went down to do some fishing from the wharf. They saw Don on the boat hanging from a rope by his neck. They dropped their fishing gear & ran all the way home to raise the alarm. Poor little buggers They must have been totally freaked out.

Nobody knew why poor Don hanged himself on Joe's boat. But I know. I could so easily have taken that same escape. Something evil was done to Don. He tried to talk to the pastor but was thrown out before he could finish his story. Did Don also wake up each morning feeling like he had been murdered? I felt that way for years. Still do sometimes. Is there any value in going to sleep knowing that you'll awake to the nightmare of losing your life all over again? Seemed to me that Don didn't want to wake up anymore. Poor bugger!

***

**Book 1 - Feb 88**

*What do we make of the man who violates someone's life &
soul with death
but the victim must visit that death every day for the rest of
their life?
We can make nothing.
There is no substance or worth in him to make even an ignoble
vessel.
He is bereft of feeling. He ponders nothing, meditates nothing,
creates nothing.
The beauty & wonder of nature are unrecognised by him.
He dwells in darkness, breathes darkness & exhales darkness.
He cloaks his victims with his darkness so that he cannot see
their suffering.
His evil smirk prevents him hearing their screaming anguish.
He delights his wicked heart by believing they want more of
him.
So fat, so incredibly ugly, so evil, so vile – there are none who
want him. He is alone.
He takes his lonely despair & plunges his rabid ugliness into
sweet innocence.
Taking sweet virtue & innocence, he smothers the young
flame with his black heart.
He rapes life. His mind & heart are foul sewers of fermentation
in his fucked-up brain.
His warped lust defiles others, but he believes it is an act of
love
it is his love for himself.*

**Book 4 - June 99**

*My lamp has gone out.*

*The oil is rancid with the foul odour of death.*

*The wick cannot burn.*

*It can only decompose*

*It will decompose for the rest of my life.*

*My life, my virtue, my innocence, are betrayed.*

*I am decomposing - but I have courage.*

*It is all I have now. It is enough. It is precious.*

*My courage will sustain me.*

*My precious courage to which I hold fast –*

*it will vindicate me & will avenge.*

*Oh courage, restore my lamp,*

*renew the oil, replace the wick.*


**Book 4 - June 99**

*I had to control my anger. I could not allow my anger to lead*
*to remorse.*

*I could not violate his life as he had so cruelly done to me.*

*He desecrated the wonderment of life.*

*He destroyed the joyous mystery & enchantment stored for*
*the untouched & unblemished.*

*Although I had been no saint, I could in no way prepare*

*to be abused by the devil posing as a man of faith & prayer.*

*No, I could not violate his life, but I could end it. I must. My*
*courage must be steadfast.*

*Even death is far too merciful for him.*

*Come my great courage, let us rise up to take back our*
*honour*

*let us once again taste the sweetness of respect & admiration.*

*we will be the conquerors now, yes,*

*we will claim our innocent inheritance.*

*So, my courage, lead me to this act to avenge those for whom*

*no mercy was shown.*

*Avenge without vengeance. Come my courage, let us remove*

*the pains, the stains,*

*the slime & grime from Don & from my own inner turmoil.*

## Book 8 - Dec 83

*Sometimes I think my life is not worth living. I'm apprehensive*

*of the future. So much damage has been done. It can't be*

*undone. I cannot retrieve the stolen years. My life was taken.*

*Everything I loved & believed is changed. Everything is*

*strange.*

*Everyone I love is now a stranger. Sometimes I think my only*

*choice is to kill myself.*

*Escape from strangers in strange places. I'm strange, I'm*

*alone.*

*I'm a stranger to myself, a danger to no one else.*

*Come courage, the time has come to release the trapped*

*torments.*

*No. No, I can't do that. That would be cowardly. Oh, isn't*

*courage wonderful.*

*Courage gives me control. I can control his life now.*

*Yes! Yes!, That's what I can do. I can't be a coward.*

*Not now. No, I won't do it to myself. I'll do it to him. He took*

*my life. But I am courageous.*

*I am strong. I will take his. No, I'm not crazy anymore. I have*

*courage - I am courage.*

But here's the funny thing. In my courage, I want to kill the fat, ugly bastard but not sure how. Then the stupid shit falls overboard during some rough weather. Surely an act of God, I surmised. All I had to do was thwart his effort to get back in the boat. Not only that, but I had noticed 1 or 2 sharks in the water not too far from the boat.

So, there's 'his fat ugliness' screaming for me to throw him a rope. I saw the panic on his face & heard it in his voice. But instead of throwing a rope, I threw a wooden crate which had a steel mesh bottom. The crazy bastard tried to avoid it, but it hit him on the shoulder. That was my contribution. But his thrashing & yelling had attracted the reason for his panic.

It was as sudden as it was terrible. The force of the attack was shocking. Joe was lifted out of the water by a big shark. It had one of Joe's legs in its mouth. He was momentarily out of the water as the shark turned in the air & fell back into the water. They both disappeared in a splash of foam. Seconds later, Joe thrashed to the surface, floating on his back, arms flailing but minus 1 leg. I saw a look of stark, naked terror on his cold, white face.

He looked at me with utter desperation while his life was bleeding profusely into the Pacific. The shark returned. The huge jaws with its rows of white razors claimed Joe head-first. It bit through his fat white belly & dispersed his guts in the midst of the whole bloody mess. All that was left was his naked, fat arse, his balls & little uncircumcised cock. A couple of smaller sharks fought over the remains. That was the last I saw of fat, ugly Joe.

I was shaking. Whether I was trembling with cold or fright, I could not tell. I just stood looking into the water at the blood & pink foam & the swirling melee of smaller sharks as the boat rolled about in the rough sea. It was mid-afternoon & now I was alone on the boat. I had no idea how to navigate back to the harbour.

The bastard was dead. I was shocked. I was elated. I was scared. I was thirsty. I had to get the story right. I needed a drink. I went down into the kitchen. I drank a bottle of orange juice.

Why was I so happy to see his utter panic? Why was I so happy to see the indescribable fear etched across his pale face? Was I throwing the crate at Joe or was someone else invading my mind at the time? Why didn't I throw a rope or a lifebuoy? Why did I throw the crate?

It wouldn't have made any difference to the outcome anyway. There was no time for the fat bastard to get back on the boat. There was no ladder over the side. How could I have lifted the fat bastard back into the boat?

My memory of everything is very clear. It had to be. To this day, I retain these pictures of what happened that day. Funnily enough, I like the pictures.

But from that day to this I am still horrified. I don't sleep easily. Nightmares force themselves into every crevice of my conscious & subconscious thoughts. I have seen something more horrible that I have yet to describe. I don't know how to tell the story.

**Book 2 - April 82**

*Do you know what it's like*
*to have a life & lose it,*
*but still have to live*
*the life that's lost?*
*Yes, this weight sinks me down*
*but I know I didn't choose it,*
*but I'm the one*
*who has to pay the cost.*
*It's a price too high to pay*
*but I pay it every day*

*& I can't seem to pray*
*the pain away.*

**Book 7 – Sept 79**

*I woke up this morning. What a tragedy. Sometimes I pray*
*that I won't wake up.*
*Life hurts & the pain searches out places in me where it*
*hasn't been & makes itself at home.*
*These are places where God should dwell.*

The relentless pressure of being pursued & harassed by hopelessness was my ever-present burden. My only comfort was the sea, even in the wildest wind or storm. I loved the storms & sometimes hoped they would claim me for the wild appetite of the sea.

**Book 3 – Oct 81**

*My life is a dark room with a high window. I can't reach to*
*see out.*
*I've been cheated.*
*My life is completely fucked up.*
*I'm fucked up.*
*I'm fucked.*
*Fuck!*

**Book 1 – March 85**

*Who wrote this wretched madness in my life?*
*Who ripped the pages from my dreams & left me future-less?*

**Book 4 – Dec 79**

*Why has this been done to me?*
*Why am I now undone?*
*Oh Lord, hear my cry!*
*Can you endure such gut-wrenching cries from a human heart?*

## Book 2 – May 85

*Lord you seated me in heavenly places but another, who was*
*also there, has defiled me.*
*I have been dashed to the earth & under the sea with*
*deliberate malice.*
*Now I lie tasting the dirt of torment & bitter salt that violently*
*shakes the*
*confidence I'd once known.*
*There are screaming thoughts in my head.*
*My heart longs to escape from me. It is breaking my bones*
*to get free.*

## Book 3 – August 88

*Once I was escaped out of the snare of the fowler but*
*now I am entwined in the deadly mesh of a fisherman's net.*
*How could you set me free only to be abused by someone*
*who calls you Lord?*
*Why did you allow this?*
*I need to drink some cool, clean water but I can't swallow.*
*Nothing good wants to enter me – torments & fears are*
*trapped inside me.*
*Hold me Lord. Love me.*
*Catch my deluge of tears.*
*Heal my agonised distress.*
*Help me!*

Why did those whom I trusted & loved, tell me it would be good to go on the boat with that man? Why did some say it was God's will? Even the beautiful young woman in my life also saw the possibilities for God to work in me through this time at sea. "You will be a fisherman," she said, "just like many of the disciples of Jesus." I loved her so much. I cry so much.

### Book 3 – September 88

*Agony, I hate you! Fuck off pain! Fuck off! Fuck off! My head is full of screams.*

The fact I have hurt someone causes my heart to ache with a pain I have never known. I can't turn back the clock; I can't take back the words. My intent & motive came from a desire to go forward, but I was foolish & unthinking. I now question my own thought processes & am convinced I have gone mad. I'm totally fucked!

Praise God! I got saved! I wanted to please God. I wanted to do what was right. I trusted God. I trusted his people. I trusted his ministers. I trusted the wrong one. I was told he would help me.

*Stay positive, brother! Remain faithful, brother! Hold on, brother! Release your faith, brother!*

*Fuckin' bullshit! I might as well pray the rosary. Why not pray the fuckin' hosiery?*

*Don't worry,*

*Everything will be okay.*

*I'm invisible now.*

*No one can see me anymore.*

# PART 2

## JAMES

Mum and Dad, Bastard Alwyn, Regret

From here, the account of my life, our lives, goes horribly awry. Actually, it went awry when Andrew, Nathan and I were young. Of course, we knew nothing about the situations and relationships in the church that were not only reprehensible but depraved and blatantly illegal. Evil furtively ensnared and assailed those whose harmless virtue should have been cherished and protected. Nobody possessed any knowledge of these tragic evils except the perpetrators and of course, the victims. Many years later, one of the victims would divulge her horrendous years of abusive ordeal to Nathan. Other victims came forward, but would not be listened to, instead they were criticised for trying to stir dissent among the people and harm the ministry.

Nathan then disclosed the details to Mum, Andrew and I, after which the largest of fans became operational and flung copious quantities of sewerage through our earliest childhood memories to the present day.

But perhaps at this stage it is appropriate to communicate some family history to hopefully introduce an understanding to the next portion of the story.

Mum and Dad had lived and were raised in near proximity to each other in Brighton. Mum's father, who we lovingly referred to as Grandpa, was a dentist. Dad's father, whom we addressed as Grandfather, was an architect. Both men were held in high regard in the community, and both were long-standing members of the local yacht club.

Because of this association and friendship between these two men and their families, Mum and Dad had known each other for as long as they could remember. Mum delighted in telling us on numerous occasions that she was only about eight years old when she decided she wanted to one day marry the man who would become our father. Dad was five years older and had never seriously considered her until he was twenty-three.

Dad finished school and decided he should enlist in the Air Force to serve 'The King, The Commonwealth and his homeland, Australia. He was sent to England to partake in a special training course with the Royal Air Force, but the war ended soon after his arrival in England. He remained in London for a further eighteen months after agreeing to take advantage of an opportunity offered by one of the English officers of the Royal Air Force with whom Dad had become acquainted.

The opportunity offered was to take a junior position in the advertising agency owned by the uncle of the English officer. When Dad returned to Australia a year and a half later, he had little difficulty securing a position in a well-respected agency in the development of the burgeoning advertising industry that flourished after the war.

Eighteen months in London prevented Dad from seeing the development from girl to attractive woman of Beth Raymond. In a little less than twelve months after Allan Darling returned from England, Mum's childhood dream became a reality. I used to love hearing Mum relating her memories of milestones that were the romantic courtship leading to the eventual proposal.

Even at a young age I decided that I too would be like my father and charmingly court a young lady as a lovely as my mother.

But, there is no explanation I can offer or rationalise how, from my mother's family, with the same background of abundance and opportunity, can emerge two wonderful children and one who would become such an evil destroyer of young innocence. I speak of my wonderful mother and older brother, Edmund and Alwyn, the youngest, a malevolent narcissist.

The new minister of our church was Pastor Alwyn Raymond. We had been attending the church for two years when he became the pastor. Although I have no clear recollection of the circumstances leading to him becoming the pastor, I do recall it being an unsettled period. There was much impassioned debate within the congregation. I am mindful of one man outside the church one Sunday morning saying, "This is not right before God," but I had little idea of what he may have been alluding to and I cared even less.

Many years later I would come to understand that Alwyn was self-appointed and had usurped the role after Pastor Tom died unexpectedly.

Even though the new pastor was my uncle, I disliked him intensely. I could not understand why Alwyn was a 'fat-pig-of-a-man' while my mother and Uncle Edmund were such affable, loving, wonderful people. Although Uncle Edmund and Aunt Claudia were not members of our church, we socialised with them regularly. Often, we would be found in the company of our cousins, Glenn and Terry. We were separated only by a fifteen-minute bicycle ride and the five of us whiled away many adventurous and fun-filled days in our younger years.

After being (self) appointed as the new pastor, Alwyn required, in fact insisted, that Andrew, Nathan and I address him as Pastor Alwyn. Prior to him assuming the pastoral role, we had called him Uncle Alwyn. I was to discover within two or three weeks, how unyielding and determined was his narcissistic vanity for this title.

It was after church one Sunday morning and my mother requested me to approach and ask Alwyn if he would like a cup of tea. I obeyed and then inadvertently made a regretted error.

"Would you like a cup of tea, Uncle Alwyn?" I asked.

In a voice clearly audible to all the family and other church members, he scalded me for not addressing him as Pastor Alwyn.

"James," he said tersely, "I HOLD A POSITION OF AUTHORITY as appointed BY GOD and YOU have to LEARN TO RESPECT my position. Now, go OUT of the room and then return and ask the question again, BUT WITH DUE AND PROPER RESPECT," he demanded.

I experienced much humiliation, but I did not realise that I was being bullied. At that age, I could not have concluded that his brutal verbal conduct was for the sole purpose of making himself appear significant to himself. Narcissism blinded him to his obvious belligerence and offences. Rather, he bestowed on himself an obstinate and authoritative self-importance and self-honour.

The previous pastor at the church had been likeable and very friendly toward everyone, from the youngest to the eldest. Even though I found church to be a boring waste of time, Pastor Tom was one of the very few who made my time in church remotely bearable. Unfortunately, he tragically died, leaving his wife and two young daughters.

That was about the time when Uncle Alwyn, who seemed to dislike children, arrived. Within a few months, certainly less than a year, he had assumed 'guardianship' of Pastor Tom's girls, Robyn and Julie. (Pastor Tom and Glenda had come to Australia from England and had no family in Australia at this time.) Alwyn was also a constant 'minister' and 'support' to Glenda, the wife of Pastor Tom. Most assumed that he would or had married Glenda, but it would be more than forty years before we would find out the truth. (Although we do not report or explore this anywhere in these pages, I can reveal this. More than forty years after Pastor Tom Phillips' death, Alwyn Raymond is being sought by police for questioning in relation to the strange and untimely demise of the beloved pastor. One wonders what secrets, long hid, may yet surface from the darkness of their hiding.)

Pastor Tom was a happy, joyful Englishman who loved God, his family and the 'flock' which he served with faithfulness. After he died, there were rumours about his unfortunate and early demise. Nobody seemed to be acquainted with the exact knowledge of how he died, but it was because of some 'mysterious illness' that proved fatal.

Alwyn told the congregation that the matter would not be talked about and suggested the best course of action was to pray for Glenda, Robyn and Julie. Although Alwyn did not actually say that God had taken Pastor Tom to prevent him from committing an evil sin, he certainly intimated that thought. He stirred up enough discomfort and alarm among the people to ensure they remained attentive to what he was saying and where he was 'leading' them.

It was during this unsettled period that my extreme dislike of church became even more well established. Up until that time, I participated in praise and worship, albeit as an appeasement to my parents and others of the congregation, rather than out of love for God. The contrasts between Pastor Tom and Pastor Alwyn were distinct, and I definitely did not like Alwyn. I remember praying that Pastor Tom would come back, which was impossible, but I prayed fervently that Pastor Alwyn would go away.

Pastor Tom had gone and a grotesquely evil man, Alwyn Raymond, usurped his role as a wonderful husband and father. A man who would many years later, be exposed as a sexual abuser; a paedophile hiding behind the pulpit and perhaps, even a murderer.

As if Mum would not have sufficient mental and emotional agony to handle hearing Nathan's ghastly story, she now had to somehow conduct a safe passage through one more bombardment. However, this final barrage fragmented her remaining tattered faith and dignity, and her health deteriorated. Our wonderful mother, a woman of honour, stability and gentle strength, was now unrecognisable. In stark reality, she had been deeply traumatised and would not recover from the intense personal turmoil generated by these disclosures.

For twenty-eight years I had no contact with my youngest brother, nearly nine years ago my father passed away and a little less than a year ago, I lost my wife. Now, in this ghastly loneliness and gut-wrenching agony, I am losing them all over again. The wheels of torment relentlessly roll over my being all day and all night long. Finally, when I was perhaps reaching a place of resigned acceptance, even anticipating that I may chance upon a way forward, my world and my life were laid waste once again.

Regret and remorse overwhelmed me in remembrance of my unexpected encounter with Robyn and Julie on Brighton Beach when I was seventeen. My prayer 'to get lucky' had been answered, but the channel by which it arrived was far removed from being a blessing. Finally, nearly forty years after the event, I understood where that sweet, sixteen-year-old girl had grasped the familiarity to perform such an act with me.

# PART 2

## ANDREW

Mum Dies, The Netherseas,
Nathan's Lost Years

I have lately realised why the three Darling brothers and many other children and even some adults at our church, turned their backs on the so-called 'things of God'. It was undoubtedly because of 'Bastard' Alwyn. That was the title by which James, Nathan and I referred to him over the years he was there, despite the fact he was an uncle.

He was a pig of a man and a pig of a pastor. He was even a pig of a pig. We hated him because we had to treat him with respect, but we could see that he didn't deserve any. Why Mum and Dad and the other adults in the church continued to support him and his position as pastor is something I will never understand. He was rude, arrogant, abrupt, abrasive and a grotesquely pathetic excuse for a man, let alone a so-called 'man of God'.

I would like to find him and bring before him everyone whose life today is in some way screwed up by his ugly, self-justified abuse. He has much to answer for but there will never be anything he can say or do to repair the damage he did; even, as it turned out, to his own sister, our mother.

Today I witnessed one of the most undignified and pathetic sights I have ever seen. I sank to my knees to hug a dishevelled, whimpering woman kneeling on the floor in the house of neighbours whom she did not know. She was calling out, "Come back! Come back! Come back, my penitent ones. I'm covered, I'm covered. Please, come back."

What madness had caused such a scene? What torment had driven this woman to bury her head in the residue of a fire long extinguished. The path of her tears had eroded pathetic pink streams down her grey, ash-covered face. Her cries were shrill, more animal than human.

The madness grew from hearing that her young brother, Pastor Alwyn Raymond, was a sex abuser who preyed on young girls. The torment followed Nathan's revelation of all this information and the horrendous abuse he had suffered, and which tragically kept him separated for so many years, from all he knew and loved.

"Andrew, Andrew, my lovely boy. Come, come on, pray, repent for them Andrew, quickly, before Jesus gets here," she lamented.

She had sought refuge in the house of a neighbour. The lady of the house had let Mum in because of her distressed state. She knew which unit Mum lived in and had gone over the street to ask a neighbour for help. Fortunately, Mum's friend, Edith, who lived next door, had my telephone number. Edith rang to inform me of the situation. I was the one who came to take Mum home to her unit.

My beautiful, loving mother was now a broken shard of what was once a beautiful vessel. She never fully recovered and deteriorated further after a mild stroke. We were now forced to find her a place in a nearby nursing home. I only wish she could have lived a little longer to see what I refer to as Nathan's final triumph. And to see the value of her years of faithfulness as a praying mother and faithful servant of the church and of her Jesus and more importantly, of her family.

What a horrible end for a woman who gave so much, was loved by so many, and served God so faithfully for so long. The Christmas that at first seemed to promise so much, was the time our mother began to die. The Christmas to celebrate Nathan's return was palpably distressing, and now even more so, because the woman who had been so expectant and excited was now distraught and deteriorating.

How should a mother react to such horrible news of the abuses perpetrated against her youngest son? What would be considered an appropriate and normal response to her learning her younger brother Alwyn, the pastor of our church, sexually abused Robyn and Julie, and apparently two or more of the other young girls in the church?

Her overwhelming joy at Nathan's return had been beautiful to see. James and I both remarked about her youthful sense of well-being and delight. Four months later, after what is believed to have been another stroke in the late morning, Mum died in a local private hospital in the early evening of the same day.

If only Nathan hadn't told his story. But I can't blame him, he had to tell us. The poor guy had lived with agony and torment for more than a quarter of a century and had received no counselling or therapy. It seemed that at last, he felt, or hoped, he was in a safe enough place to talk and finally be released from the pain, anguish, guilt, fear and devastating regret. How he survived all those years with such torment swirling like a storm in his mind, is a testimony to his gutsy determination to somehow get through it.

I know Nathan does not see it this way, but to be honest, I have the greatest admiration for him. A revolting and ghastly abuse was perpetrated against him. The damage was immediate and devastating, destroying his perception of life. As a result, he withdrew from much of society, from the church and from his family. Hearing of this tragedy sickened me and angered me. I have never been so angry. I never imagined that such anger existed.

As varied and challenging as my life has been, I've been very lucky and somewhat sheltered. I've seen a lot of unpleasant things and been in some very unpleasant situations, especially the death of our dear friend and drummer, Tony, but it still seems for the most part, that I've had a favourable existence.

But hearing Nathan's story of his 'lost years' has also left me enthralled. Certainly, the reason for the lost years is gut-wrenchingly appalling, but what Nathan did and the places he went are, in so many ways, both enthralling and inspiring.

In the days, weeks and months that followed the telling of his story, I spent a lot of time talking with him and asking many questions of his so-called 'lost years' as he now refers to them. What an incredible story! What an achievement! During these talks, I wrote down some of the things he told me and on occasions, with Nathan's permission, recorded the things he said. I read through the many notebooks in which he kept records of his tortured thoughts, along with details of places he visited and people he met.

This became a quest for me and for Nathan and I think it was good therapy for both of us. I originally thought it would make a great movie for which, of course, I would write the music. (I have already put down a few ideas.) I was rediscovering my brother and finding new qualities and new admirable traits. We laughed, cried, talked and even played some music together. Nathan had taught himself to play guitar over the many years of separation, and I was impressed with his level of competence.

Because I had recorded this part of his story in writing and showed it to a journalist friend, Derek Lenere, the idea for this book was birthed. Derek encouraged me to speak to James and Nathan about writing the history that led to such an unbelievable tale. For all its amazing colour, adventure, improbability and tragedy, it is matched so beautifully by what has only recently been made known and now takes the story in another direction.

That part of the story I will definitely leave for Nathan, but he asked me to help him write of the 'lost years' because I'd spent so much time with him researching through his fifty-five notebooks. There is another book that could be written from them.

The section I have included here is just the start of the recollections. Nathan has included other anecdotes in the parts he has contributed to the story of the Darling Brothers. We will hopefully get to write the remarkable story of more than two decades, 'missing' at sea.

All those years ago, three brothers drifted away from the faith they were raised in. Now, over forty years later, they were to discover potential reasons to again believe, trust and possibly even forgive. Not that we have returned to our faith, but I am now inclined to be less critical and less cynical. As crazy as it sounds, there are times I find myself singing some of the old praise and worship choruses we knew in our younger years.

# The 'lost years' of Nathan Darling

*(The following anecdote is written as a result of recording conversations I had with Nathan.)* **- Andrew**

Joe was dead. Although there was no body to verify his demise, there was certainly no motive to suspect anything other than a tragic end to the experienced professional fisherman. Only one man knew the truth and he'd been questioned at length by police, port authorities, a psychologist, the coroner, journalists and church people and at all times the story was exactly the same. It was also obvious the event severely traumatised the young man who witnessed it.

So many questions were asked by so many people. The attention exhausted Nathan. He was mentally and emotionally fatigued and wanted to get away from it all.

One very crucial truth to point out here is that at no time did Joe's wife or son ask Nathan any questions. According to Nathan, Joe's son Mark didn't seem to care. He stood around with his arms folded, stared suspiciously through the slits of his half-closed eyes, and kept himself aloof from any sign of emotion that might signal weakness.

Nathan did not go back to the house he'd been living in with Ross and Andrea, the youth leaders at the church. Instead, he chose the unlikely option of staying on Joe's boat. All he wanted was to spend time with

Rachel, but she'd changed so much in less than a week. She was morose and depressed and seemed unable to look Nathan in the eye. She not only avoided his gaze but avoided him altogether. No one understood why she was behaving this way. She stopped going to church and refused to speak to Nathan.

This was a time when Nathan desperately needed her, but she was not the same girl he had left less than a week earlier. Why? What had Nathan said or done to offend her? After all, she was the one whose opinion persuaded him to go in the first place. But it wasn't just Rachel who was different, Nathan was different too.

Neither of them knew of each other's horrendous abuse. Joe perpetrated Nathan's; Rachel had been violated and sexually abused by Mark, Joe's son, the day before Nathan went on the fateful voyage with Joe. Both were traumatised, but neither of them had the opportunity to talk to the other nor to anyone else. Undoubtedly there would have been a different outcome if they had been able to talk together. But what had happened to them as individuals was not an easy thing to talk about, especially when the events involved such diabolical sin. They also thought family, friends, and church would reject them if they told anyone.

I doubt very much that this would have been the case. I like to believe that someone with maturity and understanding would have recognised the abuse and offered love, support and comfort. As much as I like to believe it, often the opposite is the cruel reality. Why is it that so many victims are the forgotten sacrifices to the lusts and evils of perpetrators who hold positions of trust? Nathan and Rachel's pastor, Pastor John, offered nothing but condemnation and refused to hear what he called 'these horrid, false accusations.'

* * *

Through the remainder of the afternoon after Joe's death, the sea remained rough, but as the sun set, the wind eased and by midnight

Nathan was steering through a much calmer sea. Despite the grief Joe had caused and seeing the ferocity of a random and unpredictable sea, Nathan kept his mind focussed on returning safely. He knew Joe had taken a north-easterly course from Auckland, so Nathan monitored his return by heading southwest with the aid of the large compass set into the control panel in front of him.

The welcome sunrise revealed a clear day ahead. By now, Nathan had been awake for nearly twenty-two hours. It would be another fifteen hours before he would be back in a New Zealand port. (He would miss his intended destination by about 150 kilometres, arriving off the coast of Tauranga, south of Auckland, around 8.00pm in the evening.)

After the sun had risen, Nathan went below to get some food and returned to his position. There was a kettle, coffee and sugar in the wheelhouse and a few biscuits, so Nathan drank coffee and ate biscuits to pass the time and stay awake during the long night.

On his return from the galley, he tried the radio for the first time, wondering why he hadn't thought to use it earlier. Listening for anyone who might help him, he eventually took the headset from its hook, put it on, and using the name of the vessel for identification, began what he hoped was transmitting a message.

"This is *The Netherseas*, can anyone hear me? This is The Netherseas, is anyone there? Over," Nathan called.

"Good morning *Netherseas*, where are you? Over," came an almost instant reply. Nathan was elated.

"I'm somewhere in the Pacific," Nathan replied.

"Well, that's a long fuckin' highway bro. What's your nearest street corner? Over?"

"Not a clue mate, everything's flooded out here."

Nathan was enjoying this light-hearted exchange after his horrendous ordeal.

"Well, can you see the bottom? Over," came the response.

"No mate, but I've got a bigger problem," Nathan replied, deciding to get serious.

"What's that, bro?"

"The skipper is dead and I'm not too sure how to get back to Auckland," said Nathan.

"Fuck! Are you on your own? Over."

"Yep."

"Hang on, bro. Hey Alf!" came the shout.

Whoever shouted was away from the microphone, but Nathan could still hear him in the background.

"Hey Alf, get up here quick. Shit! Fuck me dead! What the fuck was Joe doing out there with a crew of one?" the shouter ranted.

Nathan assumed the guy did not know he was still clearly audible. The radio went quiet for a few seconds before Nathan heard another voice.

"Hello *Netherseas*, what's happened to Joe? Over," was Alf's concerned enquiry.

"He fell overboard mid-afternoon yesterday and was taken by a huge shark before he could get back on board," Nathan replied.

"Shit, mate. Are you serious? Over," came the alarmed response.

"Yes, I'm afraid so."

"My name's Alf, what's your name, son? Over."

"Nathan."

"Got much experience at sea, Nathan? Over."

"Just two very unpleasant days so far," was Nathan's response.

Again, Nathan heard the voice in the background. "Fuck! Why the fuck did that fat shit take out just one guy... and one with no experience?"

Nathan then heard Alf say, "Settle down Mick. Let's get Nathan back first, that's priority one."

Alf continued, "Okay Nathan, stay on the radio, son, and we'll see what we can do to get you some assistance. Over."

"Okay Alf, thanks."

Another voice came over the radio.

"Hey Alf, this is Bob Rittman on *Deep Strike*. Over," came the call.

Hey, Bobby on the '*Striker*'! What the fuck are you doin' up so early bro?" called Mick cheerfully in the background.

"Been listening to what happened to Joe," Bob replied before continuing, "Hi Nathan, I'm Bob. Listen mate, I think we've got you on our radar. If it's you, we should have visual in thirty to forty minutes. We'll be visible port and aft if you're where we think you are. Over."

"Thanks Bob, I'll keep watching out for you," responded Nathan.

Alf's voice came back on the radio.

"Morning Bob," said Alf. "We got back last night. Bloody glad you're still out there. Over."

"That's okay Alf. We'll do what we can. Over."

"Okay Nathan, hold your course mate and wait for a visual with Bob. Over," said Alf.

"Okay, thanks Alf," Nathan answered.

"Nathan, this is Bob again. Have you had any sleep? Over."

"No Bob, been awake for nearly twenty-eight hours," Nathan replied.

"Don't worry bro, one of my boys will take the wheel when we catch up. I suggest you slow down, okay? That way, we'll catch you sooner. Over," said Bob.

"Thanks Bob," Nathan replied wearily, as he looked for an instrument that indicated the speed. He had suddenly become aware of his exhaustion.

"Hey bro, this is Mick. Shit man, did you see the whole fuckin' thing? Did you see the shark? Over," asked Mick seriously.

"Yes Mick, from about twenty feet away," answered Nathan.

"I tell ya what Nathan, that fuckin' boat is jinxed. Did you know Donny the Canadian? Over."

"No, I didn't Mick, but I know what happened to him," answered Nathan.

"Yeah! Fuckin' awful way to go. Poor bastard. Wonder why he hung himself?"

Prompted by the reminder of Don's suicide and together with a lack of sleep, the horror and trauma of the previous day returned. Nathan began to sob. He tried to stop but couldn't control the overwhelming emotion. He had to turn off the microphone. He didn't want Mick, or anybody else, to hear him crying.

"Hey, Nathan! You there, bro? Over."

Nathan didn't respond to Mick's continued calls. It took him about ten minutes to compose himself. Mick's voice kept coming over the radio.

"*Netherseas, Netherseas*, this is *Tauranga Tora*, Over." Mick continued his calls and seemed to be getting more concerned with each one.

After Nathan stopped sobbing and composed himself, he turned the microphone back on.

"Sorry Mick, I had to go to the toilet," he offered as the reason for his absence.

"Shit man, why didn't you tell me? Over."

"Er... sorry Mick, but... um... it was a bit, a bit of a rush," Nathan replied hesitantly.

"Probably Joe's cooking mate, he was a shit cook, ay? I went out with him and Donny a coupl'a times. Twice too many fuckin' times for me mate, said Mick reflectively. "And he always perved at me when I was taking a shower on deck. I didn't like the leering, fat bastard."

The friendly chat between Nathan and Mick continued until about half an hour later when Nathan looked back and saw a boat on the horizon where Bob said he would be. It was another twenty or thirty minutes before Bob's boat was alongside. Deep Strike was a bigger boat than *The Netherseas*, and Nathan could see three men standing at the front railing as it approached.

Nathan had been awake for over twenty-eight hours, had stood at the wheel for over sixteen of them, and although he was much further south than he thought, he was at least heading in the right direction.

# PART 2

## NATHAN

A Near Miss, Joe's Abuse,
Vera's gift, Home Again

Now at last I can tell my story. Tell of how I was sinned against. How I was abused. I know it would have been better if I'd come back home to Australia after it happened. I would have had support from my family. Dad would have known what to do. But I couldn't come back because I had not been heard. I stayed away for 27 years. When I finally returned, I went to Warburton for a year. I don't know why. I lost my family. I lost my future. I lost my self.

The painful regret of not returning sooner eats into me. Obviously, it would have been better for Mum too. But it wasn't just my story that destroyed her world. Not only did I tell my mother & brothers what had been done to me, but also of the sexual abuses Robyn & Julie were subjected to by Mum's younger brother, Alwyn.

We now know that at least 1 of the other men in the church, & possibly a 3rd had also sexually abused both girls. This information was told to me by Julie. The 3rd man did not actually touch her, but she believes that he had sexually abused Robyn.

Adding to this devastation was me relating to Mum, James & Andrew what Mark, Joe's son, had done to the lovely Rachel. It was another destructive element in my life. Although I did not discover the reasons for Rachel's withdrawal from my life for 27 years, I was still broken-hearted. Not just for the finality of the end of our relationship, but it also gouged out my vision for the future.

Neither Andy, Jimmy nor I liked Uncle Alwyn, or Pastor Alwyn as he insisted we call him. We called him Bastard Alwyn. & you can't be pastored by a bastard! The 3 of us think he was the main reason we resisted & turned away from the church. Some of the other children turned away too. Some families left that church within a few months of Alwyn becoming the pastor.

Alwyn told the congregation that those who left rebelled against God. He tempered this statement by adding he would continue to pray for them. He would pray for as many years as it took for them to come back. Alwyn also told the people that the sign of their repentance would be evident when they came to him & say *"Sorry,"* for making his pastoral duties so difficult.

*"I will continue in prayer for these brethren,"* he would often say. *"I'm answerable to God for these people."* There are no words he can say now to make anything right. He preached that he was answerable to God. If God holds him to account for his words & his actions, then no amount of words will save his ugly arse from hell. Demons will squeal with delight when they discover that Alwyn's fat arse, little dick & balls are on the menu. But I had greater reason to hate him.

Mum & Dad, my brothers & I were driving home from church one Sunday when I realised, I had left my bag & books behind. Dad turned the car around, hoping someone would still be there. We got back to find that Alwyn's car was the only one there. I was in luck. I didn't want to see him, so I went around the back to the Sunday school room where I'd left my bag.

Thinking Alwyn would still be in the church; I went in very quietly only to see something that should never be seen. Robyn was holding her dress up & standing facing Alwyn with her legs apart & without her panties while he sat on a chair. He had one hand between Robyn's legs & with his other hand was rubbing his penis.

He stopped immediately & flew into a rage. My mouth went dry instantly. My feet were like lead. I wanted desperately to run. I couldn't move. I was in a nightmare. It was daylight. I was at the church.

The look on Robyn's face was one of fear. It was a look I would never forget. It would haunt me for the rest of my life.

"COME HERE, NATHAN," Alwyn demanded. I could see & hear his great anger. I was afraid. I thought he was going to hurt me. Robyn started to cry.

"Stop the silly snivelling girl," he barked. "NOW LISTEN TO ME

NATHAN, what I am doing here is good for Robyn, but you won't understand, so DON'T EVEN THINK OF TELLING **ANYBODY of** what you've seen. **DO YOU UNDERSTAND ME**? Do you want me to pray that SOMETHING **BAD** WILL HAPPEN to you & your family? GOD LISTENS TO ME. YOU SHOULD KNOW THAT BY NOW."

His demeanour, his words & his rage frightened me. All of Pastor Tom's teaching & encouragement about the love of God vanished instantly. I dared not cry. I was fearful of being spoken to like Robyn had been. I was fearful of him hitting me. I was fearful of him hitting Robyn too. I was fearful of him speaking again. He looked so fierce, even unrecognisable. His face was contorted & dark grey. To my young mind (I was 8 or 9 at the time) it seemed like I was looking at the devil himself. To this day, I have never been as scared as I was that day. I had to destroy that fear. I didn't know how...at the time. This was the same fear that chased me up the drain a few years later.

Witnessing what Alwyn was doing acquainted me with evil. For the rest of my life I tried to overcome the fear with acts of daring & wilful disregard for my own safety. My personality began to change. The search for revenge & recompense had begun.

I did not want Alwyn to hurt me. Robyn looked wretchedly unhappy. I assumed bastard Alwyn was hurting her. Something ghastly was happening inside me. Something ghastly was happening to Robyn. How do I stop Alwyn? My heart turned upside down. Alwyn has to die. I wanted to kill Alwyn, Bastard Alwyn.

"I...I...I just came back to get my bag & books," I stammered. "Can I please get them?"

"Get them & get out...&...DON'T...YOU...SAY...ANYTHING."

I collected my things & ran outside to go back to the car. I was in a state of shock. I tried not to see what I had seen. I tried not to hear what Alwyn had said. My memory was cruel. Why couldn't I forget already? Why won't my heart go back in its rightful place? As

I was running from the church everything seemed to be shaking—buildings, trees, clouds in the sky, everything jerked & swayed as my heavy feet laboured me to safety.

Because of my shock, I didn't check for traffic before crossing the road. A car came to a screeching halt. It stopped about four or five feet from me. I stood staring at the front of the car. Frozen. I didn't know what to do. The driver got out to make sure I was okay. Mum & Dad also hurried over to me. Everyone could see the terror in my eyes.

They thought it was because of the near miss with the car.

Mum walked with me back to the car. Dad & the driver of the car chatted very briefly then shook hands. As Dad was about to get into the car, Alwyn emerged from the front door of the church & crossed over the road to our car.

"What happened?" he asked Dad very abruptly.

"Nathan ran onto the road without looking. He's okay, but he's had a very big fright," Dad replied.

Alwyn glanced down at me through the car window with a punishing glare. The ferocious gaze of his eyes was hurting me. I looked away. After that day, I never looked that man in the face again. He wiped the life from my face that day. Forgiveness for him never crossed my mind. I wanted to kill him.

Something dark & horrible happened in my heart that day. What was the seed that had just been planted in my heart? Was it for murder? He hurt my friend. At the time, I had no idea of the damage he was doing. I wanted him to die. I didn't want him to pray for bad things to happen to me or my family. I told myself not to tell anyone what I'd just seen. I told my young innocent self that I would kill him one day.

How ghastly for a young mind to be tormented by thoughts of killing someone. There was something crawling within my body &

in my mind. My body was a cocoon. A newly formed grub began its metamorphosis. It would eventually emerge to darken every day.

Two or three days after this event, I began having nightmares. I dreamed I killed Alwyn. Then I dreamed I killed any man wearing a grey suit, a dark blue jumper & a yellow ochre shirt. (That's what Alwyn was wearing that Sunday morning.) I always woke to the terror of feeling evil. These dreams occurred weekly for about a month & then became monthly & from the age of 12, lessened to 4–6 times a year. Eventually, the dreams stopped. I remember the day, but it was not a good day.

I was silent on the way home & for the rest of the day too. But I was glad I caused that driver to brake so hard. It provided an obvious reason why I was so shaken & terrified. I wanted to cry, but was still too scared. From that day, I never cried again until the night I got saved. Horrible dreams & fears & tormenting thoughts followed me for years. I couldn't speak about them to anyone. Sometimes it seemed they had gone away. Sometimes they would return to plague me for a time. But I knew they would go as soon as Bastard Alwyn was dead.

Sometimes when I was alone in my room at night, I would imagine Alwyn dying. I don't think I was killing him, just watching him die. What a fucking horrible thing for a kid to live with. I lived with that for years. It became a living entity within me. It wasn't me, but it led me to greater evil.

That look on Alwyn's face was an image that would never leave me. But years later I would see that look again. On the face of someone else. This time I would have to deal with it on my own. There was no one to talk to at sea. That 'look' had to be removed. The fear had to be destroyed. Perhaps I could get my heart back after he was gone. Yes, after he was dead.

Reflecting on what had happened in the Sunday school room, I knew for certain Alwyn was not doing something good for Robyn. But I was too afraid to tell anyone. Another regret. I wish I had said something. She & Julie may have been spared years of abuse if I had told someone. But who would I tell? Who would believe me? I didn't even know what bastard Alwyn was doing. I didn't know what to call what he was doing. So, I told no one.

After that day, I became a daredevil. I don't think I had a death wish, but I don't think I had a life wish either. Everything was different. God was different. I prayed quietly in my room for Robyn on many occasions. I prayed for Julie too. Somehow, my young mind assumed that what was happening to Robyn was also happening to Julie. I was right. I also thought it was my fault. Crazy way to think, but I felt guilty for years. Nearly 40 years actually. Fuck you Bastard Alwyn Raymond.

Robyn & Julie were my friends. I prayed they'd be alright. I prayed they'd still be my friends. I prayed we would be friends forever, especially Julie, who was about my age.

One crazy little kid praying one crazy little prayer. Who could have foreseen its eventual outcome? Amazing!

* * *

Now I will recall my ordeal with Joe & what he did to me. There is no pleasant way of putting it, so I'll be upfront & blunt. Joe tore my soul. Joe stole my light & plunged me into darkness. Joe tied me down. Joe sodomised me. Joe fucked me. Is that plain enough?

We left Auckland & headed out to sea early on a Monday morning. The sky was cloudy, but there remained some open spaces of blue sky. Occasionally the sun would hit the boat for a few minutes. The sea was choppy, with waves about 3-4 feet. I was excited & was enjoying the spray & motion of the boat as we headed out on the open sea.

Joe didn't talk much & seemed to be concentrating on steering the boat in the right direction. What the fuck is the right direction! I went out on deck & stood at the stern hanging onto the railing. I looked back as New Zealand gradually disappeared from sight. My thoughts were mostly of Rachel, but I also thought about Mum, Dad & my two brothers. I sang praises to God & prayed & thanked God for those I loved. I also remember asking God for a successful catch that would return a big financial reward for Joe & me. I also prayed we would be kept safe.

I stood there for a long time praying & praising God. I thought about life & all the joys that were ahead of me. What a wonderful future I had. An attractive Christian girl who loved the Lord & wanted to serve Him, a loving family, Rachel's family & the family that Rachel & I would have.

That day I also thought of painting & drawing. I was often seeing things that gave me ideas for artistic expression. But I never fulfilled any of them. I'd dropped out of art school to be with Diana. I put my artistic desires aside when I became a Christian because I couldn't see how an artist could serve God. There didn't seem to be any encouragement of art in the church at that time. There was a place & encouragement for music. But only certain styles of music.

Andy had been in England with his band & I prayed they'd get saved & become a Christian rock band. There was much opposition in the church to rock music. I didn't play my guitar much. James was an architect in a medium-size firm. He was married to a lovely girl & recently became a father. I prayed for all of them. How great it would be for them to come to the wedding of Rachel & me in New Zealand.

"Nathan." Joe's big voice was always harsh & he rarely smiled. "I got for you somet'ink to do," he said sternly.

"Sure," I replied with eagerness as I left the rear of the boat &

headed back to the cabin.

"You get da lunch ready, okay? Make me t'ree sandviches vit cheese, tomato & ham. No salt, lots of pepper... & some sauce too," he ordered.

"Yes, captain," I responded cheerfully, although out of amusement rather than respect.

"Get vot ever you vont for yourself, okay? Brink for me a mug of coffee too, strong, two spoons of coffee, not much milk & two sugars," he demanded.

There was never a *'please'* or *'thank you'* from Joe, but I didn't really care. I was happy to be on this adventure at sea. I was looking forward to the task of fishing. But I did not enjoy being with Joe. I had always sensed a foreboding with him. I did express that on a couple of occasions. But I was brought into line with assurances that his outward demeanour was *'just Joe'* & not to mention my concerns further.

We spent all day getting to the area where Joe wanted to let out the nets. That evening, he told me what we would be doing first thing in the morning. We ate dinner & got an early night, so we'd be ready for the next day.

Joe woke me at 5.30am. I had breakfast alone because he said he had to get a couple of things ready. When I eventually went up on deck Joe called me over to where he was standing at the rear of the boat. He told me he had to wrap some tape around my wrists & hands before I put the heavy gloves on. He also held a heavy-duty long sleeve t-shirt. Joe said I should put it on under what I was wearing. I put my arms in front of me first & he wrapped the heavy-duty tape tightly around each wrist. I then took off my tracksuit top, shirt & t-shirt & was about to pick up the one Joe wanted me to wear.

Before I reached the t-shirt, Joe grabbed the ends of the tape & walked me over to a big white box that was built in behind the wall of the cabin area. It was about 5 feet wide & on either side at the back was a metal ring. Either side at the front there were metal rings too.

I had to stand facing the wall & hold the rings. Joe then tied my left wrist to the left ring & my right wrist to the right ring. He came up behind me & pulled down my tracksuit pants & jocks together. He then taped my feet to rings in front & at the bottom of the box. Now I was stretched out, leaning over a wide white box which I later discovered was a fridge & freezer.

"What's this for?" I asked, shocked at such treatment.

"Dis is just a little initiation, is vot all first timers got to do," he said with what I detected to be a degree of menace. I put it down to his arrogant manner. I was here to earn some money, so I went along with the joke.

At this stage, I was not too concerned. I decided the worst thing that could happen was to have a bucket of sea water thrown over me. I was staring at the cabin wall, waiting for the bucket of cold water to saturate me.

I writhed in protest. But I could do nothing to stop him. I was now naked, & although the sun was rising, I started to feel the morning chill. I was many miles from land on a lonely sea with a man I knew little about.

I could hear him muttering & making 'oohing' & 'ahhing' noises. I turned to see what he was doing. He was rubbing his little erect cock with his right hand. He had a large amount of white cream in his left. Joe put his cold, cream-covered hand between my legs from behind. Reaching around in front of me, he began to fondle me.

A sickening started to ooze through my entire being. I wanted to be with Rachel. I wanted to suddenly be back in Auckland. I wanted to go home. I wanted my father to be there & stop Joe. I tried to pray. I wanted to rebuke the devil. But the devil was the guy who owned the boat.

Suddenly, I felt his fat stomach against me. He fumbled, trying to push his erection into me. The shock of what was happening drained my life. I sensed a hollowness rapidly dispelling my inner being. I wanted to get hit & killed by the car that stopped short of hitting me so many years ago. My mind screamed, 'Save me, Lord.' But no words would come from my mouth. I thought of Robyn & Julie. I knew then that they were my sisters.

By the time he had finished, probably less than a minute, I was empty of life. I wanted to scream. I wanted to cry out in anguish, but I was in a deserted place. I had departed from myself. I ran away from myself. My feet searched for solid ground & fled to the depths of the sea floor to walk my life away to greater depths. I was not a good place to be. I discovered a dry, lifeless desert at sea. There are no fishermen in a desert.

Was my mouth really full of sand? Why were the dunes of this desert jostling me on this boat? Why would they not keep still? I yearned for stillness. For peace. Neither came.

I don't remember him cutting the tape. I don't remember getting dressed. I walked toward the cabin sensing that walking would never be the same again. Just before I went into the cabin, I saw a large shark in the water. I thought of throwing myself in. If the shark attacked me, at least it would be doing what was natural. That seemed preferable to what had just happened.

Everything I had been suddenly disappeared. I was deserted. I tried to cry out to God, but I was sure he wasn't there anymore. My life had passed without even waving *'goodbye.'* The boat was floating, but I could feel myself sinking. Nathan was gone. Me. My Nathan. God's Nathan. Where is he, Lord? Can you find him? I want him back. I'm not him anymore.

A cold, lonely fog encircled me. I was spinning. Out of control. How can I stand now? The real Nathan could stand. My Nathan could help. Where am I? Where is he? I understood nothing.

My head stormed with thoughts of Julie & Robyn. I thought of what Alwyn had done to them. I couldn't stop thinking of what Bastard Alwyn had done to them. I thought of his violation of their innocence. I was seasick with insanity. I thought I should do to Joe what they must surely have wanted to do to Alwyn. All my dreams of murder met me in the cabin. My head was full of celebrations of death. Alwyn had to die. I knew he was somewhere on Joe's boat. I had to find him.

But what is it that I should do? Nathan wouldn't do that. Nathan would gain victory another way. Where is my Nathan when I need him?

Blood cries out for justice, whether in the sea or on the land. Recompense demands justice. Is it justice or is it revenge? Will it be given, or will I take it?

Quite a long time passed before I went out on deck again. *Alwyn must be out here*, I thought. I didn't know where Nathan had gone. But was that Alwyn I could hear outside with Joe?

"Hey boy, get out here, ve got verk to do," came the gruff call. Joe sounded a million miles away. I didn't want to hear his voice. I wanted to sleep. Forever. I had to run away. I wanted a big bed to float up beside Joe's boat & let me sleep on a peaceful sea. But there was no peaceful sea. There was no peace. There was no bed. There was nothing. Everything had vanished & I couldn't see where I had gone.

Everything had disappeared. I wanted to be invisible too.

'I don't like that voice. *Make that voice go away, Lord! Make the voice go away, Lord!*' My screams reverberated deep into my isolation & emptiness. The sound was pitiful. Even God didn't want to hear it.

A strong breeze had sprung up & the sea was getting rougher. As

I emerged from the cabin, I saw a larger wave hit the side of the boat & knock Joe overboard. By the time he turned around in the water, the slow-moving boat was already about 10 feet away. There was no way he could reach to get back on board.

"Throw me a rope," he screamed, "turn da' boat around."

I turned around eventually, but didn't throw him a rope. Instead, I threw a wooden crate. At him, not to him. I had just heard Joe's last words. I wanted to hear him say *'sorry'*. He had no intention of saying that. Anyway, he said nothing more & then he was lifted out of the water in the jaws of a big shark. Fat, ugly Joe, the fuck-shark, was killed by a bigger shark. Is that justice? Don't know, but it sure was funny.

About 30 hours later, I arrived back in New Zealand. At Tauranga instead of Auckland. I made it back mostly on my own. Alone. Now I remained alone. Now I was the lonely desert. Nathan had run away. He wouldn't come back. Something terrible had happened to him. He hated what had happened. It was worse than he imagined when he was only 9. He did not know then that he would disappear like the shark.

In my head, I screamed out to myself. I wanted myself to come back. It was too late now. I was gone. How could a shark enter my nightmare? Why did a shark prevent my waking for so many years? Why did my dreams of murder never return after this day? (Actually, they do return later in the story) The shark ate my thoughts of murder. Nice shark. Is there one for Alwyn, too?

* * *

After Joe's death, his wife, Vera gave me a small brief case containing what she said were Joe's papers for the boat. I think she suspected I had been seriously mistreated. Vera said she wanted me to keep the boat. She didn't want it & neither did her son, Mark. This did not seem like sudden good fortune. This did not compensate in any way for the suffering Joe brought into my life.

Andy told this part of the story very well. I won't repeat it. I had just watched a man die. It was the most ghastly & horrendous thing. Beyond words. I didn't know it would be so ghastly to watch a man die. I wanted to be the shark. I wished I was the killer.

But a devastating natural killer had struck. I saw it. It was horrifying. My Nathan, my me, had run away, leaving just me to relive Joe's death. I was thrilled! Fuck you, Joe! I laughed again.

The elation of arriving safely back in New Zealand was most satisfying. But I did not recover. I felt lost. Broken. Totally fucked. Gone. Gone away. Gone away from myself. Who am I now?

Added to this anguish was Rachel's unexpected withdrawal. She didn't want to see me & wouldn't speak to me. Her parents were as perplexed as I was. She stopped going to church.

One night, Robert had to pick her up from a police station after she was arrested for being drunk & disorderly. Within 2 months, she was drinking heavily & doing dope.

Diana walked out of my life because of my drug problems. Now I was losing Rachel to the very thing she saved me from. How could this fucked-up situation be? Why had Rachel suddenly turned away from God, the church, her family & me? My pain was multiplied beyond what I felt I could bare.

I cried out for answers. None came. I could hear my screams inside my head & there was no way to stop the noise. I went to church, but everyone seemed too far away. Like looking through the wrong end of a telescope. Worst of all, Rachel wasn't there. All I wanted to do was get away from the world. A wretched black hole swallowed my world. Not only had Rachel's love ended, but it seemed that God's love had too. I couldn't relate to my church family now. They had run away from me too.

How could I tell anyone about Joe's evil rape of my life? Would I be believed anyway? He wasn't here to defend himself against anything I might say. Joe was a respected member of the church & I was a new convert.

I was broken & I kept on breaking; I was dead, & I kept on dying; I was in mental & emotional agony & the pain kept increasing. Fuck! I was fucked. Now I'm totally fucked.

But I had to speak out. I did. It turned out to be the worst thing I could have done. BUT IT SHOULDN'T HAVE BEEN.

I made an appointment to see Pastor John. I had to tell someone. I had to get some help.

Pastor John ushered me into his office at the church that Tuesday morning & invited me to sit down.

"I know this must be a very difficult time for you Nathan," he said sympathetically as we sat down, "so let's have some prayer before we talk," he added.

My mind & emotions bounced & catapulted back & forth between my head & my heart. His words, *"Let's have some prayer,"* caused me to tremble a little.

*Let's have some prayer. Have some prayer? How the fuck do you have some prayer?* I thought. I felt like screaming. *'We either pray or we don't, dickhead'*, I thought to myself.

*Why don't we have some cheese? Let's drink some cough syrup. Why not eat gherkins until we vomit?* My head was filled with madness at that moment.

Pastor John prayed. I was thinking I was in the wrong place. I was right. Pastor John was in the wrong place too. He still is. He's still a fucking pastor after all these years. The sheep don't trample their shepherd. Sheep are so fucking stupid.

Pastor John asked me what I wanted to talk about. I told him what Joe had done to me.

"WHAT?" he exclaimed very loudly after I related how Joe had abused me. Pastor Shithead displayed a fury which was beyond Christians, let alone a pastor. He stood & leaned over his desk. The knuckles of his left hand were white & pressed hard into the desktop. He held up the index finger of his right hand in front of my face.

"How dare you denigrate Joe's good name this way? Don't you know what he has done for this church?" he fumed accusingly. "How could you even imagine such a horrible thing?"

Pastor John continued to rave about Joe's goodness. I wanted to eat gherkins.

He finished his tirade against me & told me to leave.

"What, no prayer?" I asked cynically.

"Get out, Nathan," he demanded, "& don't you dare speak to anyone else of these hateful things," he insisted. Then he added, "You need to be purged of this demonic thinking." I left his office. I left the church. Jesus left too, or maybe He was never there. Maybe Jesus had gone to look for Nathan.

First, I was fucked by Joe, then I was fucked by the church. Fucked by the sanctuary of healing. I walked away from the church imagining myself stuffing cheese & gherkins into Pastor John's mouth. I would make him eat them until his arse exploded. Shit, I was a funny guy. I wondered if the Nathan who ran away would laugh at this too.

I laughed silently to myself. Then I laughed aloud. Then I cried like I'd never cried before. Huge tears of blood wept into my broken heart. I walked away dying - again.

*Where's Nathan gone? Where's God's Nathan? Where's my Nathan? Come back my funny friend!* It's too late now, I'm gone. I miss myself already. I missed Nathan. Again, I asked myself, 'Who am I now? How do I become me again?'

Bewilderment oozed through every crack in my disturbed emotions. I was more lost than ever. Lost in the church. Lost from the church. Cast out. Ripped open, left to bleed. Fuck you, Pastor Shithead!

Leaving the church office, I stared at the ground as I walked away. The bare patches of dirt in the grass soon gave way to the car park of oil-stained dirt & gravel. Dirt & gravel beckoned me. I belonged to the dirt. With the step of each foot, hope was sucked from my being. I was dead & buried in that dirt. The dirt desired me. I was repelled, but the dirt held me.

Would I ever laugh again? How long would it be before I could at least smile? By the time I reached the concrete footpath, it was dark inside my heart & mind. The 'way of truth' had rejected my truth. I was a liar, the carrier of the lie. No man could do to me what had been done. The 'truth' from Pastor John Shit-For-Brains had confirmed it.

I walked all the way back to the boat. My dark feet carried my darkness to the ever-darkening shadows as they gathered around my life. The shadows conquered me. *'Yea though I walk through the valley of the shadow of death I shall fear no evil'...* for the evil never really happened to me. It must have been my 'demonic' thinking as Pastor John had said. At that moment I realised why poor Don hanged himself on Joe's boat. I cried some more. For Don. For me. For my Nathan. They were both gone. Both dead.

Now my state was much worse. Joe fucked me: a tragic physical abuse. Pastor Shit-For-Brains fucked me: the ultimate betrayal. Trading truth for the sake of image. Denying truth to retain dignity. Praise the Good Shepherd, serve the good flock, fuck the poor lost sheep. I wanted Nathan, my Nathan, to come back.

The church held a memorial service for Joe a few days later. A celebration of his life. A celebration for the faithful servant of God.

No surprise that I didn't go. Probably wouldn't have been welcome anyway. I held my own service that day. A celebration of the death of fat, ugly Joe; arse-fucker, soul destroyer. All it cost was a bottle of red wine. I drank too much & threw up into the harbour. I hoped that every bit of my vomit would find its way to Joe's resting place. I laughed again. Joe has no resting place. Sharks ate his balls, didn't they?

There was so much more I wanted & desperately needed to pour out to Pastor John about that horrible day. I had to tell someone what actually happened. But Pastor Shit-for-Brains wouldn't listen. So, I carried a dreadful torment & further guilt. It burdened me for 27 years. I had to carry it because my Nathan ran away. He was gone. I wished I was him. Why couldn't I run away too? I had to stay with myself. I had to look after me. My heart was upside down, my head was inside out.

I stopped going to church. I was sucked into the black hole that Joe had created in my world. There was nowhere else to go, so I stayed on the boat. It wasn't Joe's boat anymore. It was now mine. Thanks, Vera.

It seemed that neither Joe's wife, Vera, nor his son knew that Joe owned 2 other boats. Mark wasn't even slightly interested in the boat. Anyway, he had just inherited 3 houses. I never told them about the other 2 boats. Joe's wife died 3 or 4 months later, & Mark sold the 3 homes, bought a house near the beach & a sports car. He apparently started buying old houses, doing a cheap renovation & selling them for a profit.

Over 27 years later, I discovered that he was the bastard who ruined Rachel's life. He is still the same sleazy, slime-ball. Evil eyes, goatee beard, unmarried, friend of the devil. Now, so many years later he is being investigated for paedophile activities. I need a shark for Mark.

Me, being funny again. Poetic too. I could have been the shark. But some of the dark clouds parted.

Before I returned to Australia, I found out what happened to Rachel. It tore me apart. The pain, humiliation & ongoing torment of what Joe did, crashed in on me again. I was so glad the bastard was dead. I wanted to see him die again & again & again. I was a mess. I was fucked in the head. Now I wanted to see Mark die an even more horrible death. My Nathan had not returned to me yet. I could have done it. I should have done it. Surely it was my calling. It is my duty to kill the bastard. Kill Mark. Kill him. Oh, yeah... gotta kill Alwyn too!

The afternoon before I went out on the boat with Joe over 25 years ago, Mark went to the hairdressing salon where Rachel worked & told her that I was ill & staying on Joe's boat. He told her that I wanted to see her, that I wanted her to visit me after she finished work. She went down to the harbour, boarded Joe's boat & went down below to where Mark told her I would be. But I wasn't there.

She entered the semi-darkness calling my name & a weak voice called her over. But it was Mark's voice, not mine. She went over to the bed. Mark grabbed her legs & pulled her down onto the bed. He jumped on top of her. He put a pillow over her face & pushed it hard. She thought she was going to suffocate. She decided, rightly or wrongly, not to fight. Mark was much bigger & much stronger.

"That arty-farty little bastard doesn't deserve you, Rachel," Mark said angrily as he pushed her dress up above her hips.

"I'm going to have what he doesn't deserve. You're going to give it to me, aren't you, Rachel?"

Rachel was terrified. She nodded in agreement as he pulled down her panty hose & panties. He felt her with his fingers. Then he invaded the most treasured possession a young woman has. He robbed her of the choice to whom she would entrust that gift. He physically assaulted & abused her. Mark dishonoured her femininity. He broke her Godliness. Then he pushed her down onto the bed & forced his erection into her. She cried out in pain—physical &

emotional. He smirked as he later withdrew his blood-stained penis.

This bastard was a self-appointed youth leader of the 10–13-year-olds. I wanted to find him. I wanted to kill him. Mark killed Rachel's life. He killed my future. He & his father destroyed my life over & over & over & over. Relentlessly, the torment bashed against my being. I was torn, ripped & lashed again & again & again.

Mark is now listed as a known sex offender. The bastard should be in jail. Preferably he should be dead. Even more preferably, I should have killed him – slowly. Praise God for the courage & conviction to show mercy. But it is not for Mark. Praise God for the courage to kill the fucking shit! Thank you, Jesus for the joy it would give me to kill the demented fucker! Praise God for sharks!

Rachel's father, Robert, told me what had happened. He too was torn. His precious daughter was dead to the family, dead to me & dead to herself. There are men in this world who don't deserve air. I would gladly cut off their cocks & their balls. I would push them down their throats until they choked on them or bled to death. I could see myself dancing around them as I sang praises to God while the bastards died. Yep, I'm still a funny guy.

*If you're reading this & you've committed such sexual abuse – fuck you. You're going to die one day. You might have been able to live with what you've done, but you sure as hell won't be able to die comfortably. You destroyed. You killed life. You killed innocence. The consequences were a lifetime of torment & pain for your victims. Reap what you sowed, you evil bastard! I hope every demon in hell walks past every day & kicks you in the balls for the rest of forever. Fuck you.*

*For those of you who did such things from positions of authority & leadership in the church, your final end will make hell seem like a holiday destination. Fuck you too.*

*Oh Lord! How can such anger exist in a human heart once*

*touched by You? Where's my Nathan gone, Lord? Where has your Nathan gone? Bring him back, Lord. Keep him safe. Help him walk from the depths of the sea. Help him find his way back to a safer shore.*

Robert was indeed a broken man & so was I. There were no positive words or thoughts that I could offer. He knew where Mark lived but had never made any attempt at contact. Mark had never been charged for what he did. Rachel could not be persuaded to press any charges. Robert believed it was because of fear.

That afternoon I decided to return home to Australia. 3 days later I took *'Diana'*, my yacht, out on my own for a final farewell sail. *(The story of the yacht is in my next section.)* I'm glad I did. I sold her within a week to a guy who made a reasonable offer. I had not advertised her for sale or told anyone of my decision. Jack just walked by one morning & stopped for a chat. I told him of my 25 plus years of sailing the Pacific & I think he was impressed with the history as much as the yacht itself.

Jack was from South Africa. He had originally come to New Zealand to watch the South Africans play cricket. He fell in love with the country & decided to emigrate. Jack was an interesting man & very likeable. I knew that *'Diana'* would be in excellent hands.

So, I finally turned my back on the sea & flew home to Australia. I bought a 3-bedroom house at Warburton. I did not have contact with my family for nearly a year although I went to Barbara's funeral. I have no idea why I read the death notices in the Herald-Sun that day. In fact, I don't even know why I bought the paper that morning. It was not my normal routine.

No one recognised me at the funeral & I left immediately after. I didn't stay for afternoon tea & I didn't talk to anyone. I don't know why. 10 months later I decided to go to Brighton Beach, a trip that required I catch a bus & 2 trains to reach my destination. I don't know why I went. I don't know why I felt I had to go.

I caught the bus from Warburton to Lilydale, a train from Lilydale to Richmond, then a Sandringham line train from Richmond to Brighton Beach. I stepped off the train & walked down to South Road toward the beach, crossed Beach Road & walked to the waters' edge. I turned & looked south toward Sandringham & saw James. Uncanny? Miraculous? Impossible? Spooky? I certainly didn't know. Why was I here? Why was James here too?

Both James & I were way outside our 'normal' routines that day. Perhaps God was at work to do something that was pleasing to Himself. Perhaps Nathan had come back to me.

*Did you find Him Lord? Is he okay? Can he come home now?*

# PART 3

## JAMES

Clarita, A New Hope, The Proposal

I suffered a grievous loss and as a consequence, life with all its hopes and aspirations for James Darling, altered course. For Nathan, however, there was to be the experience of a life-changing gain. In fact, it is a consummate boost and augmentation for all the family. It has delivered a joy and closeness that none of us could have predicted or even imagined.

Reminiscing over the happenings of the previous eighteen months since Nathan's return, I find myself considering the possibility that God may have re-entered our lives and swept away the distance we had put between us. Perhaps He did not withdraw from our lives at all. Instead, I surmise, that for all this time we may have just been hidden in the light. Perhaps.

Despite this, I was still bereft of my beautiful Barbara and there were too many times of crying and mourning in loneliness. This loneliness engulfed me in a thick fog through which I could see no way forward.

Although the grief had been horrendous and I had given little thought to ever meeting another soul mate, I am now in a relationship with a woman I encountered about three months ago. But of recent days there have emerged developments that have returned either an awareness of God, or an intrusion of God to my life, in another way.

Clarita was the wife of a former client for whom I had designed three buildings, including his home near the beach in Brighton. He left her over ten years earlier for a younger woman. Since then, Clarita had devoted herself to nurturing and raising her twin boys who were now in their early twenties, pursuing separate careers and no longer living at home.

We recognised each other as we walked in Church Street, Brighton on a tranquil autumn morning. After chatting briefly and exchanging pleasantries, we went our separate ways, but I gave a hopeful glance back to see if she was still there. Clarita stood in her bottle-green dress clutching her handbag with both hands in front of her. She flashed a brief, disarming smile before entering a café. It was just a momentary glance, surely nothing more.

I continued along Church Street with the intention of returning to my car and must have walked about ten metres before turning and going back to the cafe. Clarita was seated at a table on an upholstered bench seat against the wall. She offered the loveliest and most welcoming smile. We sat together and talked over coffee and muffins, and after chatting enjoyably for over an hour, ordered lunch as well.

As we were about to go our separate ways after our long lunch, she hesitated momentarily, and invited me to dinner at her house. I accepted the invitation and was looking forward to seeing the house I had designed more than twenty years earlier. After her divorce from Keith, she retained the house and her car.

I arrived Thursday evening two days after our lunch for a dinner that was momentous in more ways than one. I began to see a little hope for the future, that perhaps there might be room in my life to invite another woman to share it. We ate and talked and enjoyed a lovely meal with an excellent 2004 Shiraz I had selected and brought along for the occasion.

What unfolded that evening surprised and delighted both of us. We had finished the first course and Clarita was about to take the plates from the table and bring the dessert.

"Just before you leave the table, I'd like to ask something," I said hesitantly, trying to sound confident, but my confidence seemed to be retreating.

"Yes, James," she replied with a smile.

"Er, well… I'd like to kiss you, that is, if you are agreeable?" I said, surprised at how easy it finally seemed and how comfortable I felt asking the question.

"Yes James, that's okay," she replied as she smiled and looked into my eyes.

I have no idea what I saw as I looked into her eyes. We sat looking at each other for at least five to ten seconds before I moved my chair closer to hers.

Clarita was more than ten years younger than me, nearly as tall and quite attractive. Her black hair glistened under the down lights. I reached for her hand and kissed the back of it before looking into her beautiful dark eyes. As I moved forward in my chair to reach her lips, she moved toward me too.

Our lips met. We kissed each other gently for a few seconds, then opened our eyes and looked at each other again.

"James?" she questioned, with a gentle lilt.

"Yes, Clarita," I replied, feeling intoxicated by the pleasure of my first kiss in over a year and a half.

"Have you got any more of those kisses?"

"Yes, I have. Why, do you think we should try it again?" I asked as my head swooned and my heartbeat sent pulsating waves through my entire being.

"Yes, James, I think we should," she replied with her eyes closed as she moved toward me.

This time we held each other's arms and then fully embraced as we kissed passionately for what must have been only fifteen seconds but seemed like hours. The awkwardness of embracing each other from our chairs gave way as I my right knee touched the floor. We were soon kneeling together in a passionate embrace and continued to kiss.

After a few minutes, we knelt looking at each other with utter elation and surprise. She brushed her hair back gently with her fingers and slowly stood up. I knelt on the floor, looking up at her face. She was wearing a green, pink and white floral sateen dress which was just above knee-length, but from where I was kneeling, I could see a little more of her legs.

Clarita reached down with both hands. I held them as she stepped back and helped me up. She slowly tilted her head slightly to the left and then to the right and she gazed into my eyes while we held hands. She then, with a gentle shake of her head, bowed her face slightly without taking her gaze from my eyes.

"Should we have dessert now, James?" She sighed a very satisfying sigh.

"Isn't that what we just had?" I replied with a smile.

"Well, it was a wonderful taste, wasn't it?" she replied.

"Most wonderful," I nodded in agreement.

"So, what should we do now, James?" she asked with a coy expectancy.

"Continue with dessert, I suppose," was my unsubtle response.

"You mean, the one I have in the kitchen?" she asked teasingly.

"Is there another room where we can have dessert?" I replied, feigning ignorance.

"Well, we could have a look. You designed the house, James; in what other room might we find dessert?" she asked with a cheeky, yet equally innocent laugh.

I stood looking at her. I felt a shiver of expectancy tremble through me as I put my arms around her waist and drew her slowly toward me. She pressed herself into me and could obviously feel my arousal as she pushed her hips against mine. We held each other tightly for at least thirty seconds.

"Clarita, can I ask you a question?"

"Yes, James."

"Can we see if there's any dessert upstairs?"

"Yes, that's an excellent place to look."

We put an arm around each other's waist and walked upstairs to the main bedroom. She had redecorated the house since I had done the original interior design scheme. Her bedroom walls and ceiling had been repainted dark blue with white cornices. I stopped looking around the room and looked back into Clarita's eyes.

"Clarita, I haven't been with a woman for over a year, so…"

"James."

Her voice was soft as she reached a finger to my lips.

"I haven't been with a man for nearly seven years. Neither of us has any idea how this has happened so quickly, or even if it's a good idea. It might not be, but until I met you in Church Street on Tuesday, I had not even met a man who made me feel comfortable enough for me to just be myself. I don't know why you make me feel so comfortable, but I love the fact that you do," she said.

Her words held my heart with rapturous tenderness.

"Wow, I never expected in my later years to hear such beautiful words from a woman. You have a beautiful heart, sweet lady," I responded, and we held each other and kissed again.

We moved to the bed and sat down still holding each other and kissing and then looked at each other. She fell back onto the bed while I was sitting there and she let out a delighted, "Wow!"

Because she lay back, her dress was now higher. I looked at her knees and the softness of her legs and reached my hand to touch her left knee. Gently caressing her knees led to moving my fingers up her legs to the level of the hem of her dress. I dared not go any further.

As I turned to look at her face, she reached her arms up to me, beckoning me to join her. We lay there momentarily, our feet still touching the floor as we lay across the bed.

"Are you okay?" I asked.

"Uh huh," she replied nonchalantly.

She threw her right arm across me and rubbed her hand across my shirt as I lay there. Her hand moved back and forth across my chest and gradually down to my stomach, and then she ran her hand back and forth along my belt.

"What about you, are you okay?" she asked.

"I'm fine, but I'm wondering if this is a good idea," I replied.

"I'm wondering the same thing, James."

"So, what do you think, dear lady?" I asked.

"It's the craziest thing I've done in years, maybe, ever," she said with a laugh.

"Would you prefer to stop what we are doing?" I asked, hoping she would want to continue.

She hesitated for a few seconds. I had no idea whether it was on purpose or if she was thinking we should stop and go downstairs.

"James, I really think we should stop what we're doing," she finally responded and then quickly sat up.

I was surprised and disappointed but resigned myself to it being a silly idea. She looked at my face, but I had no idea what she might have seen in my look.

"We should stop lying half on and half off the bed and get into it, that's what I think," she said with a simple shrug.

I was amazed and delighted.

"Just as we are?" I queried.

"No, let's at least take off some of our clothes," she replied.

"Some?" I queried.

"Oh! Alright! But only take off the clothes we are wearing," she chirped with humorous, girlish delight as she laughed away what must have been years of lonely frustration.

She stood up, unzipped her dress and removed her bra. She then pulled back the navy and white palm leaf patterned doona and removed her panties before getting into the bed and pulling the doona up to the top of her breasts.

In the little while taken for her to complete the manoeuvres, I removed my socks and rose to unbutton my shirt, remove my T-shirt, unbuckled my belt and let my trousers fall to the floor. All the while I watched her face as she searched mine with a desiring gaze.

Standing by the bed, I slowly run my thumbs behind the elastic of my boxer shorts and relished her willing reaction as I pulled them down so that they, too, dropped to the floor. Her face beamed with delight as I joined her under the doona.

We lay in the bed together holding each other while we talked for a few minutes. We talked about how crazy the situation was and how quickly we'd moved to this stage, yet it seemed so normal, so natural, and so beautiful. For over two hours we talked, laughed, kissed, fondled and made love. I was totally amazed at her beauty, her charm, her wit and her girlish glee.

Leaving her house at about 1.30am after a long, lingering kiss in the entry hall in what was now early Friday morning, I revelled in my elation and the precious memory of an evening unlike any other I had ever experienced.

It was at 9.30am the following morning, only a few minutes after finishing my breakfast that my telephone rang.

"Hello," I said.

"Good morning, dear James. How are you?" asked Clarita with such lively cheer that the recollections of the previous evening invaded my memory of her naked beauty.

"Wonderful, dearest Clarita, how are you?" I answered, blissfully aware of her sweet voice.

"I'm still tingling all over," she said excitedly. "But I think we need to talk. Can you come over tonight please James?" she asked mysteriously.

"Sure, what time?" I answered.

"Well, I've still got some food left, as well as the dessert we didn't have last night, so come for a quick meal while we have a serious talk?"

"Certainly, what time?"

"Same as last night if you like," she replied.

"Okay, I'll see you then," I responded.

"Great. I've got to go now. See you about 7.30. Bye."

"Bye," I said.

I arrived at 7.30 that Friday evening and Clarita opened the front door allowing me to enter. After a quick kiss and hug of greeting, she seemed intent to begin asking questions.

"James, I'm so glad you're here," she began, "because I have to find out what happened last night," she added with just the slightest of hesitancy.

"Well, sweet lady." I paused briefly before continuing. "Last evening we had the loveliest dinner followed by what I can only describe as an amazingly beautiful time together. I was mesmerised and even deliriously happy the entire evening," I concluded, hoping that I had spoken words that she found agreeable.

"It was fabulous, wasn't it?" she chimed. "Oh, but James, you were fabulous too."

"Everything that was fabulous about last night was because of you, delightful lady," I replied.

"Oh, James," she responded sheepishly.

"It's the truth, Clarita. I was, and still am enthralled by all that you are and perhaps this has unfolded far too quickly. But that certainly does not diminish the absolute joy and delight that we seem to be sharing," I said, and put my arms around her, holding her close. She put her arms around me and nestled her head into my neck and we stood holding each other.

"We really did make love last night, didn't we, James?" she pondered.

"Indeed, we did," I replied before adding, "Are you okay with what happened?"

"Uh huh," she replied matter-of-factly.

"Would you like to do that again sometime?" I enquired, as I sensed a stirring up of the wonderful arousal of the previous night.

"Ooooh, yes," she said as she closed her eyes and allowed her head to slowly fall back.

"When would you like to repeat those beautiful sensations again?" I ran my hands down her back and lightly pulled her closer.

"Now please, James, right now," she said with a rapturous smile.

She took my hand, leading me into the lounge room. She turned off the lounge room light, dimmed the dining room light, and led me to the front of the gas fire.

Within fifteen minutes of arriving at her house, we were undressing each other. Ninety minutes after making love and talking and laughing naked in front of the fire, we dressed, went to the kitchen and ate dinner at the bench. She reheated some of the meal from the previous evening and we sat and talked, joked, and laughed for hours.

"What time do you want to go James?" Clarita asked with concern, but also with a gleam of hope, as we sat at the bench finishing our Earl Grey tea.

"Actually, dearest Clarita, I don't want to go, I would rather stay the night with you," I replied as I gave her a soft smile.

"Wonderful. We'll have a beautiful breakfast together in the morning then," she responded.

"If you look this spectacular in the morning my dear, it will most definitely be a late breakfast," I said.

"Hmmm!" she murmured with closed eyes. "A late breakfast would be really nice."

A little before midnight we went upstairs to bed, made love again, and had a very restful sleep. The next morning was very nice and of course we had a late breakfast. Actually, it was brunch, and we walked up to Church Street to the same café where we first had coffee together.

Driving home later that day, I was filled with what I could only describe as magnificent happiness. Another interesting and strange phenomenon was the fact that I was thanking God for Clarita and discovered myself actually praying for her to be blessed. I thought this to be somewhat absurd given that our activity had been 'sinful' as I knew Christians would label it. I do not remember giving these thoughts much credence at the time, but I could not help wondering if God was all that concerned about our behaviour. Or if he was thinking or even planning something that would delight and surprise us all. The truth is, I was not all that interested in what God thought or if He thought anything at all.

For the next few hours, my feelings wavered between elation and guilt. Not guilt for what I had done, but the guilt of not remembering Barbara. Clarita was just as vivacious and attractive, but she was not the mother of my children nor was she my closest confidante, soul mate and best friend. However, I sensed that she could be and even believed that she was indeed rapidly becoming all of those things. Our relationship sprang up so suddenly, but the suddenness was equally accompanied by such joy and beauty. I sensed healing for the pain of loss I had suffered.

Over the following days and weeks while we were together, she had my full attention. Whether it was eating dinner, going to a show or movie, walking along the beach, making love or just out driving somewhere, when I was not with her, I was thinking about her.

For the first time in a year, I was conscious that I was aspiring once again to life and all its expectancy. I had told no one about our relationship, not my children, nor my brothers. Clarita and I decided to delay the disclosure of our relationship to our families until we had a clearer understanding of where we were going. Undoubtedly though, we both knew we wanted to be together in a permanent relationship.

It was therefore a severe setback when, after three months of falling in love, Clarita telephoned one evening to express her thought that perhaps we should not see each other for a while. She thought it essential to have some space and time to explore her feelings about me. Because her announcement was a complete surprise, and because there had been no previous discussion about such a pursuit, I was aggrieved and bewildered.

Striving to sound understanding and rational, I agreed that it was probably a good idea. I cannot explain why I didn't speak my thoughts and tell her how much I appreciated her. I should have expressed my love for her. Perhaps I wrongly concluded that I did not deserve her or that she might withdraw her affections if I sounded too serious. I greatly desired for our relationship to continue. I wanted it to grow and flourish. My entire being yearned for the continuation of my healing journey out of the dark places I had been in for eighteen long months.

Hanging up the telephone upon the conclusion of our short conversation I cried for a time, but not just over Clarita, I cried for Barbara too. I cried for my father and mother and I cried for Nathan. I was hurting for so many reasons, but I realised that when I was with Clarita, my distress dissipated and almost vanished completely. Life was so much more pleasant when I was with her. Life was certainly more engaging and pleasurable, but was it easier? Pleasure is a convenient escape from hurts, but if that is all it is, perhaps it risks being a self-indulgence bringing no lasting or worthwhile benefit. Regardless, I felt that Clarita and I belonged together.

Over the following days I searched my heart and my emotions, trying to ascertain my intense desires and my thoughtful purpose for a life and a future with Clarita. What I most appreciated was her charm, companionship, intelligence and grace far more than the fabulous physical attraction and fulfilling sex. My conclusions were already well established, and I realised I was in love with Clarita. At last I had hope, but her request had dulled my optimism and I sensed myself slowly sliding back into darkness.

The more I thought about her, the more I urged myself to drive to her house and tell her I truly loved her. But for some reason I let logic rule, if indeed it was logic.

Late one morning about four weeks without seeing her, I visited the supermarket to do some shopping and returned home to prepare lunch. After I had stored my purchases, I stood in the kitchen peering out through the window at the back garden. It was mostly Barbara's input that had created that wonderful garden, and it was resplendent with many special family memories.

I stood gazing through the window for a while before venturing to my study to check if perchance any emails had been received or telephone messages recorded. As I sat down at the computer the telephone rang. It was Clarita asking me to meet that afternoon for coffee at the same café in Church Street, Brighton where we first had morning tea and lunch. My elation was boundless, and I was more than delighted to be readying myself for a rendezvous with my beloved Clarita.

Three o'clock arrived, and I was already inside the café. Clarita arrived shortly after and approached with a soft smile. I gave her a quick kiss, saying I was so pleased to see her. However, she seemed different. Although retaining her dignity and immaculate grooming as usual, she did not possess the bearing of her usual confident and vivacious self. I deferred my yearning to expose my true feelings and allowed her to start the conversation.

"James, I'm so pleased to see you again. I need to talk with you, and I hope you will understand," she started, with a tremble in her voice.

"Clarita, it is wonderful to see you again. I have no idea what you wish to say, but I want you to know that I have missed you very much. I want to tell you something I should have communicated weeks ago."

We ordered coffee and made polite conversation until the coffees were brought to our table and then she spoke.

"Well, James, I've been spending time with someone you know and..."

I did not allow Clarita to finish her sentence. I was dismayed and although not yet indignant, I perceived that I had been fooled and I knew this news had potential to do far more than just agitate me.

"Please, James, please just listen. It's not what you think," she pleaded.

I let her continue.

"About three weeks before I called for time to re-evaluate our relationship I bumped into your sister-in-law, Tanya, Andrew's wife. We chatted for a while in the street and she asked if I'd like to join her for a coffee," Clarita explained with care.

She scanned my face for assurance, which I'm sure had vanished because of her opening sentence. Clarita knew Tanya because their boys were friends with Adam and attended the same school.

Clarita continued to relate the story as she played with the cup of coffee she was yet to lift to her full, red lips.

"So, we had coffee," she continued, "and that led to an interesting discussion and an invitation to meet with some of her friends."

I was listening and trying to anticipate what would come next, but I was more than shocked by the direction our meeting was about to take.

"James, I do like you very much. I would still like to see you if you're okay with that but..."

I interjected before she could complete what she was going to say.

"Yes, of course, I'm okay with seeing you. I want to see you and spend more time with you," I responded with relief.

"Please James, let me finish," she asked with more a sympathetic resignation than desire for my company.

"Sorry, go on," I motioned.

"I began attending some meetings with the ladies; they all attend Chris's church; you know Chris who was in the band with Andrew?" she questioned nervously.

She searched my face for signs of my knowing what was to come next.

"Yes, of course I remember Chris, we grew up together in church," I responded.

"Well, a beautiful thing happened to me a couple of weeks ago, James. I met Jesus," she blurted, but with a confidence that had been missing from her voice until then.

I was stunned. I had not attended church for nearly forty years except for weddings and funerals. Yet, this lady with whom I was besotted, who to my knowledge had no experience of, or exposure to what I was raised in, has this amazing experience. I had no words to utter immediately, but the first thought or response that welled up from my inner being was, Praise the Lord! But I didn't say that. Perhaps I should have. It may have produced an easier entrance for her to convey her next announcement.

"James, I think you're a wonderful man and I know I've fallen in love with you, but I'm also in love with Jesus and I'm confused and not sure if we should continue with what we've been doing. But James, I still want to be with you," she said.

She said it with what I can only describe as a heartfelt, genuine love that was wrestling with a large degree of confusion.

Whether it was love for me or for Jesus I knew not, and although it seemed somewhat strange at the time, I felt that perhaps both Jesus and I had won the enduring love of an exceptional woman. However,

I was also perplexed and somewhat troubled.

During the preceding years of my married life, I had no contact with Chris, nor the church he pastored, except for Mum's funeral. Andrew had mentioned Chris in conversation on occasions but we rarely, if ever, discussed any subjects regarding church. Sitting in that café opposite Clarita, I began to sense that I was alone; far removed from the 'God' of my childhood and slightly distant from the beautiful woman who had transformed my sadness.

I sensed a strange emotion stirring deep within my being but had no premonition of what was about to emerge from my heart and be spoken from my lips.

"Barbara! Barbara! I'm so sorry!" I cried in anguish.

I called out the name of my beloved wife as I attempted to stifle my tears. It was undoubtedly embarrassing and uncomfortable for Clarita and also for other customers who were enjoying their afternoon coffee. I was scared of what was happening within me and still have no explanation.

Even so, Clarita remained seated with me and placed her hands gently over mine as I pressed them hard into the surface of the table. She sat willingly, holding my hands without saying anything, and I believed that she was empathising with me in my torment and pain.

"Please take me out of here. Take me for a drive somewhere. Please? Can we go?" I begged as I looked up at her through my tears.

Clarita stood up, took my hand and placed a $20.00 note on the counter without waiting for change. We walked to her car and as soon as I was seated on the passenger side, I began to sob again. She reversed out of the car space, exiting the car park onto the street, but I had no idea where we were going. I could feel the motion of the car, but my head was down, not concentrating on directions. After just a few minutes, she stopped the car, and I looked up to see that we were in the car park at Brighton Beach.

Without saying anything, Clarita opened her door and walked around the front of her car to the passenger side and opened my door. She reached out her hand and I held it with mine as I stepped out of the car. We walked down to the beach and along the sand in the direction of Sandringham. We had spoken no words to this point. I had none to say. I was bereft and agonising over the death of my lovely Barbara whilst yearning for this new woman I loved, but seemingly could not now have. All the same, I was so glad that Clarita was with me.

After walking for a couple of minutes, I suddenly realised we were near the place on Brighton Beach where I met Nathan nearly eighteen months earlier. And near where Robyn had flaunted herself before me and invited me to what became my first sexual encounter so many years ago. The disturbances and uncertainties of those two events surfaced. I began to sob again and sank down to the sand. Clarita sat with me but made no attempt to speak, and although she said nothing, her presence communicated her love and comfort.

For perhaps a minute or two, we maintained a silence before I opened the conversation.

"I'm assuming that when you said you're not sure that we can continue doing what we've been doing, that it was in reference to our sexual relationship," I offered, as an unsubtle opener to the next part of our conversation.

"Yes, James. That is what I was referring to, that's what I'm confused about," Clarita replied.

"Does this then mean that you regret what we shared together?" I enquired.

"Well, no James, no, it doesn't mean that at all. It's just that I've heard that God does not approve of sex before marriage and it certainly seems that my new Christian friends believe this, although I've told them nothing of our relationship yet," she replied. She tried to sound authoritative and convinced, but there seemed to be uncertainty in her manner.

"Clarita, I began to fall in love with you the first afternoon we enjoyed coffee together and then lunch. As I returned home late on that lovely autumn day, I sensed something new and beautiful stirring in my heart. There is no way I can now envisage that what transpired between after that meeting, is some sort of 'sin' or ungodly act," I said trying to sound dignified rather than defiant.

"Please James, can you try to understand my position? This is very difficult for me because I have fallen in love with you too," she responded with genuine concern.

"So, the God of love, the supposed creator of the most beautiful sensations and joyful vibrancy we experienced together, says that we can no longer share this beauty he created?" I said, but this time with disdain, and probably no dignity.

"I only hope and pray that we can work through this James, because I know I am in love with you and feel so comfortable being with you," she said.

I knew she was being honest in the expression of her love for me. I was aggrieved and a little angry with the news that the God of love who mysteriously disapproves of love now threatened a wonderful part of our relationship.

My early recollections of the first church services I was taken to when I was just nine, portrayed God as kind, forgiving and loving. For me, that image changed dramatically after Bastard Alwyn wrested control of the church. He left me with an impression of a harsh, vengeful God who was waiting to strike you if you stepped out of line against the doctrine Alwyn delivered.

I could not serve that God, so I walked away from the church. Who was the God that this beautiful woman was now willing to serve? At the time, I was thinking that she was responding to a doctrine of fear.

If it was God who took my beloved Barbara, surely it was God who brought the delightful Clarita into my life. If it was God who took away my best friend and lover, is he now expecting me to forgo all those joys? That seemed like a double whammy to me and a double standard too. He can take Barbara and plunge me into lonely darkness, but when a lamp suddenly burns brightly in my life after nearly eighteen months, He then wants to extinguish that too.

On the beach that afternoon, I was struggling with the thought that the Christian God was cruel. He creates such wonder and pleasure, but labels it sin. To me, that was like growing a beautiful garden but never enjoying the scene, never smelling the fragrances or tasting the fruits. Not only that, but you then you label the garden a sewer.

Comprehending the news Clarita had delivered was difficult in the extreme. What was clarified and settled in my thinking was the fact that I did indeed love her and wanted to be with her. I did not know how to deal with this new dilemma, but continued questioning.

"So, tell me what happened at the meetings, Clarita," I asked, as I desperately attempted to regain some composure.

We sat there for a long time as she warmly articulated her experiences of the ladies' meetings she attended and consequently visiting the church on Sunday mornings. I was surprised when she told me that Tanya was involved too, and even more surprised when she said that my nephew, Adam, had also been 'saved' during the same week. Andrew had said nothing to me about any of this.

But neither Andrew nor I had any knowledge that we would both be hearing similarly related information on the same day. Uncanny? Coincidence? Divine set up? God-ordained? I had no idea, but considered that this might be plain dumb luck?

I looked up at Clarita as she sat with her knees drawn up, her head resting on them and her arms around her legs. There was yet another beauty in her that I became aware of, one that, prior to now, I had not noticed. My heart was touched by her gentleness and some strange force was growing deep inside me. I was falling in love with a love I had never known or experienced and I assumed it was because of, and for, Clarita.

"Clarita, I can honestly say that I love you and although it may seem weird, I also love what has happened to you too." The words were out; my head had no say at all, and I had to assume it was my heart speaking.

Her eyes held my gaze for a while.

"I love you too, James," she said softly, as she smiled, and tears began to well up in her eyes.

"Perhaps I should delay my proposal until a more opportune moment?" I asked, almost as an apology for revealing myself as inconsiderate.

"Only if you want to wait that long for my response," she said with gentleness.

"Well, because I knew my wish was to be with you, I have been practising the words and the way to ask you to marry me," I confessed.

"Well, James, you can still ask?" she offered with loving familiarity.

I again searched the beauty I'd never seen before. I was lost for words, mesmerised. I could sense something welling up inside me. I had never encountered anything like this before, not even in my years in the church. I was not speaking audibly but inwardly I was saying, *"Yes Lord,"* but my intellect was protesting at such an illogical foolishness.

Right there on the beach I thought that I was about to float away. I had little understanding of what was happening. I heard Clarita speak and I 'returned' from 'wherever' I had just been.

"Yes, James, I will," she said with a smile.

"Er… what?… sorry," I stammered, trying to comprehend what had just happened to me and what I was now hearing.

"Yes, James, I will marry you," she replied.

Clarita accepted the proposal I had not officially advanced, and I was delirious with delight.

It was mid-afternoon by the time I arrived home. I felt so bitterly sad for Barbara but strangely comforted too. I had no idea why I thought God was comforting me. I was not sure if He was or even if He existed at all. If He did, what interest could He possibly have in me? Unless it was the inordinate pleasure of stealing from me the exquisite, joyful beauty I had shared with Clarita.

I would prefer that this comfort could not be attributable to God. Revisiting and re-evaluating all that I rejected many years ago, either through ignorance or indifference, seemed too much to contemplate. I remembered there was a verse somewhere in The Bible that said He would wipe away all my tears. Whether it was God, I still felt a warmth and joy swirling within me and caressing my cold heart.

But this was just the beginning. There was so much more in store. Andrew and I were both on a road to what Chris called 'God moments.' They were about to unfold rapidly and culminate in what we all refer to as 'Nathan's miracle.' We were all to be partakers of some incredible 'God moments' at this time. These were either the strangest of coincidences or God was revealing His incredible sense of timing, if not, an equally incredible sense of humour.

Within ten minutes of arriving home the telephone rang. "Hello," I almost sang.

"Hi James, you sound different, in a good way. What's happening?" Andrew asked.

"Been fortunate to have had an interesting day, dear brother, but more about that later. What's up?" I asked.

"Remember Robyn and Julie Phillips?" he asked.

"Of course, I do" I replied. "How could I ever forget?"

"Well Julie and her son Ricky are coming over tonight for a BBQ, and Tanya asked me to invite you and Nathan as well."

"Wow, I haven't seen Julie for over thirty-five years. Will it be alright if I am accompanied by a lady friend?" I asked, trying to conceal my excitement.

"Oh yeah, for sure, James. Wow, that's great. I am so happy for you. Bring her over, mate. It's shaping up to be a great evening," said Andrew with obvious pleasure and then asked, "Do I know her?"

"I'm not sure if you do, but Tanya knows her quite well it seems," I replied.

"Brilliant. I can't wait to meet her. Come over about six and bring a couple of bottles of red from your cellar. They should be perfect for an occasion like this," requested Andrew. "And Mitzi and Raoul are welcome too if they're not doing anything," he added.

"I'll give them a call, mate," I said, before hanging up the phone. I couldn't help sensing that this was going to be a wonderful evening.

First, I telephoned Clarita to inform her of the invitation and that I desired her to accompany me. She was thrilled at the thought of meeting together with my family.

Second, I called Mitzi and Michael. I had to tell them about Clarita before I told anyone else. Michael had visited two months earlier when he came home one weekend, but I did not tell him about Clarita, because at that stage we were still exploring our relationship.

"Hi Mitz, it's Dad," I said when she answered the telephone.

"Daddy, how are you? What have you been up to?" she asked.

Miriam had always been perceptive, and I often wondered if she knew that I was seeing someone or suspected something was happening but tactfully, had not let on. We talked via the telephone regularly, and because she and Raoul lived only fifteen minutes away in Elwood, we met together at least once a week for coffee, usually on a Sunday afternoon.

"I'm fine thanks, darling. How are you and Raoul?" I asked.

"We're great thanks, but tell me about you," she insisted.

"Well, I'm calling to see if you and Raoul would like to come over to Andrew and Tanya's for a BBQ tonight. I know it's short notice, but it seems that there are some interesting things happening," I answered.

"Sorry, we can't make it; Raoul's taking me out to dinner. But we could call in on our way home. Would that be okay?" she enquired.

"Yes, that would be great, darling," I replied.

"So, what's the big occasion Dad?" she asked with what I sensed was a knowing smirk.

I could not keep the charade going. I had to tell her.

"Mitz, I've met a lovely woman and—" I started, before she broke in.

"I knew it Dad! I just knew it! That's wonderful. I'm so happy for you. When can we meet her? Will she be there tonight? What's her name? Do I know her?" So many questions came pouring out and her excitement seemed greater than my own.

"I'll call Raoul and ask if we can change our dinner booking," she said with a laugh.

After talking with my daughter for a while, I then rang Michael, who was equally supportive and thrilled. I hadn't told Miriam that Clarita had agreed to marry me, but I did tell Michael and I also told him I wanted to announce it at the BBQ that night.

"That's fantastic, Dad. I wish I could be there. I'll come down next weekend to meet her, is that okay?" he asked.

"You don't have to come down from Canberra, Michael, you're very busy up there," I replied.

"Bugger busy! I'll be down Friday night. I'll take you both to dinner, and Mitzi and Raoul too. I'll bring Annalise too, is that okay?"

"Sure son, that will be wonderful. We would all love to see both of you again. Thank you, Michael," I replied with a grateful heart.

We chatted for another five or ten minutes. I was elated. I had the support of my children, although I had been unsure of what their response or reaction might be. Their mother had been such a precious influence in their lives, and I had been hesitant of introducing Clarita.

After speaking with Miriam and Michael, I went to the loungeroom and sat down and cried. I have no idea why I cried for so long. Perhaps I was crying for Barbara, perhaps I was crying tears of joy. Either way, it was quite confusing, but equally comforting.

As I dressed for the evening, I felt a great sense of relief. I was looking forward to driving over to pick up Clarita and then go to Andrew and Tanya's for a wonderful evening. For the most part, I was excited about surprising everyone with the announcement of my engagement to Clarita.

But my surprise announcement was to take second place, and I am so pleased it did. The major announcement of the evening was dramatically and surprisingly unpredictable, even 'miraculous'. The Darling family was about to be bombarded with an unforeseeable 'blessing'.

For most of my life I had little interest in the 'things of God.' I was sixteen when I decided I would not be attending church anymore. During my many years practising as an architect, I never gave any credit to God for my success. When I give thought to my career, I do not credit anyone with my success, not even myself. I just assumed it was 'one of those things' that happened, and I was fortunate that the success eventuated in my life.

The events of these last three months were instrumental in God getting my attention, if indeed that is what was occurring. I sensed an understanding of God's grace was developing within me, yet I remain uncertain if God had anything to do with the events. But if He had, it seemed that He was different to the God that Bastard Alwyn portrayed. Even though Pastor Tom had projected a wonderful loving father figure of what God was like, it was Alwyn's images that caused my contempt and withdrawal.

I am thankful that I am still here and planning a wonderful new journey of love. My grateful appreciation also encompasses Clarita being in love with me.

To this point everything seemed a little surreal, and not at all what I expected should happen. To my understanding, based on my early years in the church, I had been living a life of sin. Why would God choose to be good to me? I remembered the words that Pastor Tom used to often repeat.

*"God is good, God is good all the time."*

If God is real and if these events have been at His instigation, then I may reconsider all I was taught about God's judgemental nature. I may have to concede that His grace extends much further than people, especially most Christians, give Him credit for.

# PART 3

## ANDREW

Reflections – Past, Present
and Future, The Arrival

It seems that my contribution to the story of the Darling Brothers is nearing an end. What that end might look like remains to be seen, but I have read what James and Nathan have written and I feel much closer to my brothers now that we have written our individual stories.

On the surface, it seems that God did not feature much in our daily lives since our late teenage years, until the last eighteen months. But now, I think it is possible that perhaps He has somehow remained with us all these years despite ourselves.

Did God have another path for us to follow? Have we missed his 'calling'? Personally, I don't think I missed much at all. I have been very fortunate to have led such a rewarding and fulfilling life. I never sensed any emptiness or felt a need to go to church or to come back to the Lord, as Christians are often-times ready to point out. I don't think I ever thought of myself as a backslider because I've been so busy fulfilling my dreams. Also, to be a backslider, one needs to have made a personal commitment at some stage and I don't think I ever did that in a formal way.

However, I must admit, that deep down, I sometimes acknowledged that if He existed, perhaps God had indeed blessed me, although I have no idea why.

Why do some people seem to achieve great things while others who have equal or greater talent go unnoticed? I don't think I have a good answer for this question, but I have been on the speakers' circuit for a number of years and have been invited as a motivational speaker, to address various functions over the years.

I always finish these talks with these words. *"There are no great people in this world, only ordinary people who attempt great things."* Perhaps this is the only answer I can offer. I don't now nor have I ever seen myself as a great person. I'm just an ordinary guy who stepped out and had a go.

It wasn't always easy. There were many times I wanted to give up.

There were many times I failed. I got ripped off, had doors closed in my face, got knocked-back and refused, but for some reason, I kept at it. I believe that some of the things that Pastor Tom used to say possibly made a nest in my heart, and perhaps I always drew encouragement from his wisdom.

I have some wonderful long-term friendships with some well-known and some not-so-well-known people. My best friend, Wally, whom I only see once or twice a year, is like another brother. We went to school together and were in the same band for three years, sharing some highs and some lows. Through them all, we formed a strong bond built on respect and love for the talents and qualities we shared.

Not that I want to be seen as a name-dropper, but I thought it might be interesting to list some of the many people both famous and not-so-famous, that I have not just met, but actually have contact with at least twice a year. I hope I don't leave anyone out. If I have left you out, please forgive my oversight.

Ross Wilson and Ross Hannaford. I first met when they were in The Pink Finks back in the mid-sixties. Their band played in the old gymnasium at our school carnival one Saturday afternoon. I was only twelve at the time but remember being enthralled by the musical rapport and energy between both men. I think they were still at school in those days.

That was a day that changed my life. I spoke to both Wilson and Hannaford afterwards, and they seemed very approachable and friendly. I asked Ross Wilson what type of guitar I should buy because I wanted to learn.

"Choose a guitar that feels good to you and that you love holding," he said as he unstrapped his guitar and placed it over my shoulder.

He then placed my fingers on some strings and said, "Play that one, mate."

I strummed once and he said, "There you go mate, you just played **Am.** Welcome to the world of rock and roll," and he and Hannaford both laughed as he took his guitar and put it the case.

It was a moment that made a great impression. It wasn't a great musical lesson, but it was an introduction that taught me how to treat others who had dreams and aspirations. I've mentioned that afternoon to Ross on a few occasions, but he doesn't remember it.

When I started my own band, I came up with the name, 'Pink Granite', out of respect for Ross and The Pink Finks, but also because of the direction we wanted to take musically. Hard rock but with a touch of glam. Not long after we started rehearsing together, 'The Zoot' hit the scene with their pink suits and pink outfits so we had to come up with another name for our band. Nearly twenty years later, I was in Los Angeles when I met Beeb Birtles who had been in 'The Zoot'. He was one of the founding members of The Little River Band, and they were touring America doing a series of concerts.

At the time I was living in Los Angeles and spending time with a number of 'ex-pat' Aussies who were there or passing through. Olivia Newton-John was there and so was Billy Thorpe and Rick Springfield. I met so many people coming and going to and from Australia. Max Merritt, Ian 'Molly' Meldrum and Beeb to name just a few. But it wasn't just people in the rock or pop music scene who passed through.

Los Angeles was where I first met Graeme Murphy, who went on to become the founder and director of the internationally acclaimed, The Sydney Dance Company. I wrote some music for a couple of very early works that we hoped would be danced by the company, but they never eventuated. Nevertheless, Graeme and I have kept in contact and meet at least once a year, usually in Sydney, because I'm up there more than Graeme is in Melbourne.

* * *

What happens next for the Darling brothers? I suppose life will continue much as it has for me. James has found a new partner with whom he can enjoy his remaining years. As for Nathan, I am hoping that he will regain his passion and focus on his art and manage to live a productive life.

One thing I do know is that there are some interesting things happening. About three months ago, Chris told me I would be having a number of what he called 'God-moments'. He believes that God has specifically impressed upon him the need to pray for me. It was not because I was necessarily in any danger, but instead, that God was reaching out to me. Why Chris has waited so many years or why God has waited so many years is a mystery. Nevertheless, there have been some interesting developments.

Meeting Tanya in San Francisco in 1974, marrying her and having our children is by far the best part of my life. But recently I have been made aware of 'God things' happening to members of my family. Throwing another 'event' in this strange mix has been Adam's admission just last week that he is gay.

I was surprised at my reaction. I stood up, walked over and hugged him, telling him that as a father I love him no matter who he is or what he wants to do with his life. He had tears of gladness and relief in his eyes. Michelle and Giselle were equally supportive, but Tanya was shocked. She took quite a long time to compose herself. I thought it was probably because Adam had seemed to be in a relationship with a girl he met in Sydney while at the National Institute of Dramatic Arts. (N.I.D.A.)

Two days after Adam revealed he is gay, I found out why Tanya was so disturbed.

Tanya confessed she had been visiting regularly with Chris' wife, Mel, and some of the other ladies from the church where Chris was the pastor. She hadn't said anything to me, but this seemed the answer to her shock on hearing of Adam's sexuality. Added to this was the admission both she and Adam had been to services at the church and they had both been 'born again' and 'baptised in the Holy Spirit' and spoken in 'other tongues'.

She could not comprehend or connect Adam's salvation experience, and two weeks later his opening up about his sexuality.

Now I had to formulate a practical, but loving response to my wife's secret meetings and her 'born again' experience. I was happy for her I guess, but also perplexed that she kept it a secret. Tanya was so contrite about the perceived need for secrecy and constantly chastised herself for not saying anything. Both Chris and his wife, Mel, were encouraging her to tell me, assuring her that I would not reject her.

Perhaps she assumed I would reject her because of what she had seen during her upbringing in Russia. She had seen neighbours and a cousin taken away for subversive activities. Their crime was attending bible study classes in private homes and she never saw any of those people again.

Adam's conflict soon surfaced too. Both he and I were at home one Saturday afternoon while the girls were out shopping at Southland.

Adam came into the family room where I was sitting quietly reading The Saturday Age.

This would become an extraordinarily wonderful day that none of us will ever forget.

"Dad, I need to talk," he said emotionally.

"Sure Addie-boy, go ahead," I replied, as I put the newspaper aside.

He started to cry. "Dad, I'm scared and confused. I know I'm supposed to be happy, full of the joy of the Lord, but everything seems to be wrong. I seem to be wrong. I don't know what to do or say to anyone," he confessed through his tears.

Fortunately, Adam and I have always had a great father/son relationship and communication. "So, what do think the problem is and what do you think you can do about it?" I asked.

"Well, I've told you that I'm gay and now you also know I got 'saved' a couple of weeks ago at church. I've wanted to tell you about my sexuality for more than a year but didn't know how. I thought that my newfound faith had given me the courage to tell you all. But according to the church, I'm the worst kind of sinner," he said in dismay before he continued.

"I heard some guys, Christian guys, talking at church last Sunday night, saying that 'queers' are disgusting individuals who surrender their manhood to pursue evil, unnatural desires," Adam related with anxiety.

"Do you think you have surrendered your manhood?" I asked.

"No Dad, I think I'm supposed to have surrendered my whole life to Jesus, not just my manhood, but I'm not sure if that's what I've done. It's all very confusing," he responded.

"Adam," I said, looking him in the eye and moving close to him, "you are my wonderful son whom I love, treasure, adore and take great pride in. I don't know what I can say that will help. However, I was raised in a Christian environment and have a good understanding of the faith you have embraced, so let me ask you this. Do you think God really loves you? Did you experience an overwhelming sense of His love? Did you feel accepted?"

"Yes, I sensed all that and more, so much more. But I believed I was 'stepping out in faith' to tell my family that I was gay, only to find that I've stepped out in faith to plunge into an abyss," he said through tears and with a trace of fear.

"Okay, let me ask some other questions," I said as I put my hand on his shoulder. "If I, as an earthly father love you as much as I do, how much more do you think God loves you? If I love and accept you without any understanding of what you're going through, how much more does the God of all wisdom and understanding, accept and love you?" I asked compassionately.

I was in awe of the responses that were coming, not just from my mouth, but from my heart. I don't recall ever experiencing anything quite like this. It was waves of compassion and waves of love flowing through me. Was God 'ministering' through me or was I just being a loving father to my son who was facing a huge dilemma?

At this time of growing closer to my son, I was also aware of a growing closeness to God, but it was not a closeness that I had been seeking. More than that, it seemed that I was being visited. I was experiencing a 'God moment' as Chris recently suggested I would have in the coming days, weeks and months.

I didn't know why he said that at the time, but there were more to come. I also did not know why God would be interested in me because I'd had nothing much to do with Him for over thirty-five years.

"Have you made any friends at church with whom you think you could be open?" I asked hopefully.

"Yeah, I guess. There is one guy, Ricky, who I get on really well with since I started going to church with Mum. He's been a Christian since he was about five. He's a great guy. I've only known him for two weeks, but I really love him, not in a gay way though. We talk about God stuff and Bible stuff, but we also talk about theatre, music and art. I don't know if he's gay, but as soon as we met, we both felt that there was an instant connection. We haven't talked about relationships or girls or any sexual stuff," Adam said.

"Do you know what the instant connection might have been?" I enquired.

"Not really. It seemed surreal when we were introduced. Both of us commented to each other about our introduction and how it felt strange in a unique and wonderful way, but neither of us knows what it might be. We are the same height, same age, same hair colour, same eyes and a few other uncanny similarities. It seemed like we were brothers, or even twins, not identical though, who had never seen each other before," he responded with a great sense of boyish wonder. "Anyway, we are brothers now that I have accepted Jesus."

"Well, I'd like to meet him, Addie," I offered.

"Sure, Dad, that would be great," he replied with much enthusiasm. "Can I invite him over? When would be a good time? Can his mum come too? You knew her years ago," he added excitedly.

"Oh yeah? Who is Ricky's mum, and how would I know her?" I quizzed.

"Julie Phillips," he replied. "She and her older sister, Robyn, used to go to the same church when you were younger," he concluded.

He eagerly searched my face for a positive response.

"Really," I said in surprise. "Well, we should invite them over. Let's talk to Mum when she and the girls get back," I said, trying to give him some assurance and support.

None of us knew at the time how significant and enthralling the friendship between Adam and Ricky was, nor the overwhelming joy that this relationship would bring to the whole Darling family. We were about to discover something that would bring what I can only describe as a new 'God-focus', absurd as that seems, into our lives. Calling it a coincidence does not seem credible, nor does it even seem right.

Adam and I continued to talk for nearly two hours about my early experiences at home and in church and of family fun with Mum and Dad and my two brothers. We finished up sitting outside under the pergola drinking Corona beer with a lemon that Adam picked from our tree.

When Tanya, Michelle, and Giselle returned, they showed us their purchases with great excitement, seeking approval from Adam and me. We both looked at each other and smiled, sensing we had discovered something wonderful about each other, something we had never known or seen before.

After much chatter while looking at new garments the girls had bought, Adam asked Tanya about inviting Julie and Ricky over and could they come over tonight?

"Lovely," exclaimed Tanya, "Let's have a BBQ later this afternoon.

We'll invite James and Nathan too. I'm sure they would love to see Julie again. Come on, girls, we'll start making some salads."

They picked up their bags of new things and headed inside. Adam looked at me with a smirk of great satisfaction and suggested I contact my brothers and invite them over.

My first call was to James. He seemed much brighter and told me there is a new woman in his life. Tanya and I were very excited about meeting her, although James said that Tanya already knew his new lady friend. This was one more piece of information I was finding out for the first time.

I then called Nathan to ask him over to see Julie, and he was thrilled with the news. His response was very encouraging, and I was glad to hear the obvious joy and sense of expectation. We knew he'd seen Julie in the Solomon Islands, which was where she told him of Alwyn's abuses against her and Robyn.

A couple of hours later, as I was readying the BBQ, Julie and Ricky arrived, but only a few minutes before Nathan. I was both surprised and delighted to see Nathan and Julie kissing and hugging each other with enthusiastic greeting. It was as though they had been missing each other for a long time. I had no idea at that time of the relationship they shared for four months on Nathan's yacht about twenty years ago.

The arrival of James and Clarita at this time distracted me from Nathan and Julie's obvious delight to see each other again, but I will never forget how alive and reinvigorated James looked. He looked so happy, to the extent that those initial few minutes of his arrival brought a tear of happiness to my eye. Clarita seemed perfect for James, and I found myself falling in love with my entire family in a new way. Everyone was looking and sounding so happy and there was much talking, laughing and family merriment.

It seemed that the frustrations, pains and torments caused by past events would never trouble us again. Can life manifest such expectancy?

But past experiences walking with both James and Nathan through their troubles and travails should have perhaps warned me of further 'suddenlies'. It was a wonderful summer evening, but Melbourne summers produce the darkest clouds and wildest storms, and summer was not yet over.

I was standing by the bench near the BBQ as James introduced Clarita. Tanya was at my side, and she and Clarita gave each other a familiar greeting and kiss. I would be told in greater detail of their involvement at Chris's church later that evening.

While we were enjoying our first meeting with Clarita, suddenly there was a loud cry from Nathan, who was seated on the other side of the pool with Julie and Ricky. He'd fallen off the chair to his knees with his head on Julie's lap as he screamed and sobbed. It sounded horrendous and we all ran around to see what was wrong.

By the time we got there, Ricky was also on his knees with his arm around Nathan. Nathan, Ricky and Julie were sobbing and hugging each other. Nathan was incoherent. James and I tried to help him to his feet, but he didn't want to move. He suddenly turned and hugged Ricky and they fell over onto the paved pool edge. Nathan kissed Ricky on both cheeks and wept loudly.

"Nathan! Nathan! What's the matter?" called James as he knelt down to comfort his younger brother.

"Jimmy!" Nathan screamed, as he reached up and threw his arms around his brother's neck and pulled him down to the ground too.

James just lay there with Nathan and Ricky while we all waited for them to compose themselves. Ricky started laughing through his tears.

"Thank you, Jesus! Thank you, Jesus! Thank you, Jesus!" he said over and over.

I noticed Tanya, Adam, and Clarita standing nearby. They were holding hands and obviously praying in tongues. Michelle and Giselle were also there, but none of them had any idea of what was happening.

After a few minutes, Nathan began to get to his feet. Ricky helped him as Julie also rose to her feet from where she had remained on the chair. The three of them hugged each other. The sobbing and crying had subsided, and they just looked at each other and kissed each other. None of us had any idea what this episode was all about.

Nathan turned to face us all. He looked a little dishevelled but beaming, nonetheless.

"I just found out that Ricky is my son," he called loudly. "Ricky is my son. I have a boy. I am a father, and I just found out," and he began to weep with joy again.

We were all totally stunned. There was silence for a short moment before Adam went over to Ricky and hugged him, and they both cried and laughed.

"My new best friend and brother in Christ is my cousin. My brother is my cousin," he cried with a great joyful expression. It was obvious now why they both realised there was a connection when they first met two weeks earlier.

Once again, there was much hugging. Once again there was wonderment and awe in my heart. What was happening in our lives? I could only conclude this was the most amazing of coincidences, or perhaps God was working overtime in our family. I pondered whether this was His handiwork and what other wonders might also arise. I wished so much that Mum and Dad could have been with us at that moment. I also wondered if this was indeed God's doing, why didn't He do something positive and helpful years ago?

The explanation of how Ricky was Nathan's son would come later. But for the entire evening Nathan, Julie and Ricky rarely left each other's sides as they talked, laughed, and sometimes cried and we all delighted in this incredible story.

Because of the heartfelt outpouring after hearing this 'miraculous' news, we hadn't paid much attention to James and Clarita. But while we were all enjoying a marvellous celebration over dinner, Nathan addressed that issue with great delight.

"So, big brother Jimmy, it's time for you and Clarita to tell us your story. I can tell by looking at you that it's a great story," he said with warm confidence.

As Nathan was speaking, Miriam and Raoul arrived, which made the occasion all the more special for James. None of us knew James and Clarita were about to inform us of their engagement.

James and Clarita told us how they met and their brief history. They interrupted each other, finished each other's sentences, laughed, held hands and gave each other an occasional kiss. Everything about that evening and long into the night was very special in so many ways.

During the course of the evening I saw Tanya, Julie and Clarita talking together and hugging each other and laughing as they shared whatever the evening had presented for them. Nathan, Ricky and Adam also seemed inseparable and sat together on the seats near the BBQ to keep warm. Julie went over to them often, standing behind Ricky and putting her arms around his neck and then doing the same thing to Nathan.

Something dark and foreboding had broken off Nathan. He looked radiant and was glowing with this 'miraculous' blessing. I was ecstatic to see him look and act so incredibly happy, and he seemed to throw off the many years of torment and looked younger for hearing this most welcome news. At times, I was reminded of family life with Mum and Dad when they had people from church come over for a BBQ. I couldn't stop thinking how much Mum and Dad would have loved witnessing this most incredible evening.

Who could have predicted such an outcome? What an incredible joy for Nathan! What a great blessing Clarita was for James. For myself, I was surprisingly elated with what Tanya and Adam had experienced and have been speaking with Chris regularly. The fact that Clarita had the same experience may yet inspire James to explore faith anew. But I sense he still remains indifferent or even angry toward God. I think that is understandable. So do I, in many ways.

It was a remarkable evening for all of us. There is nothing more I can add to describe the strange thrill of what is unfolding in our lives. Is this the grace of God?

* * *

Later that evening Nathan asked James and I to meet with him because he had something important to tell us. The time was decided as being the following Saturday afternoon at Mum's unit and I tried to guess what the next exciting episode might be that Nathan was going to reveal. After what had recently been revealed, I was looking forward to hearing the next piece of information.

Once again, past experiences of 'suddenlies' should have warned that this may not be a welcome report Nathan was bringing us. As it turned out, it most definitely wasn't. So, now there is another change of direction to our unfolding story.

Where will the grace or goodness of God be now, if it exists at all?

# PART 3

## NATHAN

The Lost Years, Simon, My Ketch

So, what was I doing for nearly 28 years & how is it that nobody could trace me? 'Disappearing' was much easier than I expected. I simply changed my name. Fictitious name with bank account, post office box & licences. Wasn't so difficult to do back then, but almost impossible to do the same way today.

Now that those years have passed, I look back with a deep sense of loss & grief. But there are also some great memories. There's also a sense of satisfaction & a sense of awe. Not only was I separated from those who loved me, but I was also separated from myself. Joe's sexual abuse of me was an emotional, psychological & spiritual amputation of my soul.

I felt more than sorry for myself. I was in darkness. The light that was supposed to shine in my life & from my life had been extinguished. I cried, I sobbed, I howled. I called out to God for healing, but the pain kept growing. The hollow darkness was relentlessly heavy. I had gone. I don't know where I went, but I left myself to deal with my torments while I set off in search of reason. Reason is bullshit. I could find no reason. I got lost trying to find reason or meaning. I was in there somewhere, but I didn't know where.

But for now, let me concentrate on some of the good stuff. There are a lot of great stories to tell. Andrew has been encouraging me to write a book about my adventures. He thinks it would make a great movie. Perhaps when I complete my story in this book, I might write of those years in greater detail. I have over 50 books of notes, anecdotes, poetry & pain which I wrote over those years.

During the 28 years away from my family & anyone who knew me, I have travelled to many parts of the world. Primarily my visits were to the islands of the Pacific, but I also sailed to South America, Central America & Mexico. Other countries I have been to include Japan, The Philippines, Malaysia, New Guinea, Borneo (Kalimantan), Bali, Celebes, Sumatra & many other Indonesian islands & Thailand

& Sri Lanka.

This all became possible for 2 reasons. First, Vera gave me Joe's boat & an old case of documents. Second, I met Simon. More about Simon later.

After church one Sunday, a couple of weeks following Joe's death, Vera said she had something to give me. She took me aside to talk. I was totally surprised at her offer. But she was genuine. She also expressed concern for me.

"I don't know vot happened on da boat vit Joe. I don't know vot he might have done, but I vont you to have Joe's boat. Mark & I, ve are not vontink for anyt'ink," she told me.

My thoughts could find no words for my mouth to speak at that moment. Vera, possibly sensing my inability to respond, continued. "Dere are too many sad memories attached to dat boat, so I vont you to decide vot to do vit it."

I looked at her, still unable to find any meaningful words of surprise or thanks. I had no idea what to say or do. Joe's boat was a valuable asset & it was being given to me.

"Da only t'ink I ask is dat you see dis as a blessing from Got, not from Vera," she said.

"I... I... I don't know what to say," I stammered.

"Vell, vot do you say ven Got blesses you?" she questioned gently, as she looked up at me.

"Er... thank you, Lord. Thank you, Jesus. Praise God," I said, still in a daze over what was happening.

"An' dat is all I need to hear. Got is happy, I am happy & I pray dat you vill be happy too, dear boy."

With those words, she handed me an old brown leather briefcase.

That afternoon I sat at the kitchen table on board what was now my boat. I read through the documents. The envelope on top looked new, so I decided it was the one to open first. It was a solicitors' letter signed by Vera & giving me title to *The Netherseas* & all that Joe had title to aboard the vessel & all that pertained to the vessel & all income that I derived from operating Joe's assets.

Rachel's dad, Robert, had told me Joe owned at least 3 houses in Auckland & had plenty of money saved & stashed away for his retirement & a planned trip to Europe. Joe wanted to return to Holland for an extended visit to catch up with relatives he & Vera had not seen for many years.

I got myself a drink from the fridge before returning to the table. I stood looking out the small windows at the yachts & other craft moored in the harbour. As I turned to go back to the table, my eyes fell on the door to Joe's cabin. The sign on the door read 'CAPTAIN'. I had never been in that cabin. I wasn't sure if I wanted to go in. I finally decided to.

It was very neat. There was a single bed, a small desk, a single-door wardrobe & some small drawers. As I stood looking around, I opened the wardrobe & drawers. Nothing of any value to be seen, just Joe's clothes. I didn't want any of them. Finally, I approached the desk. The one drawer below the desktop was locked.

"Bugger," I said aloud. "Where did you put the key, Joe, you bastard?"

Perhaps it was on the key ring Joe kept in the wheelhouse. I went up to get the keys & brought them down below. Sure enough, the key was there. I opened the drawer. I immediately wished I hadn't.

There were a couple of folders on top, similar to the one in the briefcase. Underneath were a number of gay porn magazines & also some black & white photos of naked guys doing really gross stuff that made me feel almost physically ill.

I was immediately swamped with the memory & accompanying pain & torment of the abuse Joe inflicted on me. I wanted to cry but couldn't. I wanted to scream but was afraid someone would hear me. I wanted to get rid of the disgusting magazines & other photos but was afraid to take them outside in case someone saw me with them.

Leaving Joe's cabin, I slammed the door shut behind me. I went back to the kitchen, sat down & started sobbing. I lay my head & arms on the table trying to stifle the sounds of my bitterness in the sleeves of my jacket. Eventually I cried myself to sleep. I woke up when it was dark. I made myself a toasted cheese & tomato sandwich & sat down again. I was not enjoying the first night on board what was now, my boat. I didn't like being alone either. But I would be for the next 27 years.

I was thinking of how to get rid of the gay porn. I remembered that there was a piece of weather-worn steel on top of the fridge on the rear deck. It was about 6 inches long, 2 inches wide & about a quarter of an inch thick. I went up on deck, retrieved it & brought it down to the kitchen. Carefully wrapping the magazines & photos around the piece of steel, I then secured them in place using some fishing line. I dropped the weighted parcel over the side of the boat that faced away from the dock.

That act, I think, gave me a sense of burying Joe's evil. Unfortunately, it was not enough to give me any comfort or sense of healing.

But inside that awful drawer were 2 folders similar to the one with the papers for *The Netherseas*. Returning to the kitchen table with them, I sat down to look at all 3 folders. First, I emptied the contents of the folder labelled *The Netherseas,* which had been in the briefcase. It contained photos of the boat & documents of title which were, of course, now transferred to me.

The other 2 folders held documents & photos too. Joe owned 2 other boats. I don't know if Vera or Mark had any idea. I had no idea what they were worth. At the time, I didn't give a shit about their value. But it seemed that I was now the owner of 3 professional fishing boats. Not a fleet, but valuable assets just the same. I decided at that moment I would sell the boats. I didn't know what I would do with the money.

Now the part about Simon. It was a Tuesday morning, a week & 2 days after Vera had given me the boat. I was sitting in a folding chair at the stern of *The Netherseas* feeling very depressed & confused. In one hand I had a can of Coke, & with the other was running my fingers through my hair.

I wasn't taking much notice of what was happening on the dock. I saw a guy walking along slowly, but I paid little attention to his approach. He stopped when he reached me. I glanced up to see a friendly, smiling face.

"Permission to come aboard, skipper?" he light-heartedly enquired.

"Er, yeah, I guess so," I responded.

I remember thinking to myself that this guy must be a Christian. He had the look. Neat, tidy, well groomed, well spoken. Very straight & too friendly to be genuine. I was becoming cynical.

"What are you drinking?" he asked.

"Coke," I replied.

Now I knew he was a Christian. I figured he was making sure I wasn't drinking alcohol.

"Have you got another can? I'll pay you for it," he offered.

"Sure, in the fridge... that big white box there," I pointed, "& there's no charge."

I was feeling sick in the guts already. I was planning to tear this dickhead to shreds, verbally. It was easy to figure out what was coming next. He was going to tell me about Jesus & how much God loved me & if I trust Him, then *'all things will work together for good.'*

I'd read that verse in Romans a few times. But, as a result of what had happened just over three weeks earlier, I was having a lot of trouble seeing how God was working anything for good. I was preparing to give this guy both barrels of my 'testimony' of being fucked up the arse by a church elder, just to delight in his shocked reaction.

"Thanks, man," he said, as he reached forward to shake my hand. "My name is Simon."

I had a quiet chuckle to myself because he just gave himself away. Only a Christian trying to be cool would say "Thanks, man." He probably should have said, "Thank you, brother." Either way, my response was, & would have been the same.

"That's okay… man," I answered with a slight touch of cynicism. If he noticed, he certainly didn't show it.

"I heard about what happened to the owner of the boat," he said with a look that I took to mean he wanted more information.

Before I could say anything, he asked, "Do you want to talk about it?" This question added to my confidence in picking him as a Christian.

"No, I don't want to talk about it," I said flatly.

"Okay, man, that's cool. I'm sorry for being so insensitive," he answered.

*'I sure can pick 'em'*, I thought to myself. Every time this guy opens his mouth, he puts his foot *(shod with the preparation of the gospel of peace)* right in it.

"That's okay," I said in a half-hearted attempt to make him feel better. "My name's Nathan."

He stuck his hand out again. "Well, I'm pleased to meet you, Nathan," he said with his well- groomed, neat smile.

Suddenly I had a great idea. I'll ask him what church he goes to, then get to the nitty-gritty of why he wanted to come on board. I was far too clever for Simon.

"So, Simon, what church do you go to?" I asked confidently.

"Shit, man, are you serious?" he responded in startled amazement with a shrill cry that sounded more like a girl. "Whatever made you think I go to church?"

I was stunned. I got it wrong. My confidence abated & I began searching for a way of escape. But Simon provided that.

"No! Perhaps you better not answer that question," he said.

So that was my introduction to Simon. We sat there on the rear deck of *The Netherseas* talking about art, music, theatre, literature & the sea & the world full of all its exotic locations. We had an enjoyable couple of hours drinking Coke, eating savoury biscuits & cheese & talking about stuff that we were both interested in. After approximately 2 hours had passed, Simon said he should be going.

"Going where?" I asked.

"Back to my father's yacht," he replied with a nonchalance that seemed to indicate I should have known this already.

"Which is your dad's yacht?" I asked.

"See those yachts over there," he said, pointing to a group of sleek yachts about 50 metres away. "Which one looks the biggest?" he asked with a touch of mischief.

It was obvious which one was the biggest because it was nearly twice the size of the others.

"Hmm... ah... perhaps the white one," I replied, with equal humour because they were all white.

"Quite correct, old boy," he said, putting on an upper-class British accent & adding, "I think it would be jolly splendid if you were to join us for dinner this evening. What say ye?"

"Sure, cobber," I said with a Cockney accent. "And at wha' o'clock do ya wan' me to arrive me ol' mate?"

"I think 7.00pm will be fine... & please have a shower & shave &

most definitely wear apparel appropriate for such an occasion," he said with faked pompous pride.

"Tha' oi will do squire," I replied, continuing our charade.

"Okay. See you at 7 then," he said as a cheerful smile spread across his face while he waved & walked away.

7 o'clock arrived as I stood staring at the majestic yacht that Simon had pointed to from the deck of *The Netherseas*. I was enthralled by everything: the three tall, sturdy masts, the gleaming brass fittings, the immaculate deck, the white hull. Three thin, dark blue stripes ran the full length between the deck & the top of the shiny, brass-trimmed portholes.

"Master Nathan of *The Netherseas*, please step aboard," announced Simon.

I looked around to see Simon wearing neatly pressed white trousers, white shoes, white shirt, gold cravat & a navy-blue blazer with gold buttons. His dark hair was immaculately groomed. He stood at attention, inviting me aboard.

"Welcome aboard, dear boy," he mimicked in an upper-class British accent as I stepped onto the deck. "Drinks & entrée will be served shortly."

"Thank you, Master Simon," I toffed, "& a rather splendid maritime masterpiece you have here dear chap," I continued, fitting in with the very grand environment I found myself in.

We spent about an hour & a half enjoying a superbly presented dinner. We swapped stories of our years growing up. I said nothing of my life in the church. I said nothing at all of my experiences as a 'born again' Christian. Occasionally the awful memory of what Joe had done to me just 3 weeks earlier would surface. I'd take another drink of wine from my glass & concentrate on what Simon was telling me.

Much of the time was spent talking about girls & our experiences with the opposite sex. I thought of Rachel. Why had she suddenly walked out of our lives? I didn't say anything to Simon about Rachel. It would mean explaining my affiliation with the church. I didn't want to at the time. I was in great torment because of what Joe had done & also of his shocking death. But I was grieving far more over Rachel.

I was wondering if I was even supposed to be a Christian. My upbringing should have ensured that I stayed grounded in the basics of my faith. If that didn't suffice, my wonderful born-again experience should have.

My grasp on life was slipping from my hands. I couldn't find anything to hold on to. I wanted to hold on to Jesus, but the recent traumas made everything dark & slimy. I felt like I was a boat set adrift in a dark & stormy sea. I was at the mercy of pounding seas. They boiled in my heart & head. Sometimes I felt giddy, even as I walked on land.

"So, where are you Nathan?"

I was surprised at the question.

"Are you okay?" Simon asked.

"Yeah... er... thanks, Simon. Sorry, I guess I've had a bit too much on my mind," I replied.

"Well, I've got just the cure, come sailing with us tomorrow. Dad will be returning later this evening & we were planning to go anyway. Have you ever been sailing before?" he asked.

"A couple of times, when I was younger. My mum's father & my dad's father were both members of a yacht club," I responded. "But are you sure your dad won't mind?"

"Dad won't mind at all. I'm sure he'll be pleased that I've found a friend here in Auckland," Simon answered enthusiastically. "Besides, it's a bloody big yacht, so there's plenty of room for one more."

"Well, okay then. What time?" I asked.

"We're leaving about 9.00am, so be here about ten or fifteen minutes earlier," he said, then added, "& don't worry about bringing anything, we've got plenty of gear & food on board."

The next day proved to be decisive for me. It resulted in the opening up of a new future. Simon's father, Ron, was a very inspirational, & obviously, a very wealthy guy. He had an incredible love of yachting & of the sea. During the course of the day, I formulated what I would do with Joe's boats & with my life.

Over the next 2 weeks, I went sailing with Ron & Simon on many occasions before they had to return to Sydney on the beautiful yacht. I asked Ron many questions about yachts & learning to sail. I wanted to know what sort of yacht I should buy.

The day before they were to leave, Ron invited me to a BBQ on board. That evening, Ron introduced me to Alec, a keen yachtsman who lived in Auckland. This meeting was another important step toward my new life of adventure at sea. It was an adventure that would last for more than 25 years.

After Ron & Simon left Auckland to sail back to Australia, I spent a lot of time with Alec & other guys from the yacht club. I learned as much as I could about sailing, about yachts & about the sea. I'd always liked the sea, probably because we lived in Hampton. It was an easy walk to the beach. My brothers & I spent a lot of time on the beach with family & friends.

My friendship with Ron led to my love affair with sailing. But it was more than just sailing. It was a means of escape. What Joe had done & the events that followed left me with the urgent desire to 'disappear'. I had no idea at the time that my 'disappearance' would last so many years.

I spent a few weeks with Alec, meeting with him & other men at the yacht club. I decided to sell Joe's big fishing boats & buy a yacht. With Alec's assistance, I found a beautifully equipped ocean-going craft at a very good price. I had plenty of money left from the sale of Joe's boats. I invested some with Alec in a property development company he was a director of. He told me that Ron was also one of the directors & their interests were mostly concentrated on The Queensland Gold Coast & The Sunshine Coast.

Perhaps I should have done some research before handing over the money to Alec. There were times I wondered why I'd been so foolish. But I needn't have worried. That initial investment has grown to give me a net worth of over $3,000,000.00 today. But I'd give it all away to have my life back the way it was. Before Joe fucked me, my world & my future.

James recently made this monetary discovery. He was going through the many papers & notebooks I had in my small house in Warburton. Although both Ron & Alec had died a few years ago, I was still listed as an original partner & shareholder with full claim & benefits of my original investment of 26 years ago. I wasn't surprised to learn the current managing director was Simon. We have since re-established contact & he told me about his salvation experience. My initial 'thought' all those years ago on the rear of *The Netherseas* seemed to have been prophetic. It made me smile with amused contentment.

But for now, let me go back to my love affair with sailing. Having purchased my 54' ocean-going ketch, I set about learning everything about its history & capabilities from the previous owner.

Hugh was originally from England & had purchased the yacht in Sausalito, California in 1970. In 1976, he & five friends set sail for Australia, via Hawaii, Fiji & New Zealand. After 5 months lazily sailing across the Pacific, they arrived in Auckland. But they never sailed to Australia. Within a week of arriving in New Zealand, one of Hugh's friends died of a heart attack. Then 2 flew back home to California & the last returned to England.

Hugh was now faced with finding 1, 2 or more people for the

final leg to Australia. During this time, Hugh met a younger lady & as he put it, "I decided to dock in her harbour."

So now, more than 6 years later, he was selling his yacht. Fortunately for me, Ron had spoken to Hugh & expressed my newfound love for sailing. I was looking to fall in love with something special. Ron introduced us & Hugh asked me to join him for dinner. We talked for 4 hours, both in the restaurant & then back on board his yacht.

For some inexplicable reason, I told Hugh of my ordeal on Joe's boat. This turned out to be a good thing for both of us. After I confided in Hugh, he in turn told me of his ordeal of sexual abuse by an uncle. We were both repulsed & saddened by each other's experiences. But this openness served to ensure a lasting bond. Not only that, Hugh dropped the price of his yacht. He halved it. He wanted to ensure I got the prize. Hugh had no idea I had the money. I could have paid the original asking price. I had no idea of Hugh's extensive wealth either. He could have afforded to give the yacht away.

But the money was not his motivation. He wanted his yacht to be loved, not just owned. He also insisted I tell no one how much I paid for it. I never did. Still haven't. Won't.

Telling Hugh of what Joe had done to me turned out well. Telling Pastor John should have been a step toward healing too. It was now 8 months since Joe fucked my life. I had not been to church for over 7 months. Rachel had gone away without any explanation. All I had was this new love of yachts & the sea to lose myself in. Of course, I also had the money from the sale of Joe's three boats. I didn't even look at the other 2 before they were sold.

But there was another worthwhile discovery I made on *The Netherseas*. I searched every square inch of the boat. I wanted to ensure there were no more magazines or photos. I didn't want the new owner to suspect they were mine. I found none. But during the search, I found 3 separate places where large sums of cash were hidden. One was a black metal box wedged between the hull & one of the water storage tanks. Another was also in a black metal box locked in a small compartment below deck in the bow. I found the final stash in Joe's cabin between 2 large sheets of board that supported his mattress.

The total amount was $28,840.00. A very handy sum of money in the late 70s.

I purchased Hugh's yacht & he spent 3 months with me teaching me how to handle her at sea. We went out in all weather conditions. Sometimes we went for a day, other times for 1 or 2 nights. Often it was just the 2 of us, but at times some of the other men from the yacht club joined us. Mostly we sailed, but there were times we used the engine & he showed me everything about its operation. He had the original manuals & all the service records.

It was a complete history of his loving attention for a beautiful vessel. I assured Hugh that I would continue the same fastidious care. I did.

For nearly 26 years I followed 1 mission: to keep my yacht safe & afloat. I think it was symbolic of keeping me afloat. But for all of those years I mostly felt I was continually sinking. I would often wonder if my desire to be at sea was in the 'hope' of finding Joe. The memory was horrendous. That memory replayed in my mind every day of every week for all those years. I wanted my Nathan to come back to help me.

I kept reminding myself I wasn't going crazy. I was looking for Joe. Then I'd realise Joe was dead & think I was going crazy. This spinning thought process replayed itself over & over until I was distracted by something else. The distraction would bring a disturbing realisation. The only reason I'd want to find Joe would be to kill the bastard. Madness had become my stowaway companion. I controlled it by being a good host & a very capable sea-faring adventure tour operator.

During those years, I hosted people from all over the world. Most of them were rich & looking for adventure. Passengers included some well-known film stars & rock stars, sports identities & businessmen. There were 4 transvestites I had for 8 days. On another occasion, I had 3 gorgeous models along with a cameraman & female assistant/make-up artist. The cameraman & assistant were newly married. I was left with 3 gorgeous women in their early 20s. As we sailed from island to island, they would occasionally lie naked on the deck getting an all-over tan. They spent two weeks doing photo shoots for a range of swimwear & summer fashions.

There was also a soft-core porno filmmaker from Hawaii who booked voyages on 3 occasions. None of the porn star girls or guys were very friendly. I wished I had the 3 models back on board. They were a lot more fun. I got to have sex with 2 of them at the same time. Every sailor's dream.

Strangely, I always thanked God for any opportunity to have sex. But I felt like I was betraying Him. I wanted to be closer to Him, but I also longed for the closeness & the touch of a woman. My desire to be closer to God was always in the shadow of fat, ugly Joe. Why couldn't I get free of Joe? Why couldn't I get back? Where had my Nathan gone? I longed for Rachel too.

But there were times of comfort also, & some unexpected surprises. Like one afternoon when I'd been below getting some food. I was about 200 nautical miles north of New Zealand on a return trip. I was coming back up on deck. I looked through the glass of the cabin door window to see Dad standing aft at the wheel. He saw me & gave a big beaming smile. I ran up quickly from the cabin & opened the door. He was gone. I stood there totally bewildered. I immediately sensed that Dad had died & he was saying goodbye. I cried as all my pains & torments ransacked that balmy Pacific afternoon.

Later that evening, I diarised the event. Many years later, I would discover Dad died that same day. Andrew would confirm that Dad said I had gone sailing & he wanted to go with me. My family thought it meant that I was dead too.

Uncanny. Remarkable. Unbelievable. All that & more. But after that experience of seeing Dad, thoughts of suicide diminished substantially. After that, I used to think Dad was still on board with me. I was thousands of miles from home  but felt closer to Dad than when I had been at home. Closer to my earthly father, who wasn't really there. A million miles from my Heavenly Father, who seemed nowhere to be found, but was supposedly omnipresent.

* * *

One of the most interesting passengers I had on board was Brian, an ex-biker. He turned out to be a hardened criminal, a hit man. We had a lot in common though. He had been sexually, physically & emotionally abused, although by a violent stepfather, not a church leader.

"Fuck man, my older brother is a normal citizen," Brian lamented. "He didn't live with me & Mum & fuckin' Doug, he went with Dad. I know my life would have been different if I could have been with Dad too."

Brian grieved a loss of what might have been. I lived with the same grief.

I was back in Auckland in '81 when I first met Brian. I had sailed four Australian guys from Fiji to Auckland from where they would fly back to Sydney. I had no idea who my next passengers-come-crew would be.

I got out of a taxi that brought me back from the hotel the Australian guys had taken me to for a few thank you drinks. A man approached me with a message he said was from Simon. I hadn't seen or heard from Simon for about 5 years, but he knew where to reach me.

"There is a man from Australia on your yacht. Simon has asked if you can look after him & take him where he wants to go," the messenger explained.

I thanked him & turned to the back seat of the taxi to get the bags of things I had bought in town. By the time I grabbed my things & paid the driver, the messenger had disappeared.

I walked down the wharf to my yacht, which I had named *Diana*. I could see that someone had made himself at home inside. I rarely locked the cabin area.

"So, who are you & what are you doing on my boat?" I asked in a friendly manner.

He looked desperate. He did not look very friendly.

"My name is Brian & I'll pay you $5,000.00 to sail me somewhere," he replied. He reached into a bag, pulling out a large wad of folded money.

"It's all there, count it if you don't believe me," he said gruffly.

"I'll take your word for it," I replied & put my hand out to shake his. "I'm Nathan."

I was intrigued by this man who seemed initially to be a violent type, but also had a vulnerability that made him very human. "So, where do you want to go Brian?" I asked.

"Far, far away, sailor boy," was his response.

We sailed from Auckland later that same day after I stocked numerous supplies aboard. Brian had already brought a large number of items aboard. They were neatly stacked in four boxes under a canvas tarpaulin on the forward deck. There was a large tent, a sleeping bag, a roll of heavy-duty plastic & tools, camping gear & a large quantity of fishing gear.

"How come you want all that stuff?" I asked after I stowed it all in the forward storage bay. Brian didn't want to come out on deck.

"I'll tell you when we're out of Auckland harbour, bro," he replied. "I'm staying below until we are well out to sea. I'll tell you why soon enough. But don't worry, I'm not going to cause you any hassles," he added.

Strangely enough, I wasn't worried. I was looking forward to another adventure at sea with another stranger. Most of my passengers were easygoing, friendly & not too demanding. An important part of the adventure was for everyone to help with various duties. Brian was one of my favourite passenger/crew members, & over the years, I would catch up with him occasionally.

The balmy warmth of Auckland had cooled a few degrees by the time we were out of sight of land. It remained warm. The Pacific was offering no resistance as it rolled gently beneath the hull of my beautiful *'Diana'*. I remember thinking jealously that the sea was caressing the woman I still loved & dreamed of but would never see again. I missed Rachel too.

Brian joined me on the deck after we had been at sea for about an hour. The bright crimson sun was beginning its farewell to the edge of the Pacific. Soon we would be sailing into the starry night where sea & sky loved being the same colour. But the sky laughed at the sea because it held the stars.

"Wow! We sure are at sea now, bro. YAAAAAAAAAAAY!" he screamed with absolute delight. "Oh man, this is fuckin' incredible. You sure are a lucky bastard doing this stuff for a living. This is just beautiful. Never done anything like this before," he continued, stretching his arms out wide to hug the setting sun & embrace our unknown destination.

Standing at the wheel watching Brian enjoy his sense of freedom led me to mutter a very quiet, *"Thank you Jesus."* These moments occurred often enough but never enough to lure me back to a church & never too infrequently to forget His love for me. Although I was a little surprised by my response at that time, it seemed appropriate. Before the end of the evening, I would discover how very appropriate it was.

"So, Brian, where are we going with all this stuff?" I asked.

"An island somewhere in the Pacific," he replied with a big smile that made him very disarming & likeable.

"Do you have any particular island in mind?" I enquired.

"I want you to take me to an island that I can hide on for a long time. It has to have fresh water of course, & trees too. Preferably a place that has few or no visitors. Do you know of any islands like this?" he asked hopefully.

"Yes," I replied, "but why?"

"I'll get a six-pack & something for us to eat & sit out here & tell you my story, okay?"

"Sure man, can't wait to hear what you've got to say."

A few minutes later Brian returned with the beer, some sandwiches, some cheese & savoury biscuits & cakes he'd bought in Auckland. His grin wiped away any semblance of his previous demeanour. We sat in the stern of the yacht as we sailed north-west into the starry night, which by now was reflecting on the surface of the Pacific. The gentle movement of the ocean caused the stars to sway or spring from their orbit as they danced for the pleasure of Brian & me.

I pointed out the enthralling beauty of this starry ballet on the Pacific surface to Brian.

"Wow bro! Praise God, isn't that incredible?"

That unexpected response led to a few seconds' silence. It began a long evening that realised blessings & heartfelt brotherly love that was new, exciting & welcome for both of us. To this day, it remains one of the highlights of my 'lost years' at sea.

Brian broke the silence. "I'm on the run, bro, if you haven't already guessed."

"I figured that much," I offered.

"Crazy thing about it is I'm not running from the cops, but only because they don't know what I'm responsible for," he said. "I'm actually running from something I didn't do," he added.

"The awful truth is that I've been a hit man for outlaw motorcycle gangs & other unpleasant criminals. Done 5 hits; 2 hits in New Zealand, 2 in Australia & 1 in Hong Kong. The pay was lucrative, but the torments & nightmares take a horrible toll," he confessed.

I sat listening passively. I made no disapproving sounds or remarks & let him continue. He unloaded his burden. It was the first time he had ever spoken about his past to anyone.

"Two weeks ago, I took an assignment to knock a guy in Brisbane. It was a hit unrelated to any of the motorcycle gangs. It was over a drug deal. Apparently, the guys who wanted to buy the stuff gave my target half a million dollars to buy the dope. But he informed on them so he could keep the money. Stupid bastard."

Brian continued. "I was offered fifty thousand to do the job as well as business-class flights to & from New Zealand & five-star accommodation. I already had safe contacts for guns, explosives & poisons in Brisbane, so I took the job. Because of my reputation & not having been caught or even suspected in any of my other hits, I was paid $25,000 upfront."

"It looked straightforward enough. I knew where he lived, knew he had a pool in the backyard & figured that's where he'd be found. It would look like an accident. There would be no evidence of my involvement." he said with disgust, although I'm sure it would have once been said with a hint of pride.

"So, what happened?" I enquired.

"Before doing the hit, I went to visit my brother. He lives on the Gold Coast & I hadn't seen him in over 10 years. Not since Dad's funeral. I was pretty apprehensive, but I figured the visit would provide a good alibi. Tony, that's my brother, was really pleased to see me & gave me a big hug right at the front door. Very unusual, I thought. He'd never done that before, because he was never pleased to see me."

"He invited me in, offered beer, wine, coffee, biscuits, cake. In fact, anything I wanted. He wanted me to tell him about the 10 years of my life he had missed out on. I equally wanted to know about his. Obviously he'd done okay 'coz he had a nice big house on a canal, a 7 series BMW & a lovely boat moored in front of his house," Brian said.

I could tell he wanted to say more, so I let him continue uninterrupted.

"I couldn't tell him too much because my lifestyle was basically criminal. I was a friggin' violent bastard. I was a murderer. I felt dirty & wretched sitting on his beautiful pale green leather lounge suite. I didn't know why I was feeling that way. Was it because I was ashamed? Was it because he was my brother? I'd sat in similar & better places in the past talking with the upper echelons of the criminal worlds in Australia, New Zealand, America & Asia. But I was troubled being with Tony, yet I still felt some strange sense of comfort."

At this point Brian took a break to find out if he was boring me. I assured him that he was not boring me. Nor was he offending me or frightening me in any way. I passed him another beer & invited him to continue.

"Thanks, bro," he said as he took the beer & continued his story.

"After a while, I asked Tony to fill me in on what he'd been doing. He told me he'd got into real estate just after Dad died. He was involved with some property developers & had been very successful.

Tony told me that his wife had left him nearly a year ago, but that they were talking about getting together again. He seemed really excited."

Brian paused briefly & looked at me searchingly. I suppose he was wondering what I would think of the next part of his story. Would I laugh? Would I criticise? Would I be offended? I think I knew what was coming next. I think Brian knew that I was not only with him but had already guessed where he was going. Anyway, he seemed reassured & continued talking.

"Tony didn't wait long to tell me what had him so excited. Without any concern for how I might react, he told me he'd become a 'born again' Christian. He told me how his wife went back home to New Zealand after she walked out on him & had become 'saved' while she was in Christchurch," Brian related.

"So, here's Tony on the Gold Coast accepting Jesus mid-morning on a Tuesday at a Christian businessmen's breakfast & on the same day in the afternoon in Christchurch, Maddie is at a Bible study luncheon for women having the same experience. Even though there is a 2 or 3 hour time difference between Australia & New Zealand, they both were getting 'born again' at the same time. From then on, they each began praying that the Lord would prepare the other for contact," Brian continued excitedly.

"It was a Saturday afternoon that Tony on the Gold Coast, rang Madeline in Christchurch & told her that he still loved her," continued Brian. "She told him that she still loved him too & wanted to come back. At this stage man, Tony is crying & laughing at the same time while he's telling me this story."

"Then he tells me what he said next. *'Maddie I've got something very important to tell you. I've become a Christian. I got saved,'* &... & then he just wept with joy, man," Brian said emotionally as he continued relating Tony's testimony.

"Then, through his tears, Tony tells me that before he could finish his sentence Maddie shrilled with delight & said, *'Praise God, thank you Jesus,'* going on to tell Tony that the same thing had happened to her."

After this Brian paused again & looked at me. I could see that there were tears in his eyes. I smiled reassuringly.

"Let's go in, Brian. It's getting a little cool out here now," I suggested. "We'll have a coffee & some more food & you can continue your story. It sounds pretty incredible, man. I want to hear how it ends."

I knew in part how it would finish. I was only hoping & praying that Brian would have a better chance & future than I had. But by the time he finished, I realised we were both fucked. We sure had a lot in common.

Sitting at the table inside with a coffee & some of the cakes, I asked him to finish his story.

"Well bro, I remember thinking that his God must be pretty cool to pull this off. Tony went on telling me what happened between him & Maddie & I started to cry. I couldn't understand it. I was scared. This had never happened to me before. I was a tough bastard. I was hardened. Doug, my stepfather, had destroyed the little boy & I became a violent bastard. Violence was my escape from the torments of his abuse of my young body. But the violence I employed had its own torments. I was trapped, hedged in by torment, guilt & evil memories, with no way out," Brian confided.

He continued. "While I'm sitting there crying, Tony comes over & sits next to me & puts his arm around my shoulder. & says, *'Jesus is touching you, isn't he, Brian?'* 'Yes,' I confessed. Although I didn't have a clue what was happening to me."

Brian then went on to tell me about his salvation experience in his brother's house & how, for the next few hours they prayed & read verses from The Bible.

He told me Tony's pastor & another guy named Simon came over & spent time with Brian & his brother.

"Wow Brian, that's fantastic. Praise God," I said, & meant it too. I was excited for Brian & I could even sense some excitement for myself. I also knew who Simon was too.

"Oh, what? You're saved too?" he asked with eager anticipation.

"Yeah brother, just over 5 years ago," I answered.

"Amazing! Thank you, Jesus. Thank you, Lord. Oh man, now I know I'm on the right boat & going to the right place," Brian said with much relief.

I then told him about my joyous experience & what had happened during the first few months. Of course, this eventually led to him to questioning why I was sailing the Pacific & how God led me to this 'ministry'.

"It's not a ministry Brian, it's an escape," I confided.

"From what, bro?" he enquired with concern.

Relating my experience on fat Joe's boat was difficult, but I told him everything. I told him what happened, how it affected me, the ongoing traumas & the stumbling forward into an unknown future. I talked for about an hour. Brian listened with an understanding of every pain & torment I'd experienced.

I told Brian what I had wanted to tell Pastor John. Brian not only listened; he understood my pain. Brian is the only person who knows the depth of trauma & torments I have lived with since. He is the only person who knows why my Nathan had gone away. I gave him greater details of what really happened the day Joe went overboard.

"I'm really sorry, bro. But it seems that we're both in the same boat. Haha, sorry, no pun intended," he said, pausing briefly when I asked him to continue with his unfinished story & tell me why he was running.

"Ok, so there I was in Brisbane with the intent of killing a guy I didn't even know, but I got saved the day before I was going to do the job. Obviously, I couldn't go ahead with it. I couldn't do it. But I'd been paid $25,000.00 upfront. I can't go to these guys & give them their money back & tell them I couldn't do it 'coz I got saved by Jesus. They'd have me hit because I knew too much. So, I've got to disappear, I've got to escape, otherwise I'm a dead man," he said with firm resignation.

What a predicament Brian was in. We continued talking about it for over an hour & looking at possible islands where he might be able to stay undetected for at least 2 or 3 years. I knew of the Kermadec Islands between New Zealand & Tonga & in particular, thought that Raoul Island would be ideal. Also known as Sunday Island, it was big enough to hide on. It had fresh water & was mostly uninhabited. There was a meteorological station on the north side but we stayed well clear of it. I suggested to Brian that we should not sail across the north of the island. Despite its isolation, it was a Nature Reserve & could cause Brian problems if he was discovered.

We sailed to the Kermadec Islands & spent 2 weeks there. We looked at Raoul Island & also briefly at Macauley Island. However, most of our time on land was spent on Raoul Island. Brian eventually picked out a place in the wide, exposed bay on the south west of the island. I stayed with him for 5 days & helped him set up a comfortable camp. We put up the tent about 30 metres inland from the shore in a sheltered position. The lush forest was intoxicating.

Brian surprised me with his preparation. He had purchased a good supply of basic tools & cutlery & cooking & eating utensils. He also had a bag containing packets of seeds: cucumbers, tomatoes, pumpkin, lettuce, spring onions, capsicum, beans, peas & others. It would be at least 3-4 months before he could produce a crop. He also had a Bible, pens & pencils & about a dozen 64-page exercise books that he was going to write in each day. But I believed he was going to survive while he hid there for as long as he thought necessary.

After the 5 days onshore with Brian, we said our goodbyes. We prayed for each other's safety. I told him I would sail by whenever I had the opportunity. But it might only be once or twice a year.

We both smiled, & with a teary wave, I rowed back to 'Diana' in my 8-foot inflatable boat.

The torment & turmoil in the mind & heart of a murderer produce an anguish that keeps you running. But the longer you run, the more exhausted you become. Worse than that, if you stop running, you revisit your deeds. Then, you must surrender, go crazy or kill yourself. At least Brian could stop running now.

I hoped he would find some peace there as he read his Bible, talked to God, caught fish, hunted goats & grew his garden. God bless you, brother Brian.

Back on board 'Diana' I prepared to sail back to Auckland, leaving Brian & Raoul Island to get acquainted with each other. It would be only 4 months before I would see him again & it was a most joyous reunion.

Before leaving, he asked me to pass on a message to the woman he left behind. He had been unwilling to contact her for fear of her safety & his own. He gave me details of how to contact her. On my return to Auckland, I couldn't find the contact details. But through an amazing 'coincidence', I found her 'accidently'. Was 'something' or 'someone' else at work in this situation? It was far too unlikely to be just a coincidence.

I had booked 'Diana' in for some minor repairs & attention in dry dock at the yacht club & took a couple of days shore leave. Alec loaned me a car, so I drove south, deciding to visit Alf & Mick down in Tauranga. Was it was another one of those amazing 'coincidences' that arise unexpectedly?

Driving down on the Thursday morning, I had no idea where I might stay. I didn't know if Alf & Mick where at home or if they were out fishing. I didn't know where they lived. I only knew where Alf's boat was moored. I arrived in Tauranga at lunch time & immediately went in search of *'Tauranga Tora'*. She was tied up & I could see someone in the cabin. It was Mick.

"Nathan! Shit a fuckin' brick bro. What the fuck are you doin' here?" he yelled with glee as I stepped on board.

"Thought I'd come & check if you were doing any work, mate," I replied as I shook his hand.

"No fuckin' way mate. We've taken a coupla' weeks off before we head out again. But we had a fuckin' great season bro. Made fuckin' squillions," he said with obvious delight.

"Good for you," I said. "So what have you got planned for the next few days?"

"Well hang on to your fuckin' balls bro, 'coz you prob'ly won't believe it, but I'm gettin' married on Sat'day. Then me & Marilyn are goin' on a fuckin' honeymoon. 5 fuckin' days of fuckin'. Fuckin' can't wait bro," Mick said with wild enthusiasm.

"Congratulations Mick," I said as I gave him a congratulatory handshake.

"Thanks bro," he said, before excitedly asking, "Hey, how long are you 'ere for? You have to come to me weddin' bro," he almost demanded.

"Sure," I replied, "love to. I don't have to be back until next Wednesday."

"Fan-fuckin'-tastic bro. It's gonna be pretty casual, 'cept I'm wearing a fuckin' suit," he explained apologetically. "But no tie bro, no fuckin' tie. No fuckin' way, eh?"

Mick was obviously excited. He was being the Mick I had known him to be. I had never met anyone who could use 'fuck' & 'fuckin' in the same sentence more times than Mick.

That night I stayed at a motel. The next morning, I went out to buy Mick & Marilyn a wedding present. Bought them a matching set of purple towels, face washers & bathmat. I spent a lazy day looking around Tauranga. Bought myself a rod & reel & drove down to Waihi Estuary. Caught three fish & let them go. I was watched by a young boy who kept asking questions. "Where are you from? What do you do?" Seemed like he was a couple of slices short of a full loaf. Felt sorry for the kid. I gave him the new rod & reel because I didn't need to take them back with me. Never saw a young guy get so excited.

As I was walking back to the car, a woman ran over to me.

"Excuse me, but did you just give my son a fishing rod?" she asked.

"Yeah," I answered.

"You have no idea what you've just done," she said with a thankful smile as she tried to catch her breath.

"It's okay isn't it?" I enquired, wondering if there was some sort of problem.

"So much better than okay, so much better," she repeated as she became a little emotional.

"My son has a few mental difficulties as you probably noticed, but he never complains," she said as she started to cry a little. "He tells me, 'Mummy, everything will be alright, Jesus loves us,'" she added.

"I'm sure he does. I mean, I'm sure Jesus does love him," I replied with a friendly smile but continued to walk away.

"Yes, yes. But the miracle is that this morning Eddie, my son, told me he prayed that God would give him a fishing rod." She burst into tears of joy. "Thank you. Thank you so much."

I stopped walking, turned toward her, walked a few short paces & gave her a hug.

"God answers prayer in some strange ways," I said. I couldn't think of anything meaningful at the time. I was feeling a bit emotional myself & continued back to the car. Did God somehow prompt me to give Eddie my rod & reel?

I sat in the car for a few minutes thinking about what had just happened. I felt great & was thrilled for Eddie. Something nice was happening in my heart. Something I hadn't felt for a long time.

Driving back up to Tauranga, I was imagining Eddie catching fish & praising God for his new fishing rod. I found myself thanking God at the same time. But my time in Tauranga was not yet over. There was one more 'miracle' to come. I'm still blown away by this event. Just incredible. Even unbelievable.

The wedding was held at the reception centre & not a church. It was an open wedding & anyone was welcome. It was different. Very informal, very Mick & a lot of fun. During the reception Mick introduced me to Marilyn & the 2 bridesmaids.

"Nathan, this is Marilyn, me new missus, & this is Fiona & Fliss," he said, introducing them to me. Fliss was Marilyn's cousin & the two had been best of friends for most of their lives. It turned out that Marilyn was the only family member who hadn't rejected Fliss.

I was intrigued with Fliss because it was a very unusual name. One that I had heard of only once before.

The morning I left Brian on Sunday Island, he asked me to somehow get a message to Fliss. He handed me a sealed envelope. Her real name was Felicity. The envelope was hopefully back in Auckland on board 'Diana'. But I still hadn't found it. Surely this couldn't be the Fliss that Brian mentioned. She lived in Christchurch.

When there was an opportunity to talk to Fliss alone, I asked her if she knew Brian.

"Yes. Yes. Do you know where he is? Is he alright? Tell me Nathan, please," she pleaded anxiously but excitedly.

I told her of my time with Brian & where he was. I didn't tell her the reason why he had to get away. I think she knew he was in trouble.

"Please take me to him?" she asked. Seemed that she was about to explode with anticipation.

"Well, that's easier said than done, Fliss," I replied, knowing that she wouldn't be able to afford to get to Brian's island. I was wrong. Again. She could afford it. Don't know where she got the money. I didn't ask.

She returned to Auckland with me 4 days later. We put 'Diana' back in the water out of dry dock. Nearly 4 months after leaving Brian on Raoul Island I was returning. I was just as excited as Fliss. Couldn't wait to see the look on Brian's face when I arrived with his friend.

We were about 3 hours out of Auckland harbour when I found Brian's letter. It was under the seat cushion of a chair. Fliss read the letter Brian had written. In it, he explained why he had to get away. He also told her he had been 'born again.'

"Life sure is full of crazy shit with even crazier twists & turns, isn't it, Nathan?" she admitted.

As we sailed, she spent a couple of hours telling me her story. Brought up in church. Loved Jesus. Wanted to be a missionary. Was going to have a wonderful life. Got raped by a youth leader when she was 15. Got pregnant. Got rejected by the church for immoral behaviour. Got the baby taken from her. Raped & rejected. Fucked & forgotten.

Why was I not surprised when she told me that the bastard who fucked her is now a pastor? Why was I not surprised to learn that he wanted nothing to do with her? Her schooling suffered. She became morbid, withdrawn, sullen. She became someone else. Her Fliss had gone away, just like my Nathan.

Eventually, she drifted into the subculture world of hippies

& bikers, alone at 15. Got raped more times than she wants to remember. Got stoned. Stayed stoned for 6 years to bury the pain. But no drug can cover the abuse & degradation she suffered.

She met Brian when she was 19. Two desperados who were desperate for genuine love. Desperate for understanding. He took her away for a few days on the back of his bike. They were inseparable after that. They had been together for 5 years.

Sitting at the table that evening, I wept for Fliss. I wept for Brian. I wept for me. She sat opposite me with her hands on mine as I cried. After I had composed myself, I told her my story. We both wept. A very fine evening sailing north east on blue Pacific tears.

Our reunion with Brian a few days later was one of the best days of my life. Still is. We laughed. We sang. We danced. We drank wine & ate & talked & laughed some more. We prayed. We cried together. The fellowship of the forgotten. It was beautiful. I wished Rachel could have been there. I wished I wasn't so lonely.

One evening, Brian asked me to go for a walk with him. We went down to the shoreline & walked along the water's edge.

"Listen, Nathan. I don't want to make God angry man, but I want Fliss to stay & she wants to," he said with as much concern as hope.

"Why would that make God angry, man?" I asked.

"'Coz if she stays, we'll have sex," he replied.

"Well, I knew that, man. It's pretty obvious that you both love each other."

"Yeah, but we're not s'posed to have sex 'til we're married, isn't that right?" he enquired, hopeful of a response that would give God's blessing to what was going to happen anyway.

"Hmmm," I mused. "Well, seeing as how I'm the captain of a licensed charter vessel, I suppose I could perform a wedding," I offered, although I didn't have any qualification for such a ceremony. Didn't know how to conduct one either.

"Far out. Wow. Praise God. Do you think that would be okay with Jesus?" he asked with amazement.

"Yeah, if you're both committed to each other & to Him. Tell you what," I said, "we'll have the wedding tomorrow morning. Fliss will come back to '*Diana*' for the night & in the morning, she'll get herself ready as a bride," I continued before asking, "Have you got a ring?"

"She's wearing one that I gave her as a birthday present over a year ago. Will that do?" he asked ecstatically.

"Yep! That'll do mate," I said with assurance.

I had no idea whether it was the right thing to do. It seemed like wisdom at the time. Looking back, it still does. If this messes with your doctrinal purity, I don't care. Back then, I didn't picture God frowning down on this. All these years later I still think God remains amused by it, & approving of it.

The wedding was beautiful. I prayed God's blessing on them. Fliss accepted Jesus anew & we had a time of thanking God for His blessings. Don't know what other Christians might think of this. Don't care what they think. Two of God's lost sheep were happy. I was happy too. My Nathan came back for a while that day. He was in 'church' on a lonely island. He was in love with God again. For a short time.

I rowed back to '*Diana*', wrapped one of the double foam mattresses in plastic, tied it to the inflatable boat & swam ashore with it. I left it for them as a wedding present. They both cried.

An ex hired killer. A heavily tattooed, cruel & violent man with an horrendous past, holding hands with a victim of 'in-house' sex abuse & many rapes & abuses. Two seemingly irreparable broken lives, holding each other to make a new, unbroken entity. God held them too. I could sense that so strongly. I thanked Him too.

Neither of them was attractive. But they are two of the most beautiful people I have ever spent time with. I know why some people cry at weddings. Two misfits. Outcasts. Besieged by brutality. Concussed by conflict. Way out of their comfort zone on this island. But so comfortable together. They had peace with God. I envied their happiness.

For the next 2 years, I sailed by whenever I could. Took them a few luxuries & necessities. Always had a special time with them. I always wished Rachel was with me to meet Brian & Fliss.

The pastors of Sunday Island, I called them. They were pretty happy. Had a productive garden. Had some goats in an enclosure that Brian made & therefore they had milk. Fliss made me a Sunday Island cappuccino with fresh goat's milk. I'm one of only 3 people in the world to have ever had the privilege of enjoying one.

Sometimes I'd be sailing somewhere & often think of God smiling & rejoicing over His two precious children on Sunday Island. Every day was Sunday at Fliss & Brian's.

If I do write the story of my years at sea, I will reveal more of where they are today & what they're doing. They have two boys. They run an orphanage they set up. It's in one of the Central American countries. How they got there is 'miraculous.' I sailed them across the Pacific to this coastal town. I've been there. I've visited them twice. God lives with them. Everyone in that coastal village knows & loves them.

* * *

Jesus was my saviour & had sacrificed Himself because of His love for me. Joe was my soul-killer & sacrificed me because of his love for himself. Joe mutilated my being in Christ. I was still hurting. The loneliness pained my insides. I was still ripped up on the inside. I continued to blame Joe for the darkness.

I suffered greatly through these anxieties. I was deeply disturbed. I was the turbulent, tossing sea. As an earthquake in the depths of the sea shows no visible disturbance on the surface, my damage also was not seen. But destruction hits the shoreline soon enough. Huge waves of despair crashed upon me. I was now a battered coast.

I felt as if the sea had destroyed me. Yet I had made it my refuge. The land groaned at my ominous approach. I belonged nowhere.

I yearned for the sky.

## Book 7 - April 82

*I am the albatross.*
*I am untouched by turbulent sea.*
*I hover above the trough & crest of every wave, then dive to catch the unsuspecting fish.*
*The fish was a baited long-line hook. This cruelty dragged me under. No longer can I fly.*
*I'm hooked by the instinct to survive, to live, to thrive in my envy as royalty among birds.*
*The hooks must be unbaited.*
*Joe had to die.*
*I have to learn to fly, but I can't, so I'm sailing.*

* * *

Julie Phillips was a girl I grew up with in church back in Melbourne. She spent nearly 4 months with me on my yacht about 20 years ago. She did the cooking while I was chartering 2 Swedish couples through the islands. It was a beautiful time. I missed her greatly when she left to go to Canada. She went to visit her sister Robyn, who had married a Canadian.

I thought she would return after a few months, but she didn't. I was alone again. Every time I pulled into a port somewhere, I hoped to see Julie on the dock. I had been in love with Diana & lost her through my own stupidity. I had been very much in love with the lovely red-haired Rachel. Uncharacteristically, she left her family, the church & me. Many years later I would be told why she did this. I would once again become acquainted with a degree of anger no man should have to carry. It's too hard to control.

But, for those 4 months, I was in love with 'my old childhood friend' but she had gone to Canada.

Was I supposed to suffer with this loneliness? The loneliness stalked me. This loneliness was the whistling wind through the ropes of my yacht on a breezy day. This loneliness raged like a black-storm-sky? They all sought me as their dwelling place. They brought coldness to what should have been my place of refuge. Winter was the permanent season in my soul.

I had no lasting relationships after Julie left. People paid me to sail them to exotic places. As a result, I saw much of the world that is the Pacific rim. But most of the time I just wanted someone to love me. I knew my family loved me, but I couldn't go back until I was ready. I was waiting for my Nathan to return. What Joe did to me that morning & the way he died would haunt me for the rest of my life. With very good reason too, as I may yet reveal.

Pastor John would not hear me. I had not spoken to anyone except Brian & Fliss about my even greater pain. Could there even be a greater pain? Surely, I imagined this vileness?

### Book 11 – Nov 86

*Fuck the darkness of my thinking!*
*My mind, minus my rancid memory, would equal bliss.*
*Subtract it from me Lord!*
*Take away my nightmare!*
*Who will listen to me now?*

Until I felt I was ready to tell my family what had happened, I remained 'lost'. I couldn't go home without myself, my Nathan. 27 years after leaving Australia, I would finally return. A further year passed before I miraculously met James on Brighton Beach. I was ready. I thought I was ready. Telling my mother & brothers of what Joe had done was painful enough. Telling of the sexual abuses that Robyn & Julie suffered from Alwyn was diabolical. The effect it had on Mum was appalling. It was also tragic.

Stupidly, I didn't think about the possible consequences of revealing the information. I just wanted to get free of it all. Of what it led me to do. Of what it led me to become.

But astonishing events in my brothers' lives & those of their families were about to unfold. None of us were ready. Was it God who was going to get our attention in some incredible ways?

It seems that the greatest attention-getting event was reserved for me.

Andy rang on a Saturday afternoon about 1.00pm. He told me Julie Phillips was going to be at a BBQ at his place. He asked if I would like to come too. I was overjoyed. I hadn't seen Julie for about 20 years. She disappeared from my life just as Diana & Rachel did. I was hoping she wasn't in a relationship. I didn't think to ask if her husband or boyfriend would be coming too. But Andrew told me that she had a son, Ricky, who was coming. Andy also told me that Jimmy had a lady friend. This was the best phone call ever.

Sudden tragedy can smash into your life with destructive consequences. Also, incredible unforeseen blessing can come just as suddenly. A lifetime of hurt & grief can begin to heal. The Darling family was about to experience a beautiful 'suddenly.'

I arrived at Andy's just after 5.00pm. On the way I bought 3 bunches of flowers: 1 for Tanya, 1 for Jimmy's new lady & 1 for Julie. This turned out to be a really good idea. I just love it when I do something right. Wish it happened more often. But it's hard to get things right when life seems so wrong.

My arrival by taxi seemed to take forever. I still didn't have a car or even a licence. Giselle, Andy's younger daughter, opened the door for me & informed me that Andrew, Julie & Ricky were out on the back terrace.

First, I went to the kitchen & greeted Tanya with a kiss & gave her the flowers. She gave me a big hug. James & his lady friend had not yet arrived. I left her flowers on the kitchen table. I took the other bunch with me to meet Julie for the first time in nearly 20 years.

Julie was the first person I saw when I stepped outside. She was standing with Andy & a young guy I assumed to be Ricky. I was momentarily unable to move. She looked wonderful. Bright, happy, attractive & vibrant. She looked better than I'd ever seen her. Tears of joy found their way to my wide-open eyes.

She was about 5 metres away. Julie moved toward me, then ran & hugged me. She was crying & laughing at the same time. My head was spinning. I'm sure my heart was thumping loud enough for all to hear.

"Nathan! Nathan! Oh, it is just so good to see you, so wonderfully good," she laughed through her tears.

We held each other in a tight embrace. I didn't want to let go. I wasn't going to let go. I was going to hold her forever. I started crying & laughing too.

The look on Andy's face filled me with joy. While this was happening, James & his lady friend, Clarita, arrived. There was no hesitation or uncomfortable first meeting stuff. Everybody was hugging everybody else. It was the best family experience I could have hoped for. But it was about to get so much better. Exceeding, abundantly way better. Above anything I could have ever hoped for or even imagined.

After about 20 minutes of introductions, hugs, kisses & laughter, Julie asked me to sit with her at the table on the other side of the pool. She asked Ricky to come too, but he seemed to know already that he was to join us. He was walking beside us holding his mother's hand as Julie asked me to sit & talk with her & Ricky.

For about 20 years, I had no lasting relationships. Even my relationship with Julie only lasted 4 months. I wanted it to continue, but I think at the time she wanted more security than a life at sea with no fixed address could offer. Besides, she had perceived, no doubt, that I was 'damaged goods'. The fact is, we both were. I guess that's what brought us close.

I often regretted, even mourned, the fact that I had never had children. I think I would have been a good father. But I would not have been able to continue sailing all over the Pacific. That was a freedom I needed. It was an escape I had to keep making. Fatherhood was another sacrifice burnt on the altar of Joe's death.

Maybe I wouldn't have been a good father. I think I would have left a wife & family to continue running away. I had to keep escaping. I've been thinking of telling my brothers why I couldn't come home. I wanted to tell them the same thing I was going to tell Pastor John so many years earlier. I'm glad I didn't tell him. Brian knew, so did Fliss. I can only hope that Jimmy & Andy understand.

Over the years, I spent thousands of hours thinking about what my life might have been if I'd never gotten involved in drugs. What would my life have been if I was still with Diana? How wonderful would life have been if Joe hadn't done what he did? If only Rachel hadn't suddenly run away without an explanation?

Many nights I lay on the bed in my cabin thinking of Julie too. I could have happily spent the rest of my life with any one of these 3 women. But I was with no one. I was alone & feeling it more & more with each passing month. Seeing Julie after nearly 20 years was filling my head with thoughts & possibilities. But hearing what Julie was about to tell me was way past anything I had ever imagined.

We chatted on the other side of the pool away from the others. Initially, it was small talk & catching up on the years that had passed. Julie met a Canadian who was 14 years older than she was. Ivor had been a missionary in the Solomon Islands & I vaguely remembered him. He was on my yacht for a few days many years ago during the 4 months Julie was with me. He & Julie bumped into each other in Toronto & the result was Julie married him.

"Ivor was very good to both of us, Nathan," she said with a touch of sadness. "He was a wonderful father figure & example to Ricky," she added.

"So, what happened?" I asked sympathetically.

"He died of cancer a year & 4 months ago. After much discussion, prayer & deliberation, Ricky & I decided we would come back to Australia to live," she responded.

"Did you have any other children?" I enquired.

"No Nathan. Unfortunately, Ivor & I couldn't have children of our own," she said with what I detected as a slight hesitation.

I looked at Ricky to see if I could gauge how he was feeling about the conversation. He was smiling a slight, disarming smile. He seemed to be anticipating something but also hesitant, like he wanted to say something but couldn't.

Julie was looking at me intently & fidgeting with her clasped hands. I could tell that she was struggling with the words she wanted to say. But she courageously continued.

"Ricky was born in Canada & has never been to Australia." she said. "4 months ago, I told Ricky who his real father is. That's why we decided to come back to Australia," she added, although still no more confident with her speech.

"Wow! So, have you met him yet Ricky?" I asked.

"Y... yes, I... I guess I have," he replied, with much hesitation, before adding, "Mum has told me a lot about... about him," he fumbled.

At this point, Julie spoke. I sensed that she was scared. There was some fear & definite hesitation in her voice & on her face.

"Nathan, look at Ricky," she asked with a quivering lip.

I looked at Ricky, who was sitting slightly to my right but facing me.

"Now look at Adam," she directed with the same hesitancy & fear.

For a moment I felt sick. Up 'til now I hadn't noticed the resemblances & likenesses until Julie pointed it out. I wondered if Andrew's wife, Tanya, had noticed. What must she be thinking? I was trying to sound calm, but I don't think I asked my question that way.

"An...An...Andy is Ricky's father?" I tried to say with surprise, rather than with the disgust it came out with.

"No Nathan, No. Andrew is not Ricky's father," she replied.

She reached forward & took both my hands in hers. She was trembling. Tears filled her eyes. I held her hands tightly to give her some reassurance as she continued.

"Nathan, you are Ricky's father."

My whole being was immediately compressed into a tight ball before suddenly bursting outward with an intense explosive mix of pains, joys & shock. All I really remember of the next 10 to 15 minutes was me being a blubbering mess on the paving tiles beside Andy's pool.

The initial shock gave way to elation. Then there was more shock. Fulfilment & emptiness, absolute delight together with regret of 'the lost years'. These & many more emotions & turbulent thoughts fought for some degree of supremacy.

But in those very strange moments a light was turned on inside me. Julie had returned. Ricky had returned. My Nathan had returned. From wherever the darkness had previously scattered me over many years, the pieces came together while I lay by the pool. I knew I could now tell all of my story to my brothers. Now I could tell them everything. Nathan was home. My Nathan had come back & could now take the time to discover who he was, who I was.

In the days following the BBQ at Andy's, I dealt with a lot of anger. I also sensed that I was new. I was angry at missing the first 20 years of Ricky's life. I didn't get the opportunity to watch him grow. I was as devastated as I was elated. Even so, I still remain very thankful.

Over the days & weeks that followed, I spent a lot of time with my son. I wanted to know as much as I could discover. I spent time with Julie too & she filled in a lot of gaps for me. Julie had named our son Ricky because Richard was my middle name.

Fortunately, they had lots of photos. I loved looking at them. But there were so many times I longed to be in them. The one thing I was grateful for was that I no longer regretted being childless. I might not have had him for his first 20 years. But I wasn't going to let a day go by without him knowing that I loved him. I would always be there for him.

I was hoping I was not making that promise too soon.

# PART 4

## JAMES

No!

When Nathan asked Andrew and I to meet with him for the purpose of disclosing something of significant consequence, I eagerly accepted with assured expectation of another revealing of wonder and blessing. Although I was not leaning to the premise that God was 'doing something', I was, nonetheless anticipating more amazing news.

However, it was not a blessing in any respect. Just when our lives are being showered with a new focus and renewed direction, we are suddenly thrust back into the darkness. What Nathan confessed to us is a disclosure I could not have imagined. For me, and no doubt for Andrew too, there is a shocking numbness. My heart and gut are wrenched, twisted and desolated for our pitifully broken younger brother.

I telephoned Clarita as soon as I arrived home and endeavoured to relate what Nathan had described and what had happened, but I could not articulate with any degree of coherence. I was crying too much, and she easily discerned that I was deeply troubled.

"James? James? What's wrong, darling?" she pleaded.

I struggled with my attempt to explain but could utter nothing.

"Wait there James, I'll be over soon, okay?" she said with gentle command and understanding, although I knew there would be no words of comfort from her thoughtful, loving heart this day.

I do not remember responding, but she concluded the telephone conversation because I remember the sound of an ended call. I was standing in the kitchen, holding the telephone to my ear for an unwarranted time before sitting deeply distressed in a chair in the lounge. Although I was eagerly awaiting Clarita's arrival, I was very uncertain how to relate what Nathan had announced. I was uncertain about saying anything at all. I was uncertain of everything in life again.

About fifteen minutes later, Clarita arrived. I opened the door, and she held me, not saying anything at first. We stood in the entry hall holding each other tightly while I cried softly into her hair.

"Tell me what happened, James. What did Nathan tell you?" she asked with concern after about a minute had passed.

We walked into the lounge room and sat together on the sofa. I had informed Clarita that Andrew and I were meeting with Nathan that afternoon, and she knew also that I was charged with eager anticipation about this get-together. I began to cry again and sat there shaking my head in disbelief. The afternoon was closing in on the pending gloom of the fast-approaching evening. It was a long time before I could collect myself to convey what Andrew and I had been told.

"Do you want me to order a pizza, James? I'll get it delivered. Is that okay with you?"

She was telling me what she was about to do rather than waiting for my approval. I was more than pleased to have her with me and to be somehow taking control of the situation.

"No darling, I have plenty of food in the refrigerator which can be reheated," I replied, although food was a far distant thought at that moment.

I commenced the unfolding of everything that Nathan had related, his decision for returning home, and the reason why he stayed away so long. I cried again for my little brother. I wanted to speak to my wonderful father, but he was dead. So was Mum. I felt like I was dying too in some way, which perplexed my mental state greatly. The last few days had been filling me with hope. I wanted to believe that perhaps God had somehow re-entered my world, and I found reason to begin living again. Now I was confused, angry, regretful and decaying. Once again, I was in doubt of the existence of any god, and assuredly discounting that the God of Christians was in any way involved in our lives. He seemed callous and cruel and most unkind.

Clarita sat and listened without interrupting, and after I had concluded talking, I was mentally and emotionally exhausted. It must have been obvious to her.

"I'm so sorry for all of you, James, especially for Nathan; this is a shocking thing to hear. But I think you need to get some sleep now," she suggested with care.

Clarita was shocked, but I'm sure she was trying to stay calm for my sake.

Picking myself up from where we had been sitting, I went to the bathroom and prepared for bed. As I pulled the doona up to my chin, I suddenly remembered I had neglected to say goodnight to Clarita. I was about to raise myself from the bed when she entered.

Sitting on the bed next to me, Clarita ran her fingers through my hair. It was soothing and very comforting. Neither of us spoke, and after a few minutes, she arose and proceeded to the other side of the bed. I did not turn over, but I could hear her undressing. I did not know what to think, neither did I care. She positioned herself in the bed, wrapping her arm around my chest and held me. I could tell that she was naked at the top as her warm breasts pressed against my back.

I had no thoughts or words. I knew her confusion of the moral stand about the sexual encounters of our relationship, and the reason for discontinuing. Nevertheless, I was confused why she so readily lay in bed with me. I made no advances physically or verbally. I was most content that she decided to stay. What would Clarita have said had I made any suggestive advances? Would we have made love? I did not know, but out of great respect for that beautiful, caring woman, I made no attempt to find out. After a short while, my exhaustion quickly obeyed my body's demand for rest and I soon went to sleep.

The next morning, I awoke late, about 9.20am and Clarita was not in the bed. I could hear noises in the kitchen and decided to investigate.

"Breakfast is nearly ready, James. Are you okay?" she said

cheerfully.

"Thanks, yes, I'm okay, I guess, but still totally stunned," I answered.

"I can understand that very well, James. This has been a great shock for you," she said, and continued, "Do you have any idea what you want to do today?"

"No. No, Clarita, I have no idea at all" I replied wearily, though more from mental exhaustion rather than lack of sleep.

Clarita commenced serving breakfast as I remained seated at the table, wrestling with the turbulent dilemma that had become my very recent companion.

"I suppose you want to go to church?" I queried with an unintentional tone that was supposed to have been positive but could only have been interpreted as somewhat cynical.

"James, what I have experienced recently is very important to me, but so are you. I'm sure God is not going to feel neglected if I decide to spend the time with you," she said with a calm authority but a clearly detectable honesty.

I lifted my sad head to make eye contact and smiled a very thankful smile. I was content to have made no advances to Clarita the previous evening. I believed I acted honourably toward the woman I was continually falling in love with more each day. However, the previous afternoon and evening was in no way conducive to any act of bedroom love.

As Clarita joined me at the table, my thoughts were of Nathan and also of Andrew. How might they be coping? Should I call them?

Upon finishing breakfast, I telephoned Andrew and Nathan. My first call was to Andrew. Giselle answered and informed me that her mother and father, together with Adam, had recently left to attend church. I then called Nathan, but there was no answer.

I returned to the kitchen table and sat sullen with my hands clasped over my downcast head.

What trials may we now have to face? I am especially anxious for Nathan.

Again, it seems for me that the creator of the universe is many light years removed from us, on the far side of His creation. If He is indeed endowed with great wisdom, as supposed, then the other side of the cosmos seems the preferable place to be. I could easily wish to be that far away too.

# PART 4

## ANDREW

Great Distress

One of the things I was looking forward to so much was this time with James and Nathan. But it was not to be what I expected. I wanted this newfound joy and the resulting explorations to continue.

Now, numbness was slowly etching its cold tentacles into me, like the cold that stabs you when you step out of a warm house into a freezing winter night. For the first time in my life, I started to feel old. I was experiencing emotions and having thoughts that had never been a part of my life. I was desperate for answers, not just for myself, but for Nathan, too.

So much joy and delight had entered our lives in the last two weeks, but now we suddenly have to grapple helplessly with a new torment. I have been jolted and appalled, but equally I am trying to refuse defeat. For Nathan's sake as much as my own, I have the responsibility to remain as calm and in control as possible.

I didn't say anything to Tanya, the girls or Adam when I got home after hearing what Nathan told us. I went to my study and called Chris and he came around to see me. I know he sensed that something was very wrong. I'm sure I sounded unlike my normal self. We talked in my study for over two hours.

His wisdom and understanding, and even love, were amazing. I had grown up with him in the church. We spent three years together in the band, touring Australia and New Zealand and then to Britain. I thought I knew him well, but his years of devotion to the 'things of God' and staying true to his calling, had developed a huge reservoir of care and compassion. He seemed to bring the wisdom and calm into the situation. I am thankful that there are genuine men of God.

By the time Chris left later that evening, there was a newness of heart in me. I can't explain it any more than that at present. I don't know what I expected to occur when I initially called Chris. I just needed to talk to someone. He was the only guy I could trust with what I wanted to say. I sat alone in my study for a long time after Chris left. I felt like I had perhaps been touched by God's goodness, mercy and grace. I have no rational explanation.

I had no idea what the future held for the Darling brothers and for our loved ones now. I didn't see that there was anything I could do. There was no way I was going to solve any of the issues we now faced.

I was not trying to avoid the pains of dealing with this new circumstance and Nathan's torment, but I certainly had no idea how I was going to work through it.

After leaving my study, I went to bed. Tanya was awake, so I told her everything that Nathan had recounted. That night, for the first time in our married life, Tanya and I prayed together. I still don't know what it means or where it leads but surprisingly, I'm not concerned about it. I have not yet decided if I will go to church with her some day because I still have too many unanswered questions. But I'm not sure if the questions will ever or can ever be answered.

I have no idea how we will get through, or if we will get through what Nathan has revealed. Chris said we will have to trust God, but somehow that seems extremely trite.

# PART 4

## NATHAN

What Now?

I wanted to tell my brothers why I came back home. I wanted to tell them why I couldn't come home sooner. I wanted to tell them that my Nathan, their Nathan, had returned. I couldn't explain that to them. I couldn't even explain that to myself. But I had to try.

The damage that Joe did to me physically was sickening. But the physical discomfort dissipated sooner than I expected. However, there was severe emotional & psychological damage. It was like a relentless, marauding army marching to the next war. Never tiring of inflicting torment, anguish & death along the way. Stripping countryside & villages of food & supplies. Plundering, pillaging & raping. Taking lives of the innocent with a sword.

As cruel as these resulting pains were, there was also the spiritual damage & dismemberment. This damage led to the destruction of every foundational truth that my life was built on.

Through my teens & early 20s, I had not lived an exemplary life. I had not lived a good Christian life. I wasn't a Christian even though I was raised in that world. I had not served God. But despite this, I think there remained a solid belief structure that held me together for whatever God wanted to do.

He finally caught up with me in New Zealand & I stopped running. But before the first year of my new life was over, I was running again. This time I ran away for 27 years. I criss-crossed the magical blue waters of the Pacific Ocean. Drank lots of wine, although I never went back to smoking dope. Had sex with numerous women, but no lasting relationships. But I have finally returned. Redeemed by one decision, condemned by another.

At last, it seems, there may be some dignity. Finally, there is some resolve & a miraculous blessing. I am so thankful that I have survived. I survived a fucked-up tragedy. A tragedy that spurred me to a life of escapism. An escapism that became a great adventure. I lost my family. I lost my freedom while I searched for it in vain. I lost my way completely. But I have gained a unique & precious addition, Ricky & Julie.

I am now going to tell Jimmy & Andy why I could not come home. I will tell them what the catalyst for my return was. How I wish that the story could get better from here. I just want to live out my remaining years with my family. Just live a happy & productive life with Julie & Ricky. Probably not much chance of that. Once again, grief throws me into the confines of its darkest dungeon.

Last week I asked my two brothers to come over to Mum's so I could talk to them. I had been living in Mum's unit since she died. I rented out the house at Warburton to a young couple I met up there.

Andy picked Jimmy up on the way. They both arrived together in Andy's silver Porsche Cayenne. I stood at the door watching them get out of the car. I thought I should perhaps buy a car like that. I could certainly afford to. But I didn't even have a licence.

They both smiled & waved when they saw me & greeted me with a hug as they entered. This was something that only started after we were reunited. We never hugged each other before that. Anyway, I felt very special as the youngest brother. I was pleased to see them. After chatting about the wonderful turn our lives had taken recently, I suggested I tell them what I had been waiting many years to say.

"I want to tell you both why I was gone so long. I also want to tell you why I came home," I started.

"Great," said Jimmy.

"Yeah, I can't wait to hear what you've got to say," replied Andy.

I didn't say anything. They both looked so expectant. I knew they were not going to like what I was about to tell them. But I had to keep going.

"I've told you about Rachel, how we met, how I got saved & all that," I continued.

"Yeah, we knew about that from your letters way back when that was happening," added Andy.

"Of course," I said, before continuing.

I told them in great detail what Joe's son, Mark, did to Rachel. How he tricked her into going on board Joe's boat while he lay in wait to defile her sweet, virgin innocence.

I cried as I told them. She had been a radiant Christian girl, full of life & hopes for the future. Mark murdered her future & mine too. He raped her precious gift. I told them how destructive it had been & the toll it had taken on her family, & on me. But at the time none of us knew why she turned her back on everyone & everything she loved & lived for. Such was the consequence of the sexual abuse against her. Made all the more disgusting because someone who held a leadership position in a church perpetrated it. Even though it was an usurped position that demonstrated no call or gift of God. It was also made more disgusting because her pastor, John, the fuckwit, refused to believe her story.

As I told them of Rachel's abuse & ruin, I was crying double. Crying outwardly for her. Crying inwardly for me.

"Let me tell you what Robert told me," I said & related it to Jimmy & Andy as Robert had related it to me.

"Robert told me the story," I continued. "Rachel eventually returned home when she heard her mother had cancer. She came back home with two children to 2 different fathers. Neither father was in her life nor involved with the children. Robert took them all in. She was so fortunate to have such a loving, compassionate & forgiving father."

*"What did I do to deserve this, Nathan?"* lamented Robert, as he sat aboard my yacht that Sunday afternoon. He told me this ghastliness 26 years after these horrendous events.

*"I was a loyal & faithful servant of God. I loved God & I loved my family. But I lost my daughter. My wife died of cancer 7 years ago. My*

*son is in a constant struggle with alcohol," he continued.*

*"Now, I'm broken, alone, decrepit. I still go to church but there is no solace, no consolation & I wonder if there is any hope? It seems not. Do I have a future? Not that I can see," he said as inconsolable tears filled his eyes & he wept for his wife, his daughter, his son & himself.*

I wept with him. I was hurting for him & with him.

*"Did you know," he continued, "that shortly after Alice died, Pastor John removed me from the leadership team & took away my role of elder? He said I was draining the 'joy' from the church." He sobbed some more.*

"That information brought back my own bad memories of wasted time in Pastor John's office. What a bastard." I said.

I continued. "So, the afternoon that Robert told me this, I decided I had to return home. I had to get out of New Zealand. Anger drove me out," I concluded.

"I can understand your anger, bro," said Andy, "but why did that instigate the decision?" he asked.

"Because I wanted to kill Mark," I replied.

"That's more than understandable, Nathan. I'm really, really sorry for everyone, except Mark," Jimmy added.

"No, Jimmy. It's not understandable. It's horrendous. I wanted to kill the bastard. I wanted to watch him die, just like I watched the terror in the eyes of his father," I said with clenched fists. Hot tears of anguish welled up in me again. The centre of the earth moved into my stomach, heavy with its molten burning.

"Nathan, I am so sorry for you. Knowing what I know now, I just wish you'd come home earlier," Jimmy said almost apologetically.

I sank to my knees from the chair & began to sob. Jimmy & Andy were on their knees in front of me very quickly. I was so glad they were there. I was so thankful I had such caring brothers. I loved them. Why does it sometimes take so many years to appreciate what you have?

Jimmy put a reassuring hand on my shoulder.

"Nathan, there's not much you can do about Mark. I know you wouldn't have killed the guy. As for Joe, well he's long gone. He's out of your life now," he added.

"No, Jimmy, he still haunts me. I couldn't come home. All I wanted to do was get away. Every day was filled with the need to escape," I replied through my tears & torment.

"Nathan, there is no solace or consolation for what he did, but he's dead," Jimmy said.

"YES! HE'S DEAD. I KNOW HE'S DEAD," I cried out. "But he's dead because..." I paused. "HE'S DEAD BECAUSE I KILLED HIM." I paused again. "He didn't fall overboard. There was no shark. I was the shark. I made up the story. My imagination became a new reality. That was its danger. I ran away from it. I ran away from my Nathan. Your Nathan ran away. I've been gone from myself & it's taken 27 years to find my way back," I explained hoping they would understand my mental anguish.

I looked up at Jimmy & Andy. I knew they wanted me to continue, but I felt that they also wanted to be somewhere else. Neither of them wanted to speak at that moment. I continued.

"I hit Joe from behind with the wooden crate. He fell to the deck & slowly rolled over. As he tried to stand, he looked up at me with anger in his eyes. He saw me about to strike him over the head again. He fell, sprawled on his back. His mouth was open & his eyes rolled back in his head. I smashed him in the chest with the crate. He made some strange gurgling noises."

I paused before continuing. I looked at Jimmy & Andy. Did they want to hear any more? Maybe it was already too much. But there was more to come.

"You think this is horrible? Want to know what happened next? It gets worse."

"Nathan, if it will help you, then keep going," encouraged Andy.

"Probably won't help me. I think it's too late for that. But it's sure going to mess with your heads," I answered.

"Go on, Nathan, please continue. You have waited 27 years to purge yourself of this burden. Now is not the time to cease," said Jimmy with compassion & concern.

I started sobbing again. My angst was a tangle of writhing emotions. Guilt & confession were entwined. I was choking. I wanted to vomit. Vomit would be preferable to the words I was about to speak from my mouth. I continued anyway.

"He wasn't dead yet. He was pretty much fucked though. He moaned. I undid his belt buckle. I pulled his pants off. He couldn't resist & I didn't even have to tie the bastard up. He had toilet paper or tissues wrapped around his cock."

Both Jimmy & Andy were looking very anxious. I knew they didn't want to hear any more. But I had to keep going. I couldn't turn back now. I didn't have another 27 years.

"The lower half of his fat white belly stared at the gloomy sky," I said as I searched the faces of my brothers to gauge their reactions. "The horrible memory of what I saw Alwyn do to Robyn years ago was glaring at me. Joe was now Alwyn. I kicked Joe in the balls. I didn't know if he was Alwyn or Joe, but I was desperate for him to be Alwyn. My justification was Alwyn. I hated Joe even more because he wasn't Bastard Alwyn."

"I kept recalling the look on Alwyn's face from many years ago. I saw the anger in his eyes. I again heard his threats of praying God's revenge on me. I wanted Alwyn to be there so I could kill him. But Joe was all I had. He'd have to do. At last I would be free of Alwyn taking up space in my head."

"I had to hurry. I had to kill Joe before God's vengeance came upon me. Before the vengeance that Alwyn prayed about would find me," I offered as my pitiful excuse for my evil deed. I felt justified because I was getting rid of both of them from my mind. I didn't realise at that time that they would both haunt me for 27 years.

"At that time, I was wishing I had said something to someone about Bastard Alwyn. I wished I had said something to Mum or Dad. But I was just a kid. I didn't know what to say. I didn't even tell you guys. I didn't know how to talk about what I'd seen in that Sunday School room so many years earlier. I didn't even know what to call it, so I couldn't say anything."

"I remembered the frightening stare that Alwyn shot at me after I almost got hit by the car outside the church. But it wasn't the near miss with the car that frightened me. I was petrified by Alwyn's threats. I HAD TO KILL THE THREATS. I HAD TO RESCUE ROBYN."

I went on with recounting my fatal deed.

"Joe started making more gurgling noises. I started to shout. No, it was more a shriek. 'JOE, JOE, I'M SORRY. I'M SORRY YOU'RE NOT ALWYN.'"

"Suddenly, I felt like I was that petrified 9-year-old boy except that I'd been given the power & strength of a vengeful man. I was scared. I couldn't turn back. It was as though I was back at Dendy Beach up that dark drain, desperately struggling & clambering to get through the darkness. Once again, I was in darkness. I had to get through. Hurry, hurry, banging my knees as I crawled up the concrete pipe. I needed to breathe fresh air again."

"Courage! Courage! Victory for Nathan! Victory for Robyn! Victory for Julie too!"

"Then I rolled fat, ugly Joe over. Now he was face down. I rolled him over again so that he was hard up against the stern of the boat. I sat him up. He was fucked. His eyes were wide open. His mouth was too. Didn't know if he was dead yet. I yelled at him, *'Joe, are you dead?!'* He didn't answer. I kicked him in the side of his fat white arse. *'Answer me, fuck face! Are you dead?'* His eyes blinked slowly. *'I've got something to tell you Joe. You're fat. You're ugly. Are you listening?'* I kicked his arse again. He pissed himself on the deck. It was grotesque. He was grotesque."

"*'Fuck you, Joe,'* I yelled at him. *'Fuck you, Alwyn,'* I yelled at the sky."

I continued my confession to Jimmy & Andy.

"While I was doing all this to Joe, I felt strangely courageous. I felt strong, like I was in control. I strained to lift Joe to the wooden railing. He said nothing. But he made some more gurgles & moans. He looked at me. I could now see terror in his eyes as I pushed him over the side. He floated face down, his fat, white arse spoiling the grey, blue Pacific."

"I started to sing the chorus *'In the name of Jesus, in the name of Jesus, we have the victory...'* Then I started to laugh. I turned around & picked up Joe's pants from the deck. Wiping up his piss, I threw them as far as I could toward where he had drifted & was now beginning to sink."

"*'Hey Joe, you forgot your pants!'* I yelled. I continued to laugh, & I thought about that guy, Bruce, whose pants we found on the beach all those years ago. I fell to the deck in fits of laughter, thinking about how we fell laughing on the sand. Suddenly my laughter stopped. I couldn't laugh any more. I felt nothing. Nathan couldn't laugh any more. He had gone away. My Nathan went away. Nothing was funny anymore. Nathan was no longer a funny guy."

"His name was Joe. But it was Alwyn I really wanted to throw overboard. Uncle Alwyn, Funcle Alwyn, Fuckle Alwyn, Fuckin' Bastard Alwyn. I cried. I sobbed for Robyn, for Julie, for Rachel & for me, but it wasn't enough."

"I cried the Pacific Ocean & Joe drifted away in the salted tears. But Alwyn still remained a memory more bitter."

"I'm sorry, Joe, but you had to go, so while you're gone, prepare a place for Alwyn in the darkest, coldest depths," I continued.

"Nearly 3 decades later, sometimes, when I'm on the toilet, it feels like Joe's coming out & I've still received no healing."

I had almost concluded my confession but added one last detail.

"I went into the cabin. I was cold. I was thirsty. I needed a drink. There was orange juice in the fridge. I drank what was left of it. After I drank the orange juice, I realised my courage had drained just as quickly as the orange juice. I was left standing with an empty carton. As empty as myself. That grey day infused itself into my being. Ever since, I have always been that grey day. Grey. Dark. Cold."

"For at least an hour I sat at the table. Not caring where the boat was going as it rolled in the gloom of that day. I was stunned. I gasped for air at times. I wondered how I'd ever get to sleep again. I tried to pray. I tried to repent. I called out to God. I thought of tying the crate to myself & jumping overboard. I was tightly twisted within myself. I wished my Nathan had been there. He wouldn't have done what I did. I told myself how sorry I was. I told God how sorry I was. I've been telling myself & God how sorry I was for nearly 30 years."

"I'm still sorry. But at least I don't have to repent & be in anguish over Mark. I didn't kill him. I had to find Nathan. My Nathan. Your Nathan. I had to bring him home. I couldn't afford to be a murderer again."

"I killed Joe, the bastard. I'm a murderer. Your little brother is a murderer," I cried softly. "I sent the bastard to the depths that called him its own. Bastard! Fuck you, Joe! You bastard!" I said weakly & wept more hurting tears. I was exhausted. I wanted to go to sleep.

Jimmy & Andy were both silent. I didn't look up. I was thinking they might get up & leave, but I hoped they wouldn't. They didn't.

They stayed kneeling or sitting on the floor with me. Neither of them said anything for quite a while.

"What do you want to do? What do you want us to do Nathan?" Jimmy asked.

"Forgive me! Please forgive me. I'm so sorry. I destroyed our family," I sobbed.

"Nathan, Nathan," said Andy, who was now crying too. "You didn't destroy the family, & of course we forgive you, & it seems that God has forgiven you too. Look at Ricky, look at Julie. It seems that God is even blessing you more than you could have imagined. God has always been forgiving you."

I didn't reply. It didn't make sense. One thing I've learned is that God doesn't make sense to us so much of the time. For me, that is His greatest attraction, that I don't understand Him. That's what disturbs me about Christians, always saying what God has told them, always 'listening' for His next instruction. If God is giving instructions to His people, why are they so fucked up? But what I think I do understand is that He is not as much against our sin as He detests the consequences that invade our lives as a result.

I kept sobbing as my heart ached for life. I had been dead for years. Joe killed my hopes. I killed Joe. We were both dead. But I've had to live both deaths every day. I want to live again. I just want a chance to live again. The greatest evil, the darkest sin, had been mine. I don't deserve life, but I want to live again. I don't know what life is like. I've been dead too long. I started dying when I was 9. Alwyn started my time of dying.

After a few moments, Jimmy spoke. "Was it because you killed Joe that you felt you had to go away? Why so long Nathan? Why were you gone for so long?" he said with tears in his eyes.

I knew the answer. Now I was ready.

"Do you remember," I explained to Jimmy & Andy, "as part of

my introduction, I wrote that I was reading the book of Proverbs one morning? I read a verse which resulted in my need to run away. Nathan, my Nathan, had already gone. Now I had to try to find him."

"The verse that prompted my lost years was *Proverbs 28.17 'A man tormented by the guilt of murder will be a fugitive 'til death; let no one support him.'" (N.I.V.)*

"That verse held a brutal power on my life all those years. I believed it & concluded that God put it there to speak to me. I took it as God's will for my life."

Telling Jimmy & Andy this horrendous story finally released me from its power. All those years of running away, trying to hide from myself & my God. Yet, all the time, it seems that I was just hidden in His light. I wasn't gone at all & He never left me.

Andy spoke & I think, prayed too.

"Nathan, I don't know what to say. I'm shocked, yes, but I will support you in any way I can. I just don't know how to help you though this. I don't know if God is in this in any way, but if He is, I hope He can help you somehow. If you're there, Lord, help Nathan. Somehow do something to help Nathan, & us."

"I don't know what to say either, Nathan. I don't know if prayer will make any difference," said Jimmy. "But like Andrew, I'll stand by you, & support you," he said through more tears.

* * *

The three Darling brothers knelt together on the floor. We weren't praying, but it's the closest we've ever come to doing that together. I remember thinking God must be very patient with us. Why did he wait so long to bring about these miraculous encounters?

But then I wondered, why he didn't do something to stop Joe & Mark? Why didn't he stop me from killing Joe? Why didn't he stop Joe from fucking me? Why didn't he protect Rachel? Why didn't he stop Alwyn? I had no answers. Life happens; pain, torment & eventually death, affect us all. I sailed away, expecting to die alone. But finally, my Nathan had peace. I had peace.

My initial understanding of being a Christian was to live an ideal life, with an ideal faith, in an ideal Christian environment. I didn't get what I expected. I didn't get what I was believing for. I didn't get what I prayed for. Neither did Rachel nor her mum & dad or brother.

The Christian life is a 'lovely' ideal, lived in 'loveliness' with other 'lovely' Christians who are all so good at being 'lovely.' All I want is to be that banal & 'lovely' too. But the 'loveliness' is an illusion. Most Christians seem, to me, to be living in that illusion. But I want my torments to be the illusion. I want to exchange illusions. My illusions for theirs. Any day.

The blessing & hope that had recently come into my life was giving me no comfort as I knelt on the floor. I was glad to be home. I was glad I hadn't killed Mark. Murderous thoughts had been a daily torment. Although I believed God had forgiven me, there were times His forgiveness didn't make any difference. I was still a murderer. At times, the torments of what they had done to Rachel & to me made me feel like I wanted to kill again.

Now I pray to God for mercy as repentance demands. I rest content in His promise that He will never leave me nor forsake me. But at the same time, I want to wipe out every evil bastard that preys on the innocent.

The 'men of God' I tried to talk to over the years rejected me. They offered no comfort, no respite. Neither the Word of God nor the power of prayer could assuage the dying light. The 'men of God', the ministers of the gospel of Jesus Christ, perched like vultures on my broken heart. Their talons ripped into my bleeding mortality. Their beaks tore into my living faith. Not content to wait for my 'death,' they fed their holy disapproval on what remained of my unliveable life.

**Book 14 – Jan 88**

*Once I had a dream.*
*I died & went to a cold place.*
*I saw grey, tortured faces filled with raucous laughter.*
*They were the faces of the dead.*
*I turned to see what they were laughing at.*
*The dead were laughing at the living & the pain of their*
*existence,*
*a horrible dream in my horrid life.*
*But it's not a dream, it is my life.*

Now the truth is out. I feel relieved. But I am still greatly disturbed. I killed Joe, but only once. Joe killed me every day for nearly 27 years. Now, I've reached a place where I can finally forgive him. But I can't ask him to forgive me. Confusing really, because sometimes I feel that I'd gladly kill the bastard again. But I know I wouldn't. But Alwyn? Killing him remains an attractive thought.

Thinking back to the fateful day when I emerged back on deck after Joe abused me, I remember feeling something welling up from deep inside me. It seemed that I was growing stronger. I thought it was great courage slowly rising to help me overcome this ghastly abuse. This strange courage seemed to be protective. It was giving me an even stranger hope. It was the opposite of how I felt when Alwyn stared at me through the car window.

It was like standing close to a railway line as a train gets nearer. The noise gets louder & you have a sense of danger being very present. Suddenly the train is in front of you & you can't even hear yourself scream. Then, just as suddenly, the train is rushing by & the noise speeds away too.

Joe was in the water & I was watching him drift away. At that moment, I realised it was not courage that had motivated my action to kill Joe, it was rage. The realisation came too late. Joe paid the price for that difference. But Alwyn was the perpetrator & preferred victim.

Joe slowly sank into the Pacific. I sat at the rear of *The Netherseas* looking at the water for a long time. I was frozen by guilt until I remembered the look of anger on his face as he lay sprawled on the deck. I took my regret for courage & sailed away for more than 25 years. My courage had deceived me. It kept me away from all support.

*I, Nathan Darling, was a man tormented by the guilt of murder, a fugitive 'til death; with support from no one.*

He was gone. Rage, regret & courage fought for supremacy within me for nearly 3 decades. All these years later, I know that neither rage, regret, nor courage won the war. But I still have no answers. I'll never have any answers. Joe can never apologise. I murdered his fat ugliness. But now I would prefer the apology. Instead, the torments continue.

Is this what I have to live with now? Will I have continuous thoughts & desires to kill the bastards? They mercilessly destroyed beauty to feel good about themselves, to be comfortable with their own ugliness.

Finally, I came home to avoid fulfilling murderous intent. Would I have killed Mark? I don't know. I didn't want to find out. I didn't want to look for him. I knew what my broken, heavy heart might lead me to do. On occasions, I wish I had killed the little piece of shit.

But I didn't kill him & I know I won't. Not now. I came home. I've learned by horrendous, bitter experience that taking someone's life takes your own too. I would be twice dead, twice over.

What I have told my brothers & written in this book, I also shared with Brian of Sunday Island. My fellow murderer. My equally, or even more tormented friend. My redeemed brother. I will write of Brian & Fliss when I tell of my years at sea. *'The Lost Years.'* Telling their story will bring me some joy. There is one other experience to share. So far, I have told no one. But I now sense I am free, even compelled to reveal all.

This 'experience' has been the only thing that has kept me going. It gave me some hope of finding peace with God. There were times I sensed forgiveness & even love. Sometimes there was actually a feeling of being close to God, especially at sea. But perhaps I've only experienced an illegitimate redemption. We're all wild olive branches grafted into the perfect tree anyway.

But I had to sail away. I didn't believe anyone would help me or support me. God's Word had declared it in Proverbs.

I'm broken. I've spoken with others who are broken. The broken in the church & by the church are also the forgotten in the church & by the church. But I believe some of them will introduce a breakthrough in this world. They are perfectly positioned. The unusable. The unfaithful. The forgotten. Facing indescribable torments & pains, yet, despite it all they are still there.

So, if you're a Christian & you've read this entire book, congratulations. There are probably 'forgotten' people at the church you go to who have horrific stories. Mostly they say nothing because they know they'll be shunned. They're right. Church is for loveliness, where everything & everyone is being nice & believing God for more loveliness & more niceness.

The gaping wounds of the broken children who praise the same God as you, don't really heal. Sure, the wounds heal to where they don't fester any more. But by that time the 'nice, lovely' Christians have passed them by on the other side of the road. They don't revisit.

These victims might cover their wounds with strange behaviours. They are ignored by leadership. Each week they go to church just one more time in hope of answers. The answers don't come. They praise God anyway & go home with their broken hearts wrapped in cold silence. Their 'help' has passed over them.

They're afraid. Afraid to open up because their brothers are 'the salt of the earth' & that salt adds screams to the pain of their open wounds. Afraid to speak for fear of rejection. Afraid to serve because they feel too unworthy, though innocent.

You think you don't know who they are, but you know who they are. They are the people you don't speak to.

Raped. Abused. Bashed. Scorned Stabbed. Shot. Disfigured. Dismembered. Crippled. Betrayed. Scorned.

A price has been exacted from them. The price they paid is too high. They have been sacrificed on another altar. They pay the price-too-high every day. & they die daily. Not out of choice, but only to survive. They hope for answers they know will never come. They hope for eternity. Life has dispersed their blessings elsewhere like cold ashes blown by a cruel wind.

Ripped off. Stolen. Broken. Bewildered. Confused. Forgotten. But not by God.

What if you're not a Christian? You've read the book. You've perhaps applauded the attack on the church & some of its so-called leaders. It's not entirely unwarranted. I could give you a lot more reasons to criticise. I could recount many other instances of church abuse. I could give names too.

Don't really know why we started this book of three stories in one, but Derek urged us on. But I'm pleased that it's finished. Hopefully, I can now concentrate on writing my memoirs. The 'Lost Years of Nathan Darling'. That's the working title at present. Hope I come up with a better title for more than 25 years at sea. Lots of exciting stuff, even funny stuff & also darkness, loneliness & anguish.

But this is not a book written to make converts of the 'lost.'

Perhaps this book is for those lost in the darkness of the drain. For those lost at sea. For those accused whilst innocent. For the detached. For the broken. For your Brian or your Fliss. For your Robyn & Julie or your Ricky. For those who live in a foreboding cabin on a boat of unimaginable mental turmoil. For the misfits. For those considered as dregs. For those who are treated as dross. For those whose thoughts & memories prevent them entering any safe harbour. For those shunned by the sanctuary of safety. For those who cannot find a safe church. For those who hate the church. For those who hate God. For those who hate Jesus. For those who know they're on the wrong planet in the wrong time. I know what it's like to be you. I love you. Jesus loves you. Hold on tight, we'll survive together.

Where do I go from here? Am I going to return to New Zealand & hand myself over? Are Jimmy & Andy obliged to inform the police now that they know the truth. Either way, the truth is now out.

I told my brothers. I've written my story. What should I do now? Fucked if I know.

I used to be a funny guy. So many years later, all I've become is sorrowful & regretful. I wish my past was different. I'm not sure what my future might be. But Julie & Ricky have moved in with me. We're a family. I'm in love. Perhaps the best days of my life are still to come.

Anyway, I've written enough for now, I'm going to paint for a while.


**Nathan Richard Darling**

# EPILOGUE
## *By Derek Lenere*

Writing and then publishing your life story can be a perilous journey, especially for Nathan in this instance, as he has confessed to the crime of murder.

This was discussed at length by the Darling brothers. What are the repercussions for Nathan? What possible problems might arise for James and Andrew if they take no action in reporting their brother? Would they now legally be considered as accessories after the fact?

There can be no justification for the action Nathan took against Joe. We can debate the reasons also refer to the role that Alwyn Raymond's abuses played. But we can never condone murder. This must remain fundamental to our human law and to our existence.

I was asked to make enquiries of a legal practitioner familiar with criminal law, and specifically to how it would be applied in New Zealand.

Although I was sure the New Zealand law would be the same as here in Australia or elsewhere in the Western world, I will travel to Auckland to find out. The results of my investigations and Nathan's probable fate will be revealed after I return.

This is where I conclude my contribution to this story because

Nathan wants to write of his twenty-five years at sea and is content at present to wait pending legal decisions from New Zealand. He has realised he will have plenty of time to write if he is sent to prison.

Nathan will continue to write his memoirs and will also write what fate for his crime is meted out in New Zealand. He will return.

# ABOUT THE AUTHOR

 Ian Cameron Wood began writing this book in 2006. During the 14-year journey following, there were many times he wanted to give up. The basic story was not completed until 2010 because of the numerous interruptions and commitments. There were many re-writes and edits over the ensuing years as well as times of utter frustration and dissatisfaction that led him to abandon the project on four occasions. Nevertheless, he kept coming back and persevered through numerous rewrites and edits until arriving at a satisfied result.

The impetus for writing this book came 6 years after lapsing into severe depression after fifteen years of verbal, emotional, psychological and spiritual abuse and betrayal by a church pastor. His slow climb from deep darkness was helped by turning his focus to art and writing. He has had art exhibitions in Victoria, San Francisco and Mexico and released his first book of poetry and short stories ('the ends don't meet') in August 2018. His second novel is due for release in October 2021 with a second book of poetry and short stories to follow soon after.